DREAM COME TRUE

By
Stephen Owens

MAPLE
PUBLISHERS

DREAM COME TRUE

Author: Stephen Owens

Copyright © 2025 Stephen Owens

The right of Stephen Owens to be identified as author of this work has been asserted by the author in accordance with section 77 and 78 of the Copyright, Designs and Patents Act 1988.

ISBN 978-1-83538-516-6 (Paperback)
978-1-83538-517-3 (E-Book)

Cover Design and Book Layout by:
White Magic Studios
www.whitemagicstudios.co.uk

Published by:
Maple Publishers
Fairbourne Drive, Atterbury,
Milton Keynes,
MK10 9RG, UK
www.maplepublishers.com

A CIP catalogue record for this title is available from the British Library.

All rights reserved. No part of this book may be reproduced or translated by any form or by any means, electronic or mechanical, including photocopying, recording or by any information storage and retrieval system without written permission from the author.

This book is a memoir. It reflects the author's recollections of experiences over time. Some names and characteristics have been changed, some events have been compressed, and some dialogues have been recreated, and the Publisher hereby disclaims any responsibility for them.

CONTENTS

1

Superstar

With his back to goal, 30 yards out, Peters took one touch before passing the ball out to the right winger. Cam Peters was having the match of his life. The winger Rodriguez crossed the ball low into Peters' feet. Peters had a clear shot on goal, but he saw that his strike partner had a much better position to score. So Peters rolled the ball past the goalkeeper, for his team mate to tap in. After all football was a team sport. Besides, Peters had already scored twice in this match.

Arsenal went on to win that match 4-0, with Peters picking up the man of the match award. During his post-match interview Peters was asked about the rumours that Spanish giants Barcelona were interest in signing him. He played down these rumours, and assured everyone that all he cared about was winning with Arsenal.

Cam Peters was now the league's top scorer and he felt like nothing could stop him. He was a superstar!

That evening Peters drove his red Ferrari 458 in to London. He pulled up outside a big white building. Glass windows covered the whole front of the marvellous night club. There was a queue, a mile long, down the road. On the doors two large men, wearing puffy black jackets, stood either side of a red velvet rope. The club was full and no one else was being let in. Cam helped a young blonde lady out of the passenger side of his Ferrari. She wore a long red dress, hooked over only one shoulder, and stunning white stilettos on her feet. They walked arm in arm to the two doormen, who immediately let them in, past the velvet rope. No questions asked.

In the club Cam sat himself at a large round table. He called other women over to join him and ordered buckets of Champagne for everyone. The club's decor was dominantly white, with black marble floor. A huge chandelier hung above the dance floor and the bar stretched the entire length of the far wall.

Drinking and dancing went long into the night. Cam had kissed so many women, he'd lost count. Each woman was more beautiful than the last. He thought it was about time he took one home. He hadn't seen the blonde woman he had arrived with, for several hours. But he had caught the eye of a short Latina woman, swaying on the dance floor. She had long, dark brunette hair, smoky green eyes and wore a short black dress. Cam approached her on the dance floor, locking eyes the entire way. He ran his arm around her waist and pulled her towards him. The pair danced another song, before leaving the club hand in hand.

Cam's penthouse apartment looked out across all of London. Large windows wrapped around the corner of the apartment. His place was minimalistic but everything there was bespoke and particular. Everything matched and was laid out in a smart, orderly fashion. He had a large leather sofa, in the middle of his open plan space. Only the bathroom and bedroom were in separate rooms.

Cam led his lady friend into the bedroom and he sat on the bed. She pushed herself away from him and dropped her black dress to the floor. Still in her tall black heels, she climbed onto Cam and kissed him. Cam rolled her over onto the bed and undressed himself. He then lifted her up and walked around the bed with her. Her legs wrapped around him. He threw her back on the bed and climbed on top of her. They made love late into the night.

It was a grey October morning in Horsham, West Sussex. Cameron's eyes slowly widened, as he rolled over from his front onto his back. He rubbed his eyes and as he woke, he thought about his boring 9 to 5 job, as an accountant. He wished he could just go back to sleep and be Cam Peters, superstar footballer! Alas he sat on the edge of his bed, staring at the open door of his en suite bathroom. He slapped his hands on his knee and let out a loud sigh. He began his morning routine. Shit, shower and shave before looking in his almost empty fridge. Deciding what to have for breakfast, after all he had to eat. He buttered two slices of toast and had a glass of water. Maybe he'd grab a coffee on his way to work. He would need something to get him through the day. He grabbed his coat and tucked an umbrella under his arm, and he set off.

As Cameron strolled down the road, looking down at his feet to make sure he stepped between the cracks of each paving slab, he started to imagine what his dreams would bring that evening. He enjoyed being a footballer, but who knew if that would happen again anytime soon. He then started to reflect on his favourite dreams from the past. His imagination ran riot, and before you knew it he was at his office. Just another 8 hours to kill.

2

Cameron Peters

10 years ago

Putney, Wandsworth, June 11th, 2007

Patricia Peters, exhausted from a week of teaching 7-year olds, was cooking tea for her son and husband. Ham, egg and chips was their favourite. Her husband Barry Peters sat at the dinner table, reading the sports section of the newspaper and complaining about his back aching, after a gruelling week at work.

"Are you taking Cameron to football tomorrow?" Patricia asked her husband.

"What's the point Pat? He'll be warming the bench as always."

"Can't you let him play?"

"How is that fair? Those boys have played out their skins this season; they've grown as individuals and have become a cracking team. Cameron only comes down 'cause his dad is the coach. I'm not sure he even enjoys playing anymore. Shame 'cause the boy knows the game inside out. How long will tea be?"

"Not long. Where is he anyway? He should have been home 20 minutes ago."

In his clunky leather shoes, 13 year old Cameron was kicking an empty soda bottle along the pavement. He was almost home from school. His dark green school blazer was in immaculate condition but his smart black trousers had seen better days. He could see his house just down the street. He was running late because he stopped to watch an argument between an elderly lady and a shop keeper. He wasn't sure who won that fight in the end, but it was fun to be nosey. It should only take Cameron 25 minutes to walk from school to home, using the back routes and through the park. But he liked to walk the bus route; it was much more entertaining. He only walked through the park on Wednesdays, so he could stop and watch Harrison Harriers train. They were a local semi pro team. But right now he had the bottle at his feet.

'He dribbles past one, he dribbles round two. He looks up! He shoots! He scores!!'

Cameron sliced the plastic bottle into the front garden of his suburban home. He swung the wooden gate open and kicked his shoes off out the front of the house and his bag just inside the door.

"Mum, I'm home," he called out, slamming the door shut.

"Put your bag up in your room! Tea is almost ready," she called from the kitchen. How did she know he'd left his bag by the front door?

His mother was dedicated to her job. But she was just as dedicated to her son, as she was to her students at school. She was a tall lady. Pretty too, with long shiny brunette hair. Many of their friends would say that her husband was punching above his weight, with her. Cameron resembled his father more; square head, bad eyesight and shorter than his mother. Grey hairs were coming through his mousy brown hair; *'The stresses of life'.* It was just the three of them, Cameron's parents had tried but failed to have any more kids.

After tea Cameron and his dad went down to the pub. Barry was meeting his friends and Patricia insisted he took Cameron with him. It was a nice summer's evening, so the group sat out the front of the pub, in the beer garden. This gave Cameron a chance to people watch, while his dad drank lager with his pals. Cameron's imagination could run riot, he would create different scenarios in his head about the people walking by. He was imagining stories about everyone and what they were up to.

He saw a man roughly his dad's age, late 30's. He was wearing aviator sunglasses, a designer polo shirt and slider flip flops. He was stumbling from the pub to his car: a 2002 Audi TT convertible. Cameron imagined that he was off to a club to hopelessly attempt to pull women, before going home alone and falling asleep with half eaten kebab, slopped across his chest.

Cameron could get involved in the conversation when they began talking football. He knew his stuff when it came to the beautiful game. But mostly his dad would moan about his job as a landscape gardener and how it was destroying his body.

"So Bat, what do you think is going on with our defence this season? We're leaking more than your bum hole after a Ruby Murray." Barry thought hard at his friend, Terry's, question while glugging his beer.

"It's that new centre back. Jones! He's useless. We should never have brought him in," he replied assertively.

"What do you think, Cameron?" Terry's attention switched from Barry to his son.

"Me?" Cameron croaked.

"Yeah. Do you agree that Jones is a donkey?"

"Jones has made some mistakes. But he isn't the problem," Cameron piped up. His dad looked on confused by this statement.

"You have to look at Parker in goal, moaning constantly at his defenders. Every chance he gets. Bellowing instructions and winging non-stop. These defenders are only human. Subconsciously it has to be damaging, trying to focus on your game and the guy behind you is on your back the entire match."

"I make you right there Cammy boy. Parker doesn't shut up."

Terry beamed a smile and swigging his pint, "He's right I reckon Bat, don't you?" Barry looked away from the group with a disagreeing look on his face, before swiftly changing the subject.

"Work has been a killer this week. You misplaced anymore old ladies' doors this week, Tel?" The group laughed and Cameron sank back into his chair; watched the world go by again.

After several more pints of lager Barry and Cameron walked home. It was dark now and a light breeze swished through the trees that ran down their street.

"Look son, you don't have to play next season if you don't want to."

"Why would you say that? We might win the league tomorrow."

"I know, but it can't be much fun for you sitting on the bench every week."

"But I'm still part of the team." What he really wanted to say, and maybe would have done if they were closer, is that he loved spending that time with his father and that he felt he helped him, with tactics and formations. It was undeniable that Cameron loved football, but he knew that it pained his dad that he wasn't any good.

"Well think about it, son. I'm sure there are better things you could be doing with your time." It was clear to Cameron that his father didn't feel the same way about their relationship as he did.

The next day his football team went on to win the league title, winning 2-0. Cameron didn't play a single minute. That was the last time he was ever part of a team, although his dad continued to coach those boys for another 3 years.

Present Day,

West Sussex, 12th October, 2017

Cameron didn't particularly like his name. He did like the shortening, 'Cam', but no one ever called him that.

Cameron had recently turned 24; he didn't do anything special to celebrate. Standing at 5' 9 and sporting a dad bod these days, Cameron described himself as an average Joe. He was noticeably thin as a teenager. Not very athletic but he loved following sport. Like most young boys, he wanted to be a footballer when he was older. Unfortunately he wasn't very talented in that department. Education was more his forte. He dressed smartly for most occasions, whether he was at work, at the pub or popping to the shops. Chequered shirts and chinos were his trademark look.

Cameron was single but definitely not ready to mingle. With no girlfriend since Lucy Porter, from his years at college, he tended to keep himself to himself. Lucy was pretty but also pretty annoying. After just a few months Cameron couldn't see past these annoying traits and outright ghosted her. She eventually got the point, after texting him non-stop for two days, so wrapped up in herself, she didn't realise he wasn't responding. He saw her a few weeks later in the local Mini Mark and she gave him daggers down one of the aisles, twisting a packet of cashew nuts so hard in her hand that the bag burst, sending cashews everywhere. Clean up required down aisle three. He wasn't in contact with anyone else from college after that. He did however have one close friend. His best mate from school, Jeffrey Booker, an I.T. technician. Jeffery had a love for all things Sci-Fi. That is actually what the pair originally bonded over. Cameron didn't have much time for all that now. Jeffrey went by the online tag name, Jeffro. He claimed he could hack any computer network in the country, but Cameron thought he was full of hot air.

Cameron stopped at the same coffee shop every morning; Maicon's and ordered the same coffee. The baristas were the only people that called him Cam. Of course he told it to them, when they wrote his name on the cup. He was a regular latte kind of man. Why people put sugar or those fancy flavourings in, was beyond him. It was not because he was 'sweet enough'. Sweet isn't a term Cameron would use to describe himself.

Cameron didn't drive, although he did have a licence. Why would he need a car when everything in his life was within 20 minutes' walking distance. From his work, to his favourite coffee shop on the high street. Even his best friend's house was only a 10-minute walk from his.

After school Cameron studied Book Keeping and Accounts at college. He was fully qualified after 3 years and now worked at 'Harpers', an accounting firm in his village. The company has a sister office in London. Which boasted a much larger office space and had many more employees. The London office liaised with clients and big accounts. Whereas the West Sussex office was more for admin and local accounts.

Cameron worked in a small team. There were only 6 of them. Jane, the secretary, she was in her 60's now and waiting for retirement. A short bubbly lady, who wore her glasses at the end of her nose. She had been there forever. Then there were Sara and Leah, everyone thought they were sisters, but they were not. Both were in their late 20s. They were always dressed smart, wearing typical office attire. Josh, who sat on the desk next to Cameron, was a little annoying. But that was only because he always tried to talk to Cameron, especially in the mornings. And lastly there was Mr Kyriakos-the boss. Cameron got on well with most of them, but he despised his boss. A fat, hairy and sweaty man, his boss always demanded work, but never seemed to do any himself. He would micro manage Cameron. Constantly leering over him and wheezing while he strolled smugly around the office. Cameron was sure that he had it in for him as well. This was maybe because Cameron kept himself to himself. He didn't like to get involved in group activities and put no effort into team building exercises.

His job wasn't exciting but he'd always been good with numbers.

Cameron swung on his chair, at his work desk. His head tilting back and his eyes fixed on the ceiling fan. Which was completely distracting him from his work. At lunch Mr Kyriakos had set him a 5pm deadline to complete some spreadsheets. Cameron was nowhere near done as the clock ticked round. It was 4:50. Cameron snapped out of his daze and realised the time. He took a look around the office and Mr Kyriakos was nowhere to be seen. Cameron decided that that was enough work for today and he clicked 'save' on his spreadsheets before closing down his PC. He jumped to his feet and strolled over to the door. But just as he grabbed his coat from the pegs by the door, Mr Kyriakos walked in. "Ah Cameron, have you finished those spreadsheets, like I asked?"

"Erm, well they were a little more complex than I first thought."

"So you haven't finished them?" he quizzed disappointedly.

"Erm, no not quite," Cameron looked down at his shoes. He didn't like maintaining eye contact with people for too long. It made him feel awkward.

"This is completely unacceptable, I have been very unhappy with your work of late. You've no doubt been daydreaming this afternoon, since I left the office!" Mr Kyriakos stared at Cameron, breathing heavily. Cameron could hear a crackle in his boss' throat.

"No, Mr Kyriakos, as I said, the spreadsheet has just taken me longer than expected and a client called in to discuss their account, after you went out." This was a lie and Mr Kyriakos knew it. And Cameron knew he knew it.

"I'm sick of your excuses. We will have a meeting first thing in the morning to discuss your performance. Now go home."

Cameron left.

He started his walk home, quickly forgetting about his unproductive day at work. He walked past Maicon's on his route home, it was closed now. He popped into Budget-Mark, his local supermarket, and grabbed a microwave meal and a 4 pack double chocolate cookies. That was dinner sorted. It was dark by the time he got home, and it began to rain as he walked up the stairs to his building door. He lived in an old mansion, which had now been converted into flats. He watched the rain pour down, as he ate his dinner. He watched a little TV, which made him think. Why do only fools and horses work? He wished he never had to go back to his job. But that is life, right? As he brushed his teeth, he felt a smidge of excitement. Finally it was bed time! What a long day he had endured to get here. He rolled over in bed, switched the lamp off and rolled back on to his back. He stared up at the ceiling for a few moments, before his eyes slowly closed. Soon after he was asleep.

3

Help, help!

The sky was dark and cold. Fine rain was falling. The streets were busy with taxis and food delivery bikes. Tall buildings dwarfed the roads, with bill boards on every corner. Cam looked around at the adverts - 'The Phantom of the Opera!' - 'Casablanca' - 'Jersey Boys'. It was the West End, London. Cam expected to see bright neon lights and signs. But everything, everything, was black and white.

Cam made his way down the streets of London, he could hear buskers singing. He began to walk with a swagger as he felt the music moving through him. As he moved faster his strides became bigger. Before he knew it, he was pushing himself 6 foot into the air and landing back down again with grace. He pushed up with his right foot and he was higher than the lampposts. Could he fly?

With every step he was able to get higher. But how could he stay up here? He tried several different things - running in the air, putting his legs and arms out in front of him, Superman posing. Then he got it, he had to pump his arms up and down, beside his body. He was flying! He wasn't going exceedingly fast, but he was doing it!

He eventually had to come back to ground; he couldn't stay up there forever. As he descended he heard a lady's voice call out. "Help, help!" Where had that come from? "Help, help!" He heard again, this time louder and clearer. He pushed himself up into the air, maybe he could see better up here. "Help, help." He looked down at a side road. There! There she was. He came down to her. She looked terrified. She wouldn't make eye contact with him, so he grabbed her by either arm and shook her.

"What's wrong?" he implored. "Why are you screaming for help?" She then locked eyes with him, tears filled hers. She slowly raised her arm and pointed behind Cam. From the shadow behind some bins, Cam saw two green eyes. "What the fuck is that?" A creature then appeared behind the green eyes. Two long legs climbed over the wheelie bins, arms dragging beside it. The creature stood up tall; it was twice the height of Cam and the woman. With grey, wet skin. Its arms were so long; its knuckles scraped the pavements. Cam looked up at the creature's bright green eyes. It's the only colour he'd seen all night. The creature swiped Cam aside; flinging him down the road and onto the ground. Cam looked back and saw the creature's mouth open. A bright pink tongue emerged and snaked down towards the crying woman.

Without thought Cam jumped to his feet, bent his knees slightly and pushed himself up, towards the beast. Landing directly on its head, he wrapped his legs around the creature's neck and reached round to grab its long, thick tongue. He then jumped down off the beast, bringing its tongue with him, in his hand. The creature let out an almighty screech. Before turning and running down the road.

"Are you okay?" Cam asked, as he turned to look at the woman. She nodded but was still speechless. "It was a Kaiser Creature," a voice said from the end of the road, but Cam couldn't make out who it was. "I've been chasing it for days. It has come here from another planet, with the goal to suck out the entire colour from our planet." The voice explained. A grey- haired man appeared in the light. He wore a smart grey suit and had a grey beard to match his hair. "Who are you?" Cam quizzed.

"We believe the Kaiser Creature needs our colour to help fuel his planet. My name is Hamish, and I need your help to destroy it."

Cam was on board. He felt powerful. He knew he had what it took to bring down the Kaiser Creature and bring colour back to the world. Hamish gave him a communication ear piece and sent him to scan the area. He jumped up and looked around all evening. Then he heard it again...

"Help, help!" It had to be the Kaiser Creature. He reported the sighting to Hamish, before rushing down. "Stay back, Cam. Don't alert it that we're coming."

"Copy." Cam waited on top of a nearby building. He glanced down and saw an open park. It was still dark and without the help of the street lights, it was almost impossible to see anything. Then Cam saw it; those green eyes. It's eyes looking up at him. Cam thought that there was no time to spare and decided to jump down and confront the beast.

Sure enough under the beast's lanky frame, he saw a person. The beast had his long, pink tongue wrapped around the person's neck.

"Cam!" Cam turned around and saw Hamish at the park entrance. "Cam! Help them! Get that Kaiser cunt off him!" Cam turned to the beast and propelled himself at it, flying straight into the creature's midriff. The man was immediately released from the clutches of the creature's tongue. The man ran towards Hamish for help. The Kaiser Creature threw a long limb at Cam before turning and fleeing. As Cam turned to talk to Hamish he noticed he had his hand on the back of the victim's neck. He also noticed the victim's cheeks and neck turning from a usual tan skin colour to grey. The Kaiser Creature had sucked the colour out of him. It had to be stopped.

Cam hadn't had a sighting of the Kaiser Creature for days. But he also hadn't seen any colour for days. Had the creature stolen the entire colour in the world? Was its mission complete? Maybe he had injured the creature? He had to talk to Hamish; they needed a plan for what to do next. He began to walk before realising he could jump higher and quicker to his destination. He was only a few minutes from HQ when he heard it.

"Help, help!" someone cried faintly from behind a building. This was Cam's chance; he was going to end this and capture the Kaiser Creature. He jumped high above the building and on the other side he saw a young boy. Ginger hair, bright brown freckles across his nose. He was wearing a bright red jumper and blue denim jeans. The boy touched a car parked alongside him, which turned silver, at his touch. Cam ran up to him. "Where did it go?" he asked the boy. The boy pointed down the road. At the end of the road there was only a right turn. There it was standing taller than 2 men. It had another young boy in its grasp. This boy had blonde hair and piercing blue eyes. But his clothes were still black and white. "Release the boy!" Cam shouted. "Do you understand me creature?" The creature cocooned the boy in his grasp and ran towards Cam before leap frogging him and sprinting away at a rate of knots. As Cam turned to chase him he saw Hamish leading the young ginger boy into the HQ building. At first he thought Hamish must be taking him in there to help him. But then he noticed that the boy's clothes were black and white again. The boy's skin and hair colour began to fade, with Hamish's hand gripping his neck.

Cam entered HQ unannounced. There was no one in the lobby. He scoured the hallways but still no signs of anyone. He hadn't been here before but surely there were tons of people that worked here. After all it was a huge operation. Suddenly he heard a murmur conversation. He looked up and noticed it was coming from the vents. As he crawled through the vents he came to the end of a passage. But he was looking down at a room. There was Hamish, with the young lad tied to a surgical bed, spread eagle. In the corner of the room there were dozens of clear gas canisters. There were all different colours inside. Hamish grabbed an empty canister and put his hand over the top. Orange colour flooded from his palm, into the canister. It seemed to take almost all of Hamish's energy to do so. He fell to his knees, let go of the canister and screwed the lid on. He was out of breath, sitting against the wall. Cam couldn't work out what was going on.

While Hamish was weak from depositing the colour, Cam decided to take this time to scope out the rest of the building. He climbed down from the vent and searched the corridors, every room either an empty lab or an unused conference room. Until he turned down a long corridor. Bright lights shone off the white walls. There were no doors along the walls, just one right at the very end. It was locked. There was no window on the door, so Cam can't see inside. Whatever was in there, it could be dangerous.

Cam broke down the door with a swift kick. He found dozens of large containers, which were bolted to the wall. They were frosted over. He scoured the front of one of the containers, and looked inside. He saw frozen Kaiser Creatures inside, with surgical tubes coming from their head into a tank. He turned to face the open entrance. There stood the Kaiser Creature he had been chasing, arched in the doorway.

"Iasha hevet oo shantel," the Creature spoke. But somehow Cam understood what he was saying. "What happened here?" Cam asked. For some reason he didn't see the creature as a threat to him.

The Kaiser Creature explained to Cam, in its native tongue, that Hamish and the Kaiser Creatures were from the same planet. Hamish came to earth to steal all its colour, to help fuel his own life. Without colour he grew weak and lived a soulless life. He had already stolen another planet's entire colour. He could shape-shift into any being, and was only in human form to deceive the people of earth. The Kaiser Creatures were sent to try and stop him, and give back the colour he had stolen. Their long tongues carried the colour and their lick had the power to reinstate colour into anything they touched. But Hamish was besting each Kaiser Creature who tried to stop him, and froze them, so they couldn't hinder his plans further. But now they had Cam. He possessed the power to stop Hamish and release the Kaisers. If he helped them, the Kaisers would give back all of the earth's colour. They devised a plan.

Cam returned to the room, where Hamish had been resting but he wasn't in there. He must have sensed the Kaiser

Creature and gone after him. He was right, he found Hamish with a long steel pole, clutched to the Kaiser Creature's leg. The pole seemed to extend and disable the creature at its touch. "Hey! I know everything, Hamish! Release him and surrender!" Hamish didn't seem to like this idea, he marched the Kaiser up against the wall and left it stuck there, unable to move or help Cam. He then turned to Cam.

"You are no longer able to help me occupy these creatures. So you no longer need to be alive!" He ran at Cam, but Cam leapt over him. The pair tussled in a fierce duel. Before Hamish pinned Cam to the floor, his foot pressed down on his neck. Cam couldn't break his grip and was now struggling to breathe. His attempt to fight off Hamish weakened, before his arms flopped down to the ground and his eyes began to close.

"HELAF ETAY PEYAAA!" Hamish loosened his grip and turned to see 7 Kaiser Creatures bearing down on him. Cam had unfrozen them and now in their numbers had the power to restrain Hamish, but only for a short while. Cam got to his feet, took a deep breath and ran as fast as he could, collecting Hamish in his grip and bundling him into one of the freezer containers. Hamish tried to fight back but the door closed on him and he was frozen in his position.

The 8 Kaisers took the canisters of colour from the lab and went out to distribute the colour back to the world, before taking frozen Hamish and departing to their own planet. Cam's work was done.

Cameron was awake before his alarm sounded. He lay there and stared up at his ceiling for 10 minutes, he couldn't stop thinking about how cool it felt to jump to that height and to fight magical creatures. 'BIDDIP, BIDDIP, BIDDIP' his alarm echoed. It was time to get up.

4

Anna Davenport

It was Friday morning. Friday the 13th. As Cameron lay in bed, he began to think about work and the meeting he was to have with Mr Kyriakos that day. He dreaded that meeting. It felt like he was always having these bloody meetings. He lay in bed awhile longer, and thought to himself that maybe he should just call in sick to work? After all, it was the weekend. Hopefully Mr Kyriakos would forget about all this by Monday. He got out of bed, slid his slippers on, and pitter-pattered to the bathroom. He took his morning shit, absent of his phone or a magazine to occupy this time.

It was time to make the call.

"Good morning, Harpers, how may I help?" Jane said as she answered the call.

"Oh, good morning Jane, hope it isn't too early, I was going to leave a message."

"Good morning, Cameron, everything ok dear?"

"Yes, fine, well no not fine, I mean, erm. Sorry I didn't expect anyone to be in the office yet." Cameron spluttered as he realised he hadn't actually thought of his lie to get off work.

"You know me, in bright and early to set up the day," Jane chirped.

"Well, I was actually just phoning ahead to let you know I won't be in today. Terrible diarrhoea; hasn't stopped all night. Sick too, everywhere. Real mess." He sighed and rubbed his forehead with his thumb and index finger; he was making a right mess of this. "Yeah so..."

"Right ok dear, say no more. Please! I will note your sickness and let Mr Kyriakos know when he's in. You feel better and hopefully you'll be right as rain by Monday. Ta-ta."

"Thank you, Jane, Bye." He puffed out his cheeks, nodded his head, yeah she bought that, she definitely bought that!

Although he wasn't going to work today, Cameron still wanted to get his morning coffee. So he threw some clothes on and headed out. As he walked down towards the high street, he caught a look at himself in a car window. Tracky bottoms and chequered shirt wasn't the coolest look, even he knew that.

"Regular latte, Cam?" He loved that they knew him now, and he loved even more that they called him Cam.

"Yes please, and a pan au raisin as well. To have in this morning." Whilst he waited he flicked through the news on his phone, although not really taking anything in. He had about a hundred little red notification signs, floating above various apps.

"Cam!" the barista yelled, "your coffee." Without looking up from his phone, he grabbed the coffee off the counter and turned, straight into a young lady waiting behind him; spilling the drink all down her rain mac.

"Oh my god! I am sooo sorry!" he frantically tried to wipe the coffee off her.

"Don't even worry about it," she assured him. "It's an old coat anyway. Let me buy you a new coffee," she insisted.

"Are you serious, it was totally my fault; I'll get you one."

"Well thanks; I'm Anna by the way. And you are?"

"Hi, it's nice to meet you. I'm Camer.... Cam."

"Nice to meet you too, Camercam," she joked.

"Cameron is my name, but everybody calls me Cam," he said unconvincingly.

"Cam it is!" she had a soft, raspy voice with a hint of posh undertones.

Cameron chatted to Anna for a short while, until their coffees were ready. She had to take hers to go. Cameron stayed and ate his pastry before heading back home.

Anna Davenport worked on the high street, in a small book store called Dusty Shelf. She loved to read. Ever since she was a little girl, she always had her nose in a book. She left school with dreams of being a writer. She was now 22 and had a few unfinished things in the works, but she never stuck at any of her projects. She was always cheery and loved meeting other book worms, who would come to the store. The store itself was situated down the quieter end of the high street, which although sometimes affected footfall, this end of the high street had kept its rustic, Victorian village look. The Dusty Shelf had two large windows either side of the shop door, and wooden beams supporting the structure inside. The office/stock room was a tiny room, situated behind the counter, to the middle rear of the store.

"Morning!" Anna called out as the bell above the shop door dinged. She loved the shop's owner, Leone, although she felt a little under appreciated.

"Did you want me to organise the weekly 'must reads'?"

"Good morning Anna. No, I will sort that. Could you shelve the delivery?" Leone instructed as she carried books to the front of the store. Anna made her way to the back to unbox new books. She noticed that Leone was putting horrors out, like Anna had suggested for this week, with Halloween coming up. "I thought we would do horror books for the rest of the month, as it's October and Halloween is coming up," Leone said, beaming with inspired confidence. Anna stopped what she was doing and processed what her boss had said. That wasn't her idea. That was Anna's idea! She let it go; once again Leone wasn't giving her the credit she deserved. She felt Leone treated her like a child and she should leave the important things to the grownups.

She probably came across this way to people because of Anna's kind nature and small stature. She had short auburn hair, which reached the top of her shirt collar. A cute button nose, smothered with freckles. She loved to wear colourful clothes. Today she was wearing a yellow, long sleeved jumper, under blue denim dungarees and red sandals, with little daisies on. 99% of the time, she would have a book or two under her arm.

After work Anna headed home. It was the home she had grown up in. A forest of bushes and plants filled the front garden. And the brickwork outside was coated in pebble dashing. Inside, a hallway led to a kitchen and lounge area which was separated by a hollow alcove wall. A small garden could be found through a doorway at the rear of the kitchen. Waiting for her at home were her Mum and Aunty Maple, sitting in the front room watching TV.

"Hiya, darling," Maple said getting up from her chair when she noticed Anna was home. "How was work?"

"Work was fine. How is she?" Anna nodded her head in her Mum's direction.

"Go and sit with her. I'll make you some tea. Is that a new book I see in your hand?"

Wendy, Anna's mum had a soft, friendly face, dark brunette hair, unlike her daughter's vibrant auburn colour, dominant grey strands fluctuated through. She spent a lot of time at home these days. She was only 55 and had suffered with multiple sclerosis for many years, which the doctors believe had led to a struggle with early onset dementia. "Thanks, Maple. Things have been so much easier since you moved in." Maple looked down her glasses at Anna, with her hand placed supportively on her shoulder. Auntie Maple was older than her sister, she had wiry grey hair, although Anna's remembered it being exactly same as Wendy's before turning grey. Also, unlike her sister, Maple was a tall lady, with a slight hunched back. She walked around in little kitten heeled shoes and her little box shaped handbag. She was strict with Anna but only because she had her best interests in mind; a genuinely kind woman, under a hard exterior. Even with all this going on, Anna never let it crush her spirit and she continued to love life and tried to spread joy every day.

Cameron thought about Anna a little as he walked home. She was really nice, he thought about how she had a way about her, which made him feel good. But his thoughts soon returned to the rest of his day ahead, what he was going to do.

He could complete his half built legos. He had the Hogwarts Express half complete. Not to mention the Death Star which he'd not touched in weeks. Or perhaps he would play some PC games. Or maybe just watch TV. Whatever it was, it wasn't very exhilarating. If only he could just jump into the air and be home in two steps, like he did in last night's dream.

5

Lucky Number 13

"Welcome to tonight Lottery Draw! In just a few minutes a lucky winner will walk away with £100,000,000. And the first number out is 58, followed by 32, 16 and 29. The final 2 balls before the bonus ball are 7 and 41." Cam looked down at his ticket. 7, 16, 29, 32, 41, 58! All he needed was the bonus ball. Lucky number 13! "And the bonus ball..... 13. Those numbers again in ascending order are..." the well spoken caller's voice faded into the background. Cam looked down at his ticket, as the realisation sank in. He'd done it. He'd won the lottery!

Rain thundered against the window and woke Cameron, after he had drifted off in his armchair, in front of the TV. The lottery numbers were being called out. Looking out his window at the grey sky, he started to imagine what he would do if he won the lottery for real. It would certainly make his life so much better. He could leave his crappy job, he could move out of his shitty flat and he could do anything he wanted. His dreams could come true. Well mostly.

Friday the 13th didn't come around often, the weather was horrible and although Cameron wasn't a superstitious person, he didn't see the need to go out tonight and tempt fate. He felt like he had wasted his sick day away and hoped he hadn't just wasted a good dream on his short afternoon nap. He got to his feet, stretched his arms up in the air, moving his feet on to his tip toes. Let out a squeaky yawn and rubbed his eyes. Time for some dinner he decided.

Cameron looked long into his fridge for some inspiration on what to cook, when his phone rang. He looked down at his buzzing phone and saw 'Jeffro' flashing on the screen. He was Cameron's only real friend these days. He contemplated not answering but eventually picked it up.

"Hello?" Cameron answered with no excitement.

"Hello mate, your boy Jeffro here! What you up to tonight?"

"No real plans, the weather is terrible and to be honest with you mate, I've been off work today sick." Not asking the question in return.

"That sucks man!" Jeffro said "It feel like forever since I've seen you. We need a gaming sesh again soon. When are you free?"

"Not sure to be honest, Jeff. I'll have to check my diary. I'm actually about to have some dinner pal, so can I get back to you another time?"

"Yeah sure, don't leave it too long though! See ya soon!" Jeffro promptly hung up the phone. Cameron thought about checking his diary, but his diary was about as useful as a chocolate teapot. He never had any plans!

Before bed Cameron checked his betting app, scouring through the weekend sports. After several minutes of mindless scrolling, he stumbled across a horse at tomorrow's Derby at Epsom @ 13:00. Horse number 13, named Lucky Star with odds at 13/1. Seemed like a sign to Cameron; was definitely worth a punt. He stuck a tenner on it, and headed to bed.

Cameron has bet on the horses for years, he used to gather info about horses for his dad. So he knew the system inside out. But Cameron preferred football accumulators. Well here's hoping that 13 is lucky for him tomorrow.

6

Inked

The pack of wolves howling at the moon, surrounded by tall evergreen trees, completed the sleeve. Wincing at the pain as the needle moved its way from the triceps to the back of his arm, Cam looked down at the piece of art being printed on him. He loved it. It concluded his left sleeve; a capturing native theme. His right arm was already complete. A skull, smoking a cigar wrapped his forearm. The smoke creeped along past a bushel of roses. Before reaching another skull, wearing a crown, at the top of his arm.

This look was rounded off with a dope display of ear piercings. He had scaffolding going across, a stud in his tragus and a diamond lightning bolt in the lobe. Once the tats were done, he headed to the gym, of course.

Everyone at work was so complementary about his ink. Sara and Leah couldn't resist feeling his arms. Tickling their baby pink acrylic nails over his muscles and giggling to each other. He got attention everywhere he went. After work he went out with the girls for a couple of drinks. Two lads dressed in smart slim fit shirts leant next to Cam at the bar, while he was buying a round. They slipped him a business card 'De Luca Bros Fashion Design' printed across the front.

"We're Marco and Enzo De Luca. We are fashion designers and want you to model our stuff." They spoke assertively and confidently.

"That sounds interesting. But I already have a job." "Working 9-5 for the man? Pish! Fuck that job; you'll earn more in 1 day with us than the entire month there! Think about it and call us. Go and enjoy your night." The brothers shook hands with Cam, making eye contact throughout, then nodded at him before leaving.

What did he have to lose? The next day he told Mr Kyriakos straight. "Fuck you and your job!" he told his boss, before kissing Leah firmly on the lips, flipping Mr Kyriakos the bird and leaving.

He looked unreal in these clothes. They had him in suits, polo shirts and chinos and slick long rain jackets. But his favourite was the lounge wear. So soft. So comfy. They paid him £3000 for 2 hours work. He could get used to this life. After the day's shooting, the brothers took Cam out to the swankiest restaurant in town. Cam had the juiciest filet steak, with the creamiest mash and the crunchiest lettuce wedge. He drank an entire bottle of red wine to himself while the brothers enjoyed cocktails. They of course covered the bill. He could get used to this life style!

Before he got to live anymore Cameron woke up dying for a piss. Must have been all that wine his subconscious drank. He rolled over and checked his phone. It was 6:13am. What an annoying time, he knew he wouldn't get another good dream in at this time. He also knew he definitely won't get back to his modelling Italian clothing dream again! It was also the weekend. Why can't he ever get a good lay in on his day off?!

He lay in bed wide awake after returning from the loo. He closed his eyes and tried to get back to sleep but it was no good, he was awake now! His thoughts took over and pestered his mind. He started to think about how he always thought of the perfect thing to say... 10 minutes after an argument. And how he always smiled at people he passed in the supermarket, even though he had no idea who they were. Pointless, random thoughts racing through his head; which made returning to sleep impossible.

7

Saturday

Saturday morning TV was boring him, so Cameron decided he would get out of the house. It was time for coffee, so he walked to Maicon's on the high street. The weather matched his mood, while gloomy skies filled his walk, gloomy thoughts filled his mind; another day to get through. His early morning awakening was what had dampened his energy.

"Cam!" the calling of his name took him by surprise. He looked across the coffee shop and saw Anna sitting at a table.

"Hey... it's Anna, right?" as if he didn't know. He noticed that she had her coffee in a take away cup.

"Right. How are you? I thought I might run into you again."

"Yeah, I'm fine. Got to get my morning coffee!" Cameron said unenthusiastically.

"How's your morning?"

"Very good thanks. I'm off to work this morning. What do you have planned?" she probed.

"Oh, you know – this and that." This and that meaning absolutely sod all.

"Well if you have time, would you like to get lunch? I get an hour from 1 o'clock." Cameron paused for a second, to think. But what did he have to think about? He had no plans, Anna seemed nice and it would kill some time. "Sounds good to me, shall I see you here again at 1?"

"Perfect, see you then!" she walked away with a spring in her step. Cameron watched her leave and walk down past the coffee shop window. Her raspy voice sat with him for a while. He ordered himself a latte and set a reminder in his phone, for lunch with Anna. It began to rain, and as he had forgotten his umbrella, he decided to have his coffee in and wait for it to stop.

He passed the time between now and lunch at home, playing PC games. As he played, he thought about Jeff phoning last night and he began to feel bad for blowing him out. Cameron didn't have the energy to socialise though. His phone buzzed and flashed 'Lunch with Anna' so he needed to get off the computer and into the shower.

When Cameron got to the coffee shop, Anna was there waiting for him again. They smiled at one another as they met eyes across the room. He sat down and greeted her, before they got into conversation.

"So, where exactly do you work?" he quizzed, as if she hadn't already mentioned that the first time they met.

"Dusty Shelf; it's a little independent book store, down on the high street."

"Yes, I know it." Just then his phone buzzed. A notification from his betting app. His head slumped ever so slightly.

"What's that?" she asked.

"I had a bet on a horse; I had a dream yesterday that 13 was my lucky number, not in this case though. Anyway tell me more about your job, do you enjoy it?"

"Oh yes, I love it. Reading is my passion, I love to get lost in all different kinds of tales. One day I hope to finish my own book." Cameron listened to her go on and on about her love for books. He was fascinated. It reminded him of his dreams and how each one is a little story of their own, and so he related to her in a way. "What do you want to eat?" she asked. "The paninis here are good!"

"Yeah, I like the tuna melt, and I'll get a pan au raisin too." Anna got the same.

The pair chatted throughout the lunch date. Cameron thought to himself how easy it was to chat to Anna. While Anna found Cameron particularly interesting and uncommonly kind.

"Ok, I have a question for you," Anna jumped in with excited intent. "If you had a genie who could grant you 3 wishes, what would you wish for? And don't be boring and ask for more wishes!"

"Hmm…" Cameron took a deep breath in through his nose and he pursed his lips. "Good question. I can wish for anything?"

"Anything!" she insisted. Cameron took a few seconds longer to think.

"Apart from the obvious thing… being money, I wooould wishhh fooor a super power. Like the ability to fly or healing powers. I'll probably choose flying!"

"Yes, good one! What else?" she probed.

"For my third and final wish? I am torn; between knowing how to speak every language in the world, and being able to play every instrument in the world. That would be so cool."

"You're right it would! But what ya gonna pick?"

"You know what. I'm going to choose both, and get rid of the money! You can make good money playing music and speaking every language, right?"

"Right! I prefer that answer! Very interesting choices, I'm impressed," she said with a smile. They both smiled at one another before breaking the contact and taking another bite of their sandwiches. "What about if you won the lottery? What would you buy?" It was Cameron's time to ask the question.

"Without doubt the first thing I'd buy is my own book store. I would make it completely unique and everything would be just as I wanted."

"Would you buy Dusty Shelf?"

"No, it would have to be all my own."

"What would you call it? Have you ever thought about it already?"

"Anna's Corner," she said with a smile.

"So you HAVE already thought about it!"

"Maybe a little," she shrugged and giggled.

"What would make it unique?"

"I have a lot of ideas, too many to list."

"Why don't you voice these ideas to your boss now? Or have you and she's not interested."

"Something like that."

"What ideas would you have in your book shop then?" he probed.

"Well to start I would have a little coffee shop inside. So people can have a drink and a bite while they enjoy reading.

And I would host coffee morning book clubs, to attract regular customers, who can bond over their love of reading."

"Wow, Anna those are great ideas! Great ways of driving customers in to your store and a happy place to be, so people will want to come back. I can imagine that book stores around town are dying breeds. These plans would help keep them current and exciting. Now I'm the one who's impressed. It's a shame your boss doesn't listen to your ideas. What else would you buy with your lottery fortune?"

"Thank you, Cam. Ok, I would also buy a nice home for my mum."

"Oh, that's so nice."

"Yeah, with lots of people to help look after her."

"Look after her? What? Is she sick?" he asked sympathetically.

"Yes, she is. She has MS." Cameron looked muddled.

"What is MS?" he said with a tone to indicate he sort of knew.

"Multiple sclerosis; it's a condition that affects her brain and spinal cord. It makes it hard for her to do things. Her body hurts and she gets tired a lot these days." Anna surprised herself with how open she was being.

"That's sound nasty," Cameron sympathised.

"Well along with that she also suffers from dementia. It has gotten worse lately, the doctors say it's Alzheimer's. I see a change in her more and more, as time goes on." A croak replaced the rasp in her voice. She didn't really talk about her mum to people. But she felt comfortable speaking about it with Cameron.

"That's sad to hear. How are you coping?" he asked. No one really ever asked her that.

"My auntie has moved in with us, that's helped a lot. Let's talk about something else though, before I have to head back to work."

"Sure, no problem. Do you have any siblings?" They chatted a while longer, getting to know each other, a little better. Anna looked down at her phone on the table and checked the time. "I need to get back to work. I've had a great time. Maybe I'll bump into you here more often."

"Absolutely, I'm here pretty much every morning," Cameron said with a smile on his face. He paused before she got to her feet. Should he ask for her number? Should he offer her his? "Anna," he stood and locked eyes with her.

"Yes?" she said hooking her coat onto her shoulders.

"Have a great day at work," he copped out. He grit his teeth and lowered his head as she turned away to leave.

"Thanks again." She waved over her shoulder at him and walked out. Cameron grabbed his coat and left not long after.

As he walked home still upbeat from his lunch date, he thought why waste the rest of his day. So he grabbed his phones, from his pocket and called Jeff.

"Jeffro! I've been thinking. Gaming session sounds good. Are you around tonight?"

"I am indeed," he replied with excitement.

"Why don't you come over later? I have something to show you, as it happens," he added.

"I'll text you when I'm on my way," Cameron confirmed before hanging up the phone.

8

Jeffrey Booker

Jeffrey only lived a 10 minute walk from Cameron's apartment. He lived in the house he inherited from his grandmother, and it hadn't been renovated for 40 years. The same dusty maroon plush carpet throughout, which was so worn down that Cameron was certain it used to be a different colour all together. Even the kitchen was the same, although it was so worn away, you could see the flooring underneath in patches. But the worst of all was the bathroom. Avocado painted walls with the bath and basin to match. It was revolting. Cameron felt dizzy sometimes looking at the old, green Aztec style tiles around the bath. Like an optical illusion from another dimension. Jeffrey moved out here to live with his grandma during college after he lost his mum to cancer. He travelled back to London every day. His dad disappeared years before; Jeffrey hadn't seen him since he was little. Fortunately he was a strong individual and in his words, "life goes on". Cameron wanted to move out here, following college. Jeffrey really was a great friend and Cameron trusted him completely, so when a job came available here, Cameron took the leap. He knew he wanted to leave London and get away from his parents.

Jeffrey himself was a tall slender man, with shaggy hair. He looked like he was stuck in the 90's with his bifocal glasses, which had a strong, black frame, made his eyes look ginormous. A real tech wiz; an aura of nostalgia, with a roam of his bedroom, he had a collection of vintage video games, from old arcade machines to consoles from through the years. Online he went by a different handle. He was known as 'Jeffro' on the net. He had dismantled and put back together his PlayStation, when he was just 7 years old. He and his little brother Tomas were creating firewalls and encryption codes by the time they were teenagers.

It was dark out now, as Cameron arrived.

"Come on in man, you want a drink? Tea, coffee, beer?" Jeffro uttered as Cameron came in.

"Yeah, sure, I'll take a beer," he replied as he took his coat and shoes off. He then followed Jeffro down a dingy corridor, to a brightly lit kitchen. Jeffro didn't smoke, but the kitchen walls and ceiling were stained yellow. This was from years of tobacco smoke, when Jeffro's grandmother and her friends, chained smoked in that room. The pair exchanged pleasantries and both gave the "same old" reply to "how's things". Before Jeffro moved onto more pressing matters. In his opinion.

"Follow me to the study, pal. I wanted to tell you about this over the phone last night, but you know... you don't know who's listening." As he led Cameron back down the poorly lit hallway and into an even more poorly lit study room, Cameron saw the excitement building in Jeffro. His shoulders were raised and he rubbed his hands together. He turned to look at

Cameron and held one arm out to display what looked to be a very old and dusty computer. The mouse and keyboard were eggshell white, along with the monitor. The screen was barely 10 inches. It was deeper than it was wide.

"What am I looking at here, Jeff?" Cameron asked confused. Dejected, Jeffro puffed out some air in frustration.

"That is a Maghurt F4 50," he replied. It dawned on Cameron; Jeff had been talking about it for years. "This may not look like much to any Tom, Dick or Harry, but if I can programme this right, then I will be able to link to any computer in the world." Cameron squinted as he stared blankly at this machine. He had heard rumours online of its capability, but always assumed it was hear-say. Something said by nerds to catch some nerdy high.

"Where did you get it? How much did you pay for it?" Cameron quizzed, as he processed about 100 thoughts at once. Surely Jeff had been scammed, surely this thing wasn't real?

"I can get anything on the black market, I used an alias, and routed through several different servers to find it. But then I did. And I had to have it!" Money was no object for Jeffro after inheriting his grandmother's house and all of her life savings. He also earned good money as an I.T consultant, which surprisingly came with very little work load and was mainly contract work.

Cameron was very impressed. He wanted to know if it would work. "What do you plan to do with it? Spy on people?" Cameron asked unsupportively.

"What? No! Of course not; I just want to see what it's capable of, and you know... one day... you never know... we might need it." Cameron always thought although Jeff was incredibly smart and kind; he did live in his own little cyber conspiracy world. He left him to it because he was never harming anyone.

"Well this is really cool, when are you going to get to work on it?"

"This weekend, I wanted to show you first."

"I can't wait to see it working. You'll have to keep me posted."

"Yeah, I will. Anyway, any chicks on the go? You haven't had a girlfriend since Lucy at college, although you did well to get out of that one. She was psycho!" Cameron laughed awkwardly.

"Actually, I met a girl. Anna. She's pretty cool. Still early though."

"That's great mate, I feel you've been a little detached recently, but it's great to catch up. Let's not leave it so long next time."

As Cameron walked home in the cold, he felt warm inside. The night sky was jet black and the stars beamed brightly. He had had a brilliant day, the best he'd had in ages. He hadn't thought about his dreams all day. Guess he didn't need to when his day had been occupied. As he yawned walking up the stairs to his front door, he did start to wonder what adventures he would come across tonight, in the land of nod.

9

Clown Birthday

There were red and blue balloons in each corner of the room, with an arch over the door in matching colours. A food spread of all of Cam's favourite party snacks, on the kitchen island. These included sausage rolls, mini pizzas, chicken sticks and samosas. Not forgetting the range of mini desserts; cupcakes, cheesecakes, brownies just to name a few. A banner hung high above the TV in scripted 'Welcome to Cam's Birthday'. Upbeat orchestra music was playing softly across the room. Cam had a brand new chequered shirt on; red and black and grey skinny jeans. He felt really smart.

People began to arrive with gifts of wine and other booze. There were party games for everyone to play, such as penis ring toss; where players wore a blow-up dick around their waist while other players threw rings around it. Balloon belts; which players wore while other players used their bodies to burst the balloons. Of course, beer pong set up on the dining table, oh! and giant Jenga. Cam mingled and laughed with his guests, making sure everyone had a drink on the go, when there was a knock at the door.

The guests gathered in a huddle as Cam opened the door. Before him in the doorway stood two clowns, Cam leant forward with excitement, a huge beaming smile on his face. Clowns were his favourite growing up. His mum and dad always hired a clown on his birthday. These clowns had bright green hair, smiles painted wide across their faces. Big red bow tight finished off the green and white waist coat and ginormous red shows, that balled at the toes. The clowns sauntered around the room performing tricks and making balloon animals for individuals, before setting up for an act to put on for the party.

Everyone gathered round on chairs to watch the show. There was a red curtain at the back of the staging area, with golden glitter scattered across the floor in front.

"Well hello there everyone! We're Ernie and Burnie! Don't ask him how he got his name! Just remember never play with matches! And definitely don't use them for a clown performance!" Jolly party music played as the two clowns bumbled out from behind the curtain.

"Wow, I sure am hungry," Ernie jested to Burnie.

"Here, take my lunch, Ern." Burnie handed him a can and winked at the audience.

"Mmm, nuts! My favourite." POP! Snakes shoot out the can and hit Ernie square in the face. "Hey, Burnie! You tricked me!" he grumped as the crowd laughed. "Very funny prank. Kudos, very funny. Here would you like some cheese?" handing Burnie a box labelled 'Stinky Cheese'. Burnie slid the box open and a giant plastic spider pinged out; nipping Burnie's finger.

The two clowns laughed hysterically with one another. The audience was in stitches too. Cam sat with both hands on his knees, rocking back and forth laughing. Both clowns turned and looked at Cam when their laughter started to sound more sinister. Then lightning struck outside. Cam turned to look out the window. Black skies and rain were out there. The music stopped as he turned back to face the room. The clowns' smiles were now frowns. He turned his head even further to notice all of his guests were gone.

The room turned very gloomy and cold; Cam could see his breath out in front of him. He sank low into his chair, his arms hanging beside him. He wanted to stand but he found it extremely hard to move his body. He could move his head but it feels like slow motion. Now Ernie and Burnie stumbled towards him, with tilted heads. Both their eyes glued to Cam. They seemed to be moving in slow motion as well. Cam dropped his head to avoid eye contact, before lifting it to his right and seeing the window again. He felt his chair slowly pulling towards the window; thunder and lightning ignited the room every few seconds. Sound of evil cackles could be heard from the clowns. Cam was now completely paralysed, his body felt so heavy, as he breathed deeply to try and remain calm. He was dragged across the room until his face was pressed up against the window. It was freezing, he felt as though his face was fusing to the glass. He started to feel his hands coming to life; he could clutch them. Shortly after he felt warmth coursing through his arms, he could lift them. Pushing against the wall he tried to free his face, but he was still fixed against the cold pane.

The storm settled outside. Cam's face detached itself from the glass, leaving a printed smudge outlining his forehead, nose, lips and chin. Cam searched the room but there was no sign of the clowns. What had just happened? He looked across the room and saw the impression left on the window, by his face. He slowly approached until he could see his reflection in the window. He leant in and the reflection of his face perfectly aligned with the imprint. Just then a huge flash of lightning sparked behind the glass, thunder rumbling a second behind. The image of Cam's reflection was replaced by Anna's outside and the smeared face on the glass came to life. The face levitated towards Cam and he heard a woman's voice eerily echo through the walls, "You don't belong here! We don't want you here!"

Cam was frozen with the printed face still drifting towards him. He couldn't move; he couldn't stop it, so he just closes hid eyes until it met his face. He let out a loud gasp as the face imprinted back on to Cam's face.

The gasp woke him. He was sweating in bed and disorientated. He was confused for a few seconds, wondering where he was. He launched himself up into the seated position before realising. What was that dream all about? He hadn't had a nightmare in months. What brought that on? Why was Anna there? Did this mean anything? So many questions raced through his mind. How irritating to have a horrible dream; after having such a great day. Then Cameron wondered if that had anything to do with it? Surely not.

It was 3AM. He took off his sweat drenched vest and threw it on the ground before flopping back down and sinking his head into his pillows. He rolled onto his side and hoped for no more horrors. He closed his eyes.

The next morning Cameron was in a foul mood. He couldn't get last night's nightmare off his mind. He pottered around his flat, doing some of his chores. He got carried away yesterday and forgot to wash his work clothes. He stuck a load in the machine before making himself a cuppa; he didn't often drink tea but home coffee just wasn't the same as Maicon's. He tried to distract himself from thinking about the nightmare he'd had to endure, last night. He texted Jeffro to see if he had had any luck with the Maghurt F4-50. He tried to remember if Anna said if she worked Sundays. Was a little shop like that even open today? He wouldn't find out moping around the house, so finished his tea and jumped in the shower.

Cameron grabbed his umbrella before heading out. Not to make the same mistake twice and got caught in the rain again. When he got to Maicon's he couldn't see Anna inside and there weren't many people there at all right now. Cameron looked down at his watch. It's 10:21. Surely the book shop would be open by now, if it was opening at all today. He made the short walk from Maicon's to the Dusty Shelf book shop. He saw on approach that no one was there, all the lights were off. As he got closer he saw the CLOSED sign hanging in the door.

Feeling like a wasted journey, he turned back, when he heard someone calling his name.

"Cam! Cam!" he thought to himself that could only be Anna. Or it was the barista from Maicon's. No one else called him that. He turned around and saw Anna waving at him from outside the Dusty Shelf entrance. Cameron picked up a light jog to meet her. "What are you doing here? Looking for a book?" she chuckled to herself.

"Actually I was looking for you. Wasn't sure if you were working today."

"Yep, every Sunday. But the store doesn't open 'til 11," she began chatting away. Cameron zoned her out. His gaze was distracted away from hers. It created a flash back of seeing her face in the window last night. He shook it off just in time to reply to her. He cleared his throat. "Anyway, I was just heading to town and thought I'd say hello." He dropped eye contact with her once more.

"Oh right, well, hello!" she smiled and ducked her head to try and catch his eyes again.

"Well, have a great day at work. See you around."

"Thanks, have a great day off," she replied as he turned to walk away. "Cam!" she snapped. He turned to face her.

"Yes?"

"Could I take your number? Maybe I can text you this evening when I'm done with work." Cameron froze, something felt off. Was it the lingering fog in his thought about last night's nightmare? Did he blame Anna for the horrible scenes that filled his subconscious reality? This was silly of course it wasn't because of her.

"Absolutely, drop me a message later." His cheeks blushed as he typed the digits into her phone.

"Great, I will. See ya."

"See ya."

That cheered him up a little. He walked back toward Maicon's, checking his phone along the way. Still no message back from Jeffro. He was usually very prompt with his replies. There was however a message from Cameron's mum. The same 'checking in to see if everything was ok' text once a month, to then not hear from her again for 30 days. He in turn replied with the same 'Everything is well, hope all is well with you and dad'. Now to grab a latte and get on with the rest of the day; the rain stayed away, typically as he had his umbrella.

As Cameron tucked into his jacket potato, with beans and cheese, his phone buzzed on the arm of his chair. An unknown number had texted him. He took a large fork full of spud before resting his cutlery down on his lap tray and lifting his phone up. He thought surely it had to be Anna. It was!

"Hey, Loser! It's Anna. See I told you I would text you! Hope you've enjoyed your day as much as I have! Text me back and I'll tell you all about it xx."

He smiled and locked his phone. He'd reply once he finished his food.

After dinner Cameron felt so stuffed. He cleared up the cooking trays and washed up the dishes; grabbing himself a chocolate mousse from the fridge, on his way back to his armchair. Later that evening Cameron woke up slouched in the chair. Yogurt pot still rested in his grasp. Feeling lost and groggy he grabbed his phone and took himself straight to bed; completely forgetting about texting Anna back.

Crawling into bed he hoped to God that tonight would be a good dream. It had to be after what he went through the previous evening.

10

A Day at the Beach

The sun was shining and the weather was sweet. 2 eggs, 3 bacon, a sausage, hash brown and baked beans occupied Cam's morning breakfast plate. A cold glass of OJ on the side. A latte for after. What a perfect way to start the day! Cam looked out the cafe window, with the sun beaming through the panes, igniting the whole restaurant with an orange glaze. Cars searched for places to park up and down the road. Families frantically unpacking copious amounts of luggage from their boots. Seagulls flocked at lamppost height and quarking nonstop in unison. Cam could smell the crisp sea breeze creeping in through the front door. Accompanied with the seagull's mew bellowing through the streets. Across the road slowly being packed out by holiday goers, was a long, pebbled beach which stretched 3 miles long. Cam was in Brighton!

Taking a stroll down the beach front to walk off his hefty breakfast, Cam was enjoying the views and the weather very much. As he quickly approached the famous Brighton Pier, Cam sensed someone was following him. He had that all too familiar feeling that someone's eyes were fixed on him. He stopped abruptly and slowly scanned his surroundings, but there was nothing out of the ordinary. Some kids playing with their parents, laughing and screaming, on the beach to Cam's left. There was an old couple out for a stroll on the opposite side of the road, but they were minding their own business. Straight ahead there was a group of teenagers, roller skating, but they were off in the same direction as Cam. And behind him there was just a dog, a retriever with a long golden coat. He was about 30 metres back, sitting like a good boy. He was probably waiting for his owner to come out from the kiosk nearby. Cam shrugged off this feeling of being watched and continued on his walk.

Inside the pier Cam played all the games in the arcade, collecting as many tokens as possible. He sat on the 2p slots for ages, trying to make the towers fall. He went from basketball hoops to whack-a-mole, then on to ring toss. He also jumped on the simulated motorbikes. But his favourite was the Down the Clown! He loved launching the balls at the little clowns. He got himself a book, a keychain and a photo frame, with 'Brighton' bowed over the top and 'Pier' across the bottom, and he still had enough tokens left to get some sweets. After all that fun Cam was dying for a drink, but as he left the arcade he saw that same dog again, the golden retriever, sitting at the end of the pier. As if he was sitting and waiting for Cam. Cautiously Cam approached the dog. He held his hand out for the dog to sniff but the dog swiftly turned and walked away. How strange, Cam thought to himself but not letting it dampen his day he ignored it and strolled further down the beach front, to find a drink. Ice cold lemonade quenched his thirst. He downed a third of the bottle before looking at the bottle and releasing a refreshed, "AHH!"

In the shop next door they sold fun novelty beach toys. This was definitely worth a look. He came out with bat and ball, an oversized football, a bag of tennis balls and a rubber ring round his stomach. Ready to hit the beach Cam looked down the road which he'd come from. There it was again! The dog was back again! Only this time he had a friend, a tall black and brown Doberman with fierce pointed ears. What was going on? Cam asked himself. He shook it off and restarted his walk along the beach. Every couple of minutes he would stop and look back, and there the dogs would be. Just sitting and looking. They must have been following Cam, as they were the same distance from him every time he looked. So Cam tried to catch them out by stopping and looking quicker, but every time they were just sitting and watching. Cam brought himself to another abrupt halt. He slowly crouched down and pretended to tie his shoe lace; he then sharply turned his head, around the corner and caught the golden retriever, with one foot in-front of the other. "Ah-ha!" he calls out "Saw ya!" when Cam noticed two more dogs were on his trail. A black and white Springer spaniel and a brown and white Jack Russell had joined the pack following.

Finally Cam found a spot where he wanted to set up camp for the day, on the beach. But now Cam had 7 dogs on his tail and he needed find out why. So he decided to make contact with the group. He was a little apprehensive at first, as some of the dogs looked pretty mean. He squatted down to eye level with the golden retriever. "Are you the boss here?" he asked. The dog locked eyes with Cam and his left eye brow rose. The dog's head tilted to one side. "Where are your owners? Why are you here?" Cam was asking questions to an animal who could not answer him back. "Right! Well, would you like to come to the beach with me?" the dog's mouth opened and he began to pant, but within that pant Cam saw a smile. "Come on then, let's go to the beach."

As Cam stepped out on the pebbles of Brighton beach the stones underneath the pressure of his foot burst into sand. And then in a rapid wave every pebble on the beach burst into dark golden brown sand. Cam watched in amazement. As he looked up from the newly laid sand he noticed all the people on the beach slowly vanishing. The families, the cute couples, the elderly groups, everyone was gone. It was just Cam and the dogs.

He pushed the rubber ring down his body and stepped out of it. A little King Charles spaniel curled up inside the ring and dozed off. Laying a towel out on the sand, Cam sat, he brought his knees up to his chest and wrapped his arms around them while he looked out on the open sea. The golden retriever plodded up to his left side and Cam put his arm around the dog and scratched his ear. Some of the other dogs lay close by while some others snuffled their noses in the sand. Two of the bigger dogs went exploring the beach, looking for signs of other life. There was no sign of anyone else. Cam brushed sand off their snouts when they returned to him. Cam jumped to his feet, lifted his arms high in the air, arching his back and stretched his whole body out. He dropped his arms sharply, patted his hands on his hips and began to undress, down to his yellow and black flowery swimming shorts.

"Gather round, gather round," Cam looked left and right huddling the dogs around him with his arms. "On the count of 3 we all run and jump into the sea! Ready? One.. Two.. Ahhhh." Cam bolted towards the water prompting the dogs to follow him a moment after. They all sprinted through the low waves, before a bigger wave crashed Cam in the torso. While the dogs leapt elegantly into the strong water. Cam swam around with the dogs, throwing balls around for them to retrieve.

What was that!? Cam looked frantically around him, the dogs oblivious to any distraction. Cam was sure he saw something swim past him. He speedily tried to gather the dogs. Calling them out of the water. He swam back to shore and looked out at the now calm water. He scanned for over a minute and then he saw something! It was the Doberman! Cam desperately tried to call him out of the water but to no avail. So Cam decided he had to go in and get him. "Stay here everyone!" Cam swam as quickly as he could out to the Doberman, who looked frantic when he reached him. "Wooah boy! What is it?" Cam noticed that the Doberman kept looking past him over his left shoulder. Treading water at this point Cam slowly turned to see what was there. Focusing on the bobbing water, the sun making it harder to see, he squinted his eyes and saw a few air bubbles surface the water about 10 metres away. The Doberman hid behind Cam, clinging to his back to stay afloat. The air bubbles hit the surface of the water again, just this time much closer to Cam, when he saw a pair of black eyes emerge and two round nostrils shortly after. Then a whole head appeared just a few feet from Cam, followed by a leathery grey body. It was a seal, the dogs of the sea. "Don't fear the seal," Cam said to the cowering Doberman, "come and say hi." So the Doberman cautiously let go of Cam and swam around beside him, and waited for the seal to come closer. They touched noses and the tension dropped. Cam wondered if there were any other animals out there.

Cam swam around the sea for hours with the dogs on the search for other creatures, as well as walking the beach front.

They came across a variety of animals that joined the quest for other companions. There was a bale of turtles, a fever of stingrays, and a pod of dolphins and of course a colony of seals. They stumbled across a herd of walrus as well, but they weren't as friendly as the others, so Cam kept his distance from them. Cam surfed the waves on the back of the dolphins. Deep dived with the turtles and the dogs became best buds with the seals. Life was good.

However through the midst of everything, a persistent thought in the back of Cam's mind was telling him of danger ahead; he sensed sharks and crocodiles in these waters. He had to keep on the move to avoid these dangerous creatures and he had to keep the others safe. He could see shadows lingering in the distant water. It had to be the sharks. But as long as he and the dogs kept moving they didn't swim any closer. "Beware those sharks and crocs," Cam shouted every time one of the animals stopped swimming or playing.

The thought of the dangerous creatures swimming nearby, started to startle the dogs. They kept stopping to stare and every time they did the shark and croc silhouettes stopped their casual circling and began to dart towards Cam and the others. This became too risky now and Cam decided it was time to leave the sea. He circled up the dogs and they said goodbye to the other animals but as they dawdled around the sharks found time to approach and corner the group.

A dim ringing started to echo through Cam's head, he shook it off and made a plan. He decided to sacrifice himself and hopefully create a diversion long enough for the dogs to make their exit from the water. "I'll swim out and left and you guys wait here. They'll come for you. But on my signal I'll stop, turning their attention to me, and that's your window to go!" Everyone knew their assignment. But just as Cam was about to swim another sound started to rattle in his head, just this time louder and higher. He battled through the pain from the screech and he started to swim. The dogs waited and the shark and crocs hustled closer to them, when Cam gave his signal. The sharks sharply turned their attention to Cam and the dogs swam to safety. Once Cam saw the dogs all safely on the beach he started to swim back but this time the sharks didn't stop when he started.

They were after him now and nothing was going to stop them from this free meal. Cam matched the sharks stride for stride. He was managing to get away when the screeching in his head rang through his ears again. This time it was unbearable; he couldn't swim through this pain. He clutched his hands to his head, his eyes screwed shut from the pain. He was afloat in the salty ocean with an entire shiver of sharks fast approaching. Cam composed himself, released his head from the shackle of his grasp and looked out on the incoming threat, ready for their dinner. The excruciating sound still roaring through his head but he accepted his fate and braced for impact as the sharks swam ever closer. The shadows in the water, were no more. Now Cam could see the sharks clear as day, mouth unlatched, teeth exposed. Cam locked eyes with the shark as the ringing in his head was now white noise. It was Cam's alarm clock. This was a dream. All he had to do was wake up. In the blink of an eye he was no longer staring down a fatal end but his dusty ceiling fan.

What a thrill that was! A truly wonderful dream to see out the weekend. Cameron shut off his alarm and gave himself a few minutes to take in and reminisce on the great adventure he had just had. But he couldn't ignore the fact that it was

Monday morning and he had to go back to work. It was time to face the music. He had to face Mr Kyriakos today; he would surely want to have that performance review.

Cameron pulled the covers off himself and sat on the edge of his bed. He rubbed his face forcefully, waking himself up and stretching his legs out in front. He got to his feet and cracked on. After his triple S routine; shit, shower and shave, he spent the morning thinking about his trip to Brighton last night and other amazing adventures he had over the years, in his dreams. It distracted him from the inevitable. But eventually it was time to head to work. A quick pit stop at Maicon's on his route, where he bumped into Jeffro with a carrier bag full of shopping.

"Morning Jeff!" Cameron said sounding chipper.

"You sound like you're in a good mood."

"Yeah, I guess I am. What you got there? Healthy meal prep?" Cameron joked. Jeffro smirked and looked down at the white plastic bag he was gripping in his fist. The handles had become thin stretched and were digging into the palms of his hands.

"This? Just some handy bits and bobs and snacks to fuel me through the week." Cameron knew there wasn't anything healthy in that bag. He assumed Jeff hadn't eaten a single vegetable since he was left living on his own. His kitchen cupboards were always filled to the brim of pot noodles, packets of crisps and multi packs of party sized chocolate bars, and the man lived off canned energy drinks. How he was so slim still was astounding.

"I need to head to work, but catch up with you soon?" Cameron insisted.

"Absolutely, catch ya later." Jeff reached his other hand up in a fist, which Cameron reciprocated, and touched fists with him.

Jeffro threw his keys on an antique table which sat on its lonesome in his hallway; chucking his jacket over a rickety looking banister at the foot of the stairs. He unpacked the shopping onto his kitchen side. Cameron was right, packs of crisps and cookies was hardly a balanced diet. He also had interrogate looking tools; pliers and screw drivers, along with blank CDs and 5 rolls of red electrical tape, which he pushed to one side, stuffing the food into the kitchen cupboards. He flicked on the kitchen light and collected the bits off the side, taking them through to his office.

There was mess everywhere, like a mechanics work shop, only electrical components everywhere not grease and car parts. There were crushed cans of energy drinks, of all different flavours sprawled around the room. Empty snack wrappers overflowed a wire tin bin, by the desk. The desk itself covered in separate pages of notes, spread out around the monitor of the Maghurt F4:50 which lay on its back, in the middle of the table. Jeff cracked a split in the blinds to allow some natural light in, opening the window slightly to let some fresh air in, and the musky stale smell out. He sprayed a couple blasts of his cheap deodorant, that he had acquired as a gift last Christmas. It was still going strong almost a year later. Grabbing some of the notes off the table, he cracked a can of drink, slumped down on his office chair, leant back and slammed his feet up on the desk.

"Right! Let's get to this," he said softly, kicking his feet down and finishing off the last few drops of liquid; crushing the can in his hand and tossing it onto a nearby filing cabinet. Another day of work on the computer was about to commence.

11

Return to Work

8:45 on the dot, Cameron could see Jane perched at receptions as he approached the front door. One deep breath in before opening the office door. "Morning, Jane."

"Oh, Cameron dear, good morning," Jane called out as she looked up from her desk. "How are you feeling today? All better I hope."

"Much better," Cameron replied as he jotted down his name on the staff sign in sheet. "Is 'erm, Mr Kyriakos in yet?" "Yes dear, he's in his office."

"Great, thanks." He laid the pen down on the clip board and gave an eye brow raising smile toward Jane. She in turn tilted her head a little and screwed her face up smiling back at him. "Just get on with things as normal, keep yourself to yourself and keep your head down." Cameron thought to himself.

"Cameron!" boomed across the office. "Cameron could you come into my office, right away!" Well that lasted long. Cameron threw his coat over the pegs on the rack and walked over to drop his bag on his desk. "Better get this over with," Cameron said under his breath.

Although most of the office was alit with natural sunlight, shining through the tall glass windows, Mr Kyriakos' office wasn't as well lit. He had two small windows behind his office chair and one L.E.D office style bulb on the ceiling. He had a big oak desk in the middle of the room, covered in files and paperwork. Some people would say this was organised mess, but knowing Mr Kyriakos it was all just carnage. Probably mostly work in which he'd ask for, and then moaned he never received it. In the corner of the room he had a coffee machine on top of a fridge. He spent a lot of time in this office. He wouldn't socialise with the others in the staff break room. He only left his office to lurch around the main office, demanding work to be done.

"Good morning, Mr Kyriakos. You wanted to see me?" "Yes, come in and close the door, will you." Cameron closed the door, closed his eyes and gave himself a second, before opening his eyes, putting a smile on his face and turning to face his boss. "Take a seat. We just need to go through this sickness report and sign off that you're fit to return to work. Shouldn't take more than 5 minutes, then you can go back and carry on with your work."

Just a return to work form! No bother, no bother at all to Cameron. Had Mr Kyriakos completely forgotten he wanted to have a performance meeting with Cameron today? It wouldn't be the first time. Perhaps he was just delaying it until later. Make Cameron ponder on it a while.

Cameron decided it was a good idea to keep his head down and crack on with his work for the rest of the day. Every time Mr

Kyriakos left his office, he would catch Cameron glancing over. Cameron would quickly look away to look busy. Hours went by and Cameron remained unbothered by his highly critical boss. Cameron found himself clock watching throughout the day. He was sure if Mr Kyriakos didn't say anything today then that would be the end of it and Cameron would have got away with it, and avoid any performance review- for now at least.

The clock struck 4pm. Mr Kyriakos emerged from his office once more, carrying a mug of hot coffee. He took a sip and pursed his lips tight together. He scans the floor, inspecting that all was well and everyone was still working hard. He then potters around the office breathing heavy and glugging his coffee. "Good work ladies," he called out to Sara and Leah. He plodded over to Josh's desk and stood between him and Cameron.

"Josh my boy! Keeping busy with those clients? Make sure you let the London office know about Morgan & Filmon. They're hosting them next week. I'll be going up there as well. So make sure everything is arranged."

"Absolutely, Sir. I have already emailed the London office. The wheels are certainly in motion," Josh replied with some confidence.

"Good!" Mr Kyriakos boomed in a commanding voice, "Very Good!" He turned to look at Cameron. Cameron's eyes fixed on his computer screen. He could feel the sweaty heat coming off Mr Kyriakos' fat belly and he could smell the coffee stench on his breath. "Cameron," he said snappily and nodding his head once before leaving them to it and returning to his office.

"What's all this about London next week?" Cameron asked Josh.

"He told us all on Friday. Morgan & Filmon are sending representatives to the London office for 3 days. They're one of our biggest clients and they're doing all sorts of events with our big boys. I think we are planning on putting on a big show for them too."

"Wow, sounds like a big deal. I've had contact with Morgan & Filmon over the years. They became a client shortly after I joined Harpers. They're a great company to work for; or so it's said."

"Well rumour is that we were all invited to go to London but Mr Kyriakos declined that offer and is just going by himself. Whether that's true or not remains to be known." Cameron sat there staring at Mr Kyriakos' office door. That probably is true. That is the kind of man he was. He never looked out for this team. He never encouraged progression and never promoted opportunity. He would take all the glory for his office's performance. He selfishly hid the team away, when the big bosses occasionally visited from London. Restricting his subordinates' face time with those important folk and taking credit for their ideas; offering them up as his own. Cameron stared and stared, eyes fixed firmly on his boss' door. He daydreamed walking up to the door, barging into that office and demanding to know if these rumours were true. He pictured yelling at his boss and telling him exactly what he thought of him. But Cameron snapped out of the trance and averted his gaze towards the clock. It was 4:47pm, time to gather his things and head on home.

On his walk home, Cameron kept revisiting the idea of him and the team heading to London. It could be fun and beneficial. A chance to learn more about the business and meet some important people. But on the other hand it would be a lot of hard work. Getting to know new people and having to suffer the endless small talk. Also he'd have to spend an awful lot of time with his work colleagues and this seemed like a lot of effort. If he cared more about this job then he would be upset on missing an opportunity like this. But he didn't. So no biggie.

As Cameron climbed the stairs to his flat, fumbling with his keys, it dawned on him that he hadn't replied to Anna's message! How rude of him. Was it too late to now? He could lie and say he'd been too busy. Maybe he should just wait until he bumped into her again; play it cool. For now he was starving. So he'd wait 'til after tea to decide. Winding down the evening was Cameron's favourite part of the day. Soon he would be off on another adventure and he couldn't wait. Who knew brushing your teeth could bring so much excitement. He stared at himself in the mirror as he manoeuvred the electric brush around his mouth, excitement building up inside of him. He leant down to the sink as he spit and rinse. Then took one last look in the mirror, raising a smile and headed for bed.

Today wasn't so bad in all honesty. Nowhere near as bad as he'd first imagined. He'd gotten away with things at work but now it was time to start living, in the figments of his subconscious imagination.

12

The Heist

"Gather round, I won't be repeating myself. We have one shot at this, but follow my instruction exactly and we will all be very rich, by the day is out." Stood in what looked like a half-built office block, all open plan, no windows had been put in yet. Concrete pillars flowed through the structure throughout the building. Clear tarpaulin laced the door ways, some blowing around in the light breeze. There were tools and materials scattered around the place. Camp chairs were set up in a cluster and wooden pallets lay across matching trestle legs, to form a make shift table; blue prints and binders laid out across it.

Cam gave out instruction. There were 11 people involved in the operation, with Cam leading things. "These 3 companies have been getting rich off the backs of the little people. Poor pay for labour, avoiding taxes and they have no regard for safety. They have blood on their hands and they couldn't give two shits about it." The companies that Cam was referring to, run by Mr Thatcher, Mr Cameron and Mr Johnson are illegally buying land, building tall office buildings and selling the estates to large corporate businesses. "It comes to an end today. I have inside information that each company is moving high amounts of cash and damning documents, to a secret location. These transfers are being made at 3 different times, from 3 different locations but to 1 same destination; a shipping container at the docks. Once it leaves the docks, there is nothing we can do. So we don't hit them on the move. We hit them when they're there, at the docks." Cam went on to explain that his source, is to be kept nameless, but is highly involved in these illegal operations. They have given detailed descriptions of the vans being used for this mission.

In the team there were three get away drivers- Ronnie, Tramp and Carlisle. There were also 3 decoy drivers- Arietta, Clark and Milo. Then there were two tech engineers- Jazz and Clara, who were running systems at base and communicating responses with the team. And lastly Tom and Tommo, two experienced con men. No one was even sure that Tom was their real name. They would join Cam in engaging with the enemy and recovering the goods. The plan was airtight. Now time to execute it.

The two Toms and Cam had identified the workers being used on the container. They dropped a sedative in each of their coffees, before stripping their uniforms and being there in their stead. Cam and the two Toms helped load the containers throughout the day. No-one from the company's organisation suspected a thing. The six drivers all made their way to a hidden location, less than a mile from the dock. They had identical vehicles to the three being used for the drop offs. Jazz and Clara stalked each drop off and its route; keeping the team involved up to date. Each van just had one driver. The two Toms radioed over once the last drop had been made. But the container was still being guarded by three heavily armed men. Cam radioed over to Ronnie "move in now". Cam then radioed Jazz back at base "Block all radio connection from now. Everyone, you know what to do."

Ronnie, Tramp and Carlisle drove the vans round to the docks in tandem. The guards waved them to a halt; one of them approached Ronnie's van, which was at the front of the convoy. "What's going on?" the guard asked.

"Ask him," Ronnie replied, pointing at Mr Thatcher sitting in the passenger seat.

"Move aside lad, there has been a security breach. We're transporting everything to a second safe location for now," Mr Thatcher instructed. He was Cam's inside man all along.

"Start loading the vans and I'll radio Mr Johnson to confirm all this." The guard turned and nodded at the other guards to open the container. The guard walked 10 yards away and tried to radio to the other company heads, but he couldn't get through to anyone. He looked back at the team loading everything into vans, and Mr Thatcher smiled at him. Something didn't seem right, he tried to radio through again but nothing was working. "Stop!" he yelled. "Stop! I can't get through on the radio," the guard told Mr Thatcher.

"How strange!" Mr Thatcher assumed. "Here let me get through to them on the phone." As he lifted his phone to his ear Cam and the two Toms sneaked up behind each guard and sank a syringe into their necks, simultaneously and injecting them with a sedative, rendered them helpless. They continued to load the van.

All six vans departed the docks together. One of the guards came round just as he saw the crew of cars off in the distance.

He pulled himself together and shook off the foggy feeling in his head. He grabbed the radio and tried it again, it worked.

"CODE RED! I repeat CODE RED! Mr Thatcher has taken everything. Three vans are heading east."

As the convoy made its way down busy streets Tramp who was in the back vehicle noticed a tail. "A black civic is on our six, people. It's been with us for a few miles."

"Our drone has picked up 2 more," Clara informed. "Looks like Mr Cameron and Mr Johnson's men."

"Stay in single file until my signal," Cam demanded, riding in the middle vehicle with Ronnie. "We wait until all 3 of them are on us. Then we split. They'll have to choose which of us to follow. Then we pray." They all continued their neat formation when Clara let them know all 3 chasing cars were close. "Now SPLIT!" All 6 vans broke rank immediately, some diverting down side roads, one screeching a hard turn and going back the way they came, and one continued on route. The chasing pack had to make a quick decision whom to follow. It was pot luck. One civic continued straight. The second car followed a van that veered off right and the last turned and went back the way they came, this was Cam and Ronnie and they had goods in the back.

"Who still has a tail?" Cam radioed to everyone. Clark and Milo responded, "Both decoy vans, which are empty. That's a result."

"Keep them busy as long as you can, we don't want them to find out you're both decoys. Tramp and Carlisle get your vans to the safe drop as soon as possible. Ronnie and I will try to shake these and meet you there when safe to do so."

After miles of high speed chasing, Cam and Ronnie took a turn down a dead end side road. There was access from the other end but there was a gated fence half way down. Ronnie looked over his shoulder, planning to reverse. But they were being blocked in. Cam took a moment to think.

"What do we do?" Ronnie frantically asked. "We need a plan now or we're dead." Cam looked out around the van. There were back entrances to restaurants up and down the road, and big dumpster bins outside. There were tall building blocks either side of them, with flats above the shops. Each flat connected by a fire escape stair case. If they made a run for it that meant leaving the merchandise in the van.

"How many do you see in the car?" Cam asked Ronnie while staring out the window into the van wing mirrors. Ronnie checked his rear view mirror. "I think there's four. Two in the front and two in the back."

"The lock on the van doors are all secure and there's a two inch thick bar across the inside of the back door. They can't access the back from this cab either. It'll take them at least 10 minutes to break in. I have a plan, break off the steering wheel." Ronnie removed the steering wheel while Cam gave his further instruction. "Stuff that wheel down the back of my trousers. Let's go!" Cam opened his van door and was met with immediate gun fire. He held out a black white piece of paper as a sign of surrender and the gun shots ceased.

"Step out of the van with your hands above your head!" a gun man called out. Cam did just that, scanning his surroundings as he did. 6 feet down the road, there was an open door, hidden behind a huge silver garbage bin and out of sight of the gunmen, who were stood about 10 metres further down the road. Cam slowly stepped towards the car, hands aloft high above his head. "Unlock the van!" they demanded. Cam stopped walking when he reached the back of the van. He turned his head right to look at the lock and then made a darted run for the open restaurant door.

"You two chase him down and bring him back!" the driver of the civic instructed. "You come with me. The driver is still inside. Let's take the van." Two of the gunmen followed into the restaurant in pursuit of Cam and the remaining two men approached the driver side door of the van. In formation they prised the van door open and each pointed their guns at Ronnie.

"Put your hands in the air!" Ronnie slowly lifted his hands revealing the empty space, where the van's steering wheel was meant to be. "Fuck! Right, get out the van! Open the back!"

Cam had run through the restaurant and out the other side onto a main road. The pavement was crowded with pedestrians. He turned right and saw an old lady walking into her flat door, about 15 metres down, which was locked by a pin pad. He sprinted to the door as it closed behind the old lady. He reached out his arm and jammed it between the door and frame, just in time, before it closed. He pulled the door open and looked back through the crowd to see for the chasing men. They were walking briskly through the pack of people looking all around to try and catch a sight of Cam. He quickly entered the flats and closed the door, before standing up straight with his back up against the hall way wall. He looked out the front doors and saw the two men wander past, still searching for him and oblivious to his whereabouts.

"Excuse me. What floor do you live on?" Cam called out to the old lady, who is now waiting for the lift.

"Second," she replied.

"And do you have a fire exit in your flat?"

"I do."

"Perfect," Cam muttered to himself with a grin on his face.

Back at the van, Ronnie was pinned up against the side of the van. He explained to the two gunmen that he didn't have the key to the van. They believed him as he didn't flinch when they pressed their guns against his head. They tied Ronnie's hands behind his back and pushed him down to the floor.

"Wait there!" one man screamed, while the other made haste back to the car. He returned with tools, ready to break into the back of the van. They got to work by drilling through the lock. This wasn't easy to break but they got it done. The door still wouldn't open.

"Why won't it open?" they asked Ronnie, who was still sat on the floor. He refused to answer.

"Why won't it open!?" they screamed as they struck him across the face with the handle of their gun.

"There is a steel bar across the door inside." The two men looked at each other to think.

"We are going to have the saw through the roof."

"I wouldn't do that if I was you," Cam said after sneaking up behind them. He hit them each across the face with the van's steering wheel, knocking them unconscious. He pulled Ronnie to his feet and cut him free. He then handed the steering wheel to him. "You're going to be needing this. Get us to the safe location."

One of the decoy vans that was being chased managed to get away. While the other was stopped but left alone after they discovered the van empty. So everyone managed to get to the safe location unharmed and the mission was complete. They had the money and the documents to expose the companies. Cam estimated £8,000,000 in total.

Cam gave Mr Thatcher £30,000 and told him to leave the country and never return, as a good will gesture for helping bring Mr Cameron and Mr Johnson down. The remaining money was used to pay to turn the office blocks built by the companies into flats, which they gave to people who had suffered at the hands of the companies and other folk who were less fortunate.

A job well done.

13

Investigate

Buttering 2 slices of toast and eating them over the sink. Cam was running late for work. He had wanted to get in early and find out more about this London situation, before Mr Kyriakos got in. Why was this bothering him? He didn't care about going to London but something didn't feel right about the team being left behind. It got Cam thinking about a time when Mr Kyriakos had asked him to forward some account details over to him, instead of directly to the London office as usual. He had never done this before. He usually didn't get involved at all. But these accounts belonged to some of their biggest local clients, and Mr Kyriakos was adamant those files were sent to him to forward. Strange behaviour, but Cam always found him to be odd.

Cam arrived at the office half an hour earlier than usual, without stopping at Maicon's on the way. He always stopped at Maicon's! Jane was there of course. He paced through her upbeat welcome. He was obviously in a bit of a hurry.

"Yes, morning Jane. Is Mr Kyriakos in yet? He asked me to drop in an assignment first thing this morning."

"He isn't in yet, dear. But drop off whatever you need on his desk."

"I will, thanks, Jane." Cam threw his coat over the peg and hastily wandered over to Mr Kyriakos' office. He looked around and there was no one else in the office; just Jane, busy at the front desk and oblivious to anything else. Cam didn't know what he was looking for, but he knew something wasn't right. He clutched the door knob and took one more scan of the office, before slowly turning the knob. It was locked! Damn!

Cam sat at his desk and stared across the room at his boss' door. He knew something was in there.

"Good morning, girls!" Jane called at the front desk, as everyone else arrived to work. Sara and Leah first, shortly followed by Josh. No sign of Mr Kyriakos. Cam got on with his work as best he could, but his attention kept being dragged back to that office door.

"Josh, you're Kyriakos' lap dog. Have you noticed anything unusual recently? Seen him working on anything strange or anything?"

"Unusual how?" Josh asked confused.

"Just anything he's been keeping secret. Or has he mentioned anything about any clients' accounts?"

"Nah, I ain't noticed anything. Seems normal to me."

"Alright, thanks." Cam was still suspicious.

He waited for everyone to head out for lunch. Mr Kyriakos still was nowhere to be seen. Cam took this opportunity. He had to get in to that office! He approached the door and once again searched around for anyone. The coast was clear. He grabbed a paper clip out of his pocket and dissembled it. He then jammed it into the key hole on the door knob. He'd seen this countless times in the movies, surely it wasn't that difficult. It was very difficult, nothing was happening. As Cam decided to give up, he slid the clip out of the door and he heard a click. The door was unlocked. Cam took a deep breath and slowly turned the handle. He swung the door open to find his boss sat behind the imposing oak desk.

"Ah! Cameron!" Cameron? Who is he calling Cameron?

"It's Cam!" he implored.

"Come in boy, take off your clothes!"

"My clothes!? What the hell!"

"Come in and join me, take a seat on my lap boy!" What the hell was going on! Cam turned to look out into the office and everyone was back and staring at him, motionless.

"Boy! Come here now! Boy! Boy! BOY!"

Cam let out a gasp and next thing he was in his bed again! Panicking, he sat up and looked around frantically. It was just a bad dream. He must have fallen back to sleep, after his alarm had woken him up. He looked across at his alarm clock. He had massively over slept. He needed to hurry. That was weird.

Cameron butters 2 slices of toast and eats them over the sink. This time he was really late; he had to hurry and hope he's at work before his boss. He power walks to his office without stopping at Maicon's. He always stops at Maicon's!

He is 15 minutes late. "Morning, Jane. Is Mr Kyriakos in yet?"

"Yes, dear, he's in his office." Cameron hangs his coat on the peg and rushes to his desk. His computer lets out a loud jingle as it switches on. It does the same jingle every morning; it just seems louder when you're late. Mr Kyriakos emerges from his office. "Cameron boy! There you are!" the way he called him 'boy' now made Cameron feel ill. He shakes it off. "Can you forward the accounts for Whitehalls, Jolly Hoppers and Saint Claries. No need to send them to London, I will do it."

"Sure thing Sir. I'll get on it straight away." What did he want with these accounts? Cameron wondered. London requested this detail from Cameron by the end of the week. Never the less Cameron does as his boss commands, completes the accounts and forwards them to him. Cameron swings from side to side on his chair, procrastinating work. He grabs his phone off his desk and decides to reply to Anna.

"Hey Anna, reeeeeaaally sorry for the delayed reply. I've been manic since being back at work. Would you fancy meeting for lunch? 1pm at Maicon's? You can tell me all about the great day you had? I'll be there anyway so hopefully see you there!"

It felt needed to have lunch at Maicon's today, after missing his morning coffee, as he rushed to work. Cameron orders a latte and grabs a seat in the corner, by the window. Clouds gathered outside and rain started to spatter the shop windows. Cameron gazed out the window, while sipping his coffee. He grabs his phone off of the table and checks the time. It is 1.15pm. He then checks his messages, but no new messages to read. It doesn't look like Anna is going to make it. He looks out down the road at the increasingly heavy rain full, when he sees a little beam of light, walking down the path. Dressed in a yellow flowery rain coat, and a bright blue denim skirt, was Anna. She had shiny, red, low cut wellies on. Cameron wondered if she was wearing them all day or just put them on to walk in the rain.

Anna shook the rain off her coat before hanging it by the door. She caught Cameron's eye across the room and waved, with a beaming grin on her face. She gestured one finger to him and headed to the counter. She locked eyes with Cameron again as she waited for her latte. She rolled her eyes humorously and tilted her head from side to side.

"Wow where did that rain come from! It's been bright all morning. How are you?" she plonked the drink down and pulled a chair out from under the table.

"Yeah it's horrible out there. And of course, I didn't bring an umbrella out with me! I'm good, just needed to get out the office. Sorry about my delayed text reply by the way. I'm not usually that slow at getting back to people." He questioned that statement to himself. To be fair he didn't often text anyone so didn't have to worry about replying much.

"Well it's a good job your office isn't far, as you'll get very wet without a brolly. Honestly it's fine, I'm just glad you're not ignoring me totally. What's going on at work? Is it stressing you out?" Cameron told her all about his boss' weird behaviour and his intuition the he had something to hide. It was obvious Cameron needed to let off some steam.

"He does seem a bit shady, but you may be over thinking things?" she asked.

"Yeah, very possible I am over thinking it. But something just doesn't seem right, you know. I would love to do some digging and investigate what's really going on. But I don't have the guts, and it's easier for me to just forget it. Like you said, it could be nothing."

"It's difficult 'cause he's your boss and you want to trust him. And you don't want to piss him off. Keep your eyes open. If you really suspect something then buck up the courage and investigate."

"That's what I'll do. I'll keep a close eye on things and see what develops, if anything. How are things with you anyway?"

"All good. The shop is busier than usual. At the weekend a customer introduced me to a new series of books. It's called Cold Fighter. It's a fictional series about a vampire who fights to extinct the world of vampires. It's very gripping and quite sad. If you like to read, you should give it a whirl."

"If he's a vampire then why does he try to rid the world of vampires?" he challenged.

"You'll have to read it and find out! Gosh, look at the time; we had both get back to work."

"You're right, we should. We haven't even eaten anything."

"It's been great to catch up. I'm here if you need to vent about work some more. Or about anything for that matter."

"Thanks. I'll text you later on, nice to see you. Oh what was that vampire's name? From the books you're reading."

"Louis, You gonna read it?"

"I might!" he said with a rise smile as Anna tucked her chair back under the table.

"Catch ya later," she grabbed her coat and headed straight out. Cameron grabbed a pastry for his walk back to the office. Unfortunately for him the rain persisted. He'd be drenched by the time he got back to work.

Very wet indeed! He hung his coat over the peg and hastily took himself to the toilets where he tried to awkwardly position himself, to dry his soaked suit trousers under the hand dryer. He really must remember to take his umbrella everywhere. His hair was still dripping when he returned to his desk. He took a selfie and sent it to Anna, captioned 'SODDEN!' Now time to crack on with his work and keep an eye on Mr Kyriakos!

14

Cold Fighter

Everything was cold. Cam could see his breath fog out as he exhaled. He ran his tongue along his teeth and noticed enlarged and razor-sharp canine teeth. He raised his hands out in front; he had long pointy nails with blue half-moon shapes lunulas instead of white. He looked around but could not see far through foggy and dark woodland. The night sky was jet black and he was standing on a dirt track, surrounded by hundreds of tall, blustery trees. He could smell smoke. Most likely from a wood burning fire, roughly a mile away, he wagered. He started to run in that direction, he was whipping through the trees at a tremendous speed. His reactions so sharp, he could navigate around the oncoming trunks, along the way. He was hungry. But this was a hunger that he'd never experienced before. He could taste copper in his mouth and his stomach yearned for food.

He reached a log cabin in seconds. It wasn't big but he could smell life inside. The doorway was an open structure. He looked inside and found two children asleep in the corner and a grand arm chair with its back to Cam, in front of the crackling fire. The fire was the only light in the hut. A hand flopped down beside the chair and Cam heard a murmur of snoring. Dinner time. He tried to walk in but bounced back out of some kind of imaginary door. He reached out to the hollow arch and felt pressure pushing back on his palm; he couldn't get in. His meal would have to wait.

There was a lake behind the cabin, Cam discovered as he explored around. The moonlight bounced off the water to provide some clarity of the area. He leant down over the water to see his reflection, but there was no image looking back at him. His hunger burnt more intensely. He began to feel weak. He sat down on the pebbles cross legged, resting his hands on his knees. It was time to conserve his energy. He looked out over the horizon of the lake; it was beautifully calm, when he saw off in the distance, a silhouette of a man. He got himself back to his feet and when he looked out again the unidentified man was moving quickly closer; he was running across the water. This didn't seem good to Cam and he felt too weak to defend himself. He had to face whatever this was. He had no choice. Before he knew it, the man was standing just yards from him. Long, dark slicked back hair. Examining Cam through squinted eyes and moving his head slightly from side to side as he took him in. "Who are you and what do you want?" Cam called out assertively. Lifting his chin and puffing out his chest, speaking in a deep and smooth French accent the man replied,

"Bonjour, je m'appelle Louis, et toi?" exposing his long canine teeth as he spoke. They looked twice as big as Cam's. Cam looked puzzled at him. "Do you not speak French?" Louis pressed as he slowly stepped closer to Cam.

"No."

"Then why are you in France? Those are some lovely teeth you have." He gestured at his own, to show Cam's inferiority. "Are you here for dinner as well? They smell delicious, don't they?" Louis swayed around Cam, running his long thick nails across his chin, ensuring Cam turned and watched him.

"There's plenty for both of us, how do we get in?"

"We don't; we are vampires. And I'm not here to eat." Louis stared intensely at Cam, with a wicked look, "but they are," pointing past Cam. Cam sharply turned to see 4 other vampires running straight towards him and Louis, and they looked fierce. Cam prepared himself to fight. He looked back over his shoulder and yelled to Louis, "Are you going to fight with me?"

"No, it's a lot more fun watching. After all I am the vampire slayer. I'll deal with them, once they've dealt with you."

"Arghhhh! Come on then!" Cam engaged in a vicious duel with the other vampires. Every time a damning blow was landed, Cam healed almost instantly. Cam managed to land some brutal blows himself and the others seemed to not heal as quickly. Cam was knocked to his knees. He looked up and saw one of the huntsmen bearing down on him; Cam thrust his arm through his enemy's chest, landing a fatal strike, and pulling out his heart. It turned grey and dropped to the ground. The other three vampires circled him. One by one they took Cam on; one by one he prevailed.

"Well... not bad, for someone who looks like they haven't eaten in days," Louis announced, slowly applauding Cam's efforts, "no matter, I will finish what they couldn't. Don't worry... I'll make this quick." His mouth ajar, flexing his enormous fangs and extending his sharpened finger nails;

semi clenching his fingers. He elegantly advanced on Cam, cutting him across the face, before Cam even knew what was happening. A thousand thoughts processed in Cam's mind. Should he try and run? Louis was probably quicker than him. Should he fight? Louis was probably stronger than him. Before he knew it Louis had struck another heavy blemish across his back. The pair contested in the duel for several minutes before Louis' long talons lacerated Cam's neck. The damage was excessive and Cam was badly wounded. Louis took a step back, searching on the floor for a sharp tree branch.

"You've fought valiantly. I respect that. I don't take pleasure in killing other vampires. But the humans pay me well to do it. Ah-ha!" Louis picked up a sturdy but pointed branch but when he turned to face Cam, he wasn't there.

"Behind you, cunt; guess I am just as quick as you," Cam said smugly before plunging his own pointed branch through Louis' chest. Shocked, Louis threw his arms out and sank his long nails into Cams shoulders, but it was too late. He then evaporated into nothing.

The sun was coming up and Cam could sense a meal wouldn't be far behind. He hid himself away and bade his time. They'd have to come out at some point and when they did; he'd be ready!

Cameron could taste blood as his eye widened; he'd left a crack in his curtains and the morning light was hitting him straight in the face. He reached into his mouth and pressed both his thumbs into his canine teeth, they were back to normal. Not long and too sharp to touch. How boring! He sat himself up in bed and stretched his legs and arms out in front of him. Letting out a long exhale, he released his limbs from their stretch. He wondered to himself if Anna's book series were anything like his dream. He also moved his head quickly around, locking eyes with different objects in his room; to see how fast his reactions were. Not as fast as Cam, the vampire's reactions. He stumbled to the toilet to take a piss; not even lifting the seat in the process and covering it in yellow droplets. He wiped the seat with a cut of toilet roll and headed back to his bedroom. No work today, so maybe he could get another dream in. He pumped his pillows and climbed back into bed. He could hear the birds chirping outside but managed to drift off to sleep.

The shower turned cold. How long had he been in there? Cam asked himself. He looked down at his hands and saw severely wrinkled tips looking back at him. He turned the water off and reached out to grab his towel. He aggressively and only partially dried his hair, leaving it in a spiky mess. He swung the towel around his waist and headed into the kitchen. The room was gloomy. He opened his fridge but there was nothing but leftover takeaways, in there. The fridge light began to flicker. Cam stared at the flickering light and a cold shiver ran down his spine. All of a sudden, a wet, sticky tentacle looped itself around Cam; dragging him backwards to the ground. More tentacles came breaking through the floor boards and pinning him down. He felt powerless against this force. Just as he tried to call out for help a tentacle wrapped around his mouth. He could feel the tentacles' grip pulsating through him. When an eerie voice called out in the distance. "Youuu don't belong hereeee!"

15

Pressure

Maicon's was busier than usual. There were golden balloons hanging from the ceiling. Above the counter a white and gold sign read *'5 YEARS OLD'* and there was a white collection bucket next to the till, with gold tinsel around the top rim. On the collection pot it said, *'Today's tips will be donated to the Paw House, dog shelter. So please tip generously!'* There were also leaflets beside the bucket with info about the charity and how to donate or adopt, a rescue pet.

"Hey, what can I get you?" the barista asked Cameron with a beaming smile on his face.

"The usual; latte and pan au raisin, please. What's this with the charity?"

"We're working in partnership with them now. We'll be opening a Maicon's at their rescue home. Have you ever thought about adopting?"

"I haven't. But great work. I'll take a leaflet and be happy to donate."

Cameron found a table right in the corner. He looked around at the couples and families bustling in the room, it was nice to see the place so alive and thriving. It had been a long week and Mr Kyriakos hadn't done anything out of the ordinary, which was very disappointing. But for now, Cameron just wanted to forget about work and get on with his weekend.

A little boy approached Cameron at his table in the corner. "Hello little man, what are you doing?"

"Waiting for my parents; they're over there, chatting to Paul and Sue. They will be ages."

"My parents use to chat for hours with their friends. Boring isn't it?"

"Yeah, so boring. Can I sit with you?

"Sure, as long as your mum doesn't mind."

"She don't. As long as she can see me."

"How old are you?"

"7 and a half."

"Wow, and what's that you've got?"

"My 5 times tables."

"I see and have you learned them all? I'm good with numbers and could help you."

"No, I know them. But that's not the problem. I can't stand up in class and say them," the boy said with his head hanging low.

"Why's that?" Cameron asked, lowering his head as well to catch the boy's gaze.

" 'Cause I get scared and can't speak proper."

"What's your name kid?"

"Archie," he said with a sad expression across his face. "I don't like the pressure."

"Well Archie, it's normal to feel pressure. But when you get older you'll learn what real pressure is. When you get to my age there are so many more pressures in your life."

"There is!?" Archie asked, looking back up at Cameron.

"Oh, yeah! For example, when you're walking through a busy park on a Sunday, there's a group of lads playing football and the ball rolls to your feet as you're walking by. And one of the players shouts 'Kick our ball back' that's pressure!" The little boy begins to giggle. "Then you have the thoughts racing through your mind 'what if I slip over on my bum or shank the ball in the wrong direction!' the pressure grows even more."

"You're silly!"

"I am silly. But try to remember it's natural to worry about these things. You might slip on your bum, or you might ping the ball straight to their feet. You just need to be confident. Think of something funny before you stand up in class."

"Like you slipping on your bum?"

"Exactly!" Cameron said with a click of his fingers and rise smile.

"Come on, Arch, let's go," the boy's mum called out across the cafe.

"Coming Mum! I have to go, but thanks Mr."

"I'm Cam, was nice to meet you Archie."

"Fanks Cam! See ya!" he grabbed his homework off the table and slung a tiny backpack over his shoulder. He waved to Cameron as he raced away.

Cameron checked his phone as he saw he has a message from Anna.

'Hey Loser, sorry I'm running late. I had a thing with my mum but it's sorted now. See you in 10 x.'

Sent 7 minutes ago. So, he expected her any moment. Cameron finished his coffee and gazed out the window into nothing, watching the world go by.

"Cam! You ready?" Anna hollered, snapping Cameron out of his gaze.

"Oh hey, Anna. Sure. Where are we going?"

"Ok, hear me out here. But what about Mr Tom's Golfing World? I'm pretty good at mini golf," she said confidently. Cameron began to remember walking round the golf course with his dad, when he was 11. Carrying his clubs and giving him advice. His dad never taught him how to play though.

"Sure, sounds fun," he said in an agreeing tone.

"Great, let me just grab a coffee to go and we'll head off?" Cameron looked up at her, nodded, and smiled through closed lips.

As Cameron finished his coffee he thought to himself that this could be a fun day out. He also thought about a great dream he had a few weeks back, where he could drive golf balls over 400 yards! He was taking bets with everyone down at the driving range. He made an absolute fortune. Now that was a fun day out, one evening, while he slept.

Mr Tom's Mini Golf was a candy land themed course. 9 holes of colourful mayhem. Hard candy obstacles throughout. One hole even had a wooden chocolate fountain, in which you had to decide to hit right or left, whichever way you went decided how the ball would travel down the fountain and where it would land at the bottom. The sand bunkers were bright colours like pink, blue and yellow to represent sherbets instead of sand.

The sun had come out for their round but it was still chilly. Being the weekend it was a little busy with families, so the pair got stuck behind a few at times. Cameron teed off first on a straight course, but with the hole hidden behind a scatter of plastic penny sweets. He hit the ball past the obstacle and putted in two from behind the hole. Anna went a different route and tried to hit the ball straight over the collections of fake confectionery, causing the ball to ricochet off and away from the hole; meaning she finished it off in three.

It came down to the last hole but Anna did beat him by one stroke. She pulled off a hole in one on the 6th hole, while Cameron was leading. He admitted at the end that she was a worthy winner.

"Do you want to keep the score card to remember your victory?"

"Yes, I think I will!" she replied as she tried to grab the card from his grasp. But he hooked it away and stuffed it in his pocket.

"Tough! I'm keeping it. So I can dispose of it later!" he said as he turned his back on her. She tried to wrestle him and get her hand inside his pockets. Finally, she gripped the corner of the paper and pulled it out.

"Ha! Got it!" she smirked and stuffed it into her pocket.

"Fine! You can keep it," he laughed and rolled his eyes.

"Tell me about your parents, you've never mentioned them," she asked as they strolled back to the welcome hut.

"What do you want to know? I don't really see much of them anymore," Cameron replied very blasé, swinging his club beside him as he walked.

"Well to start with, what are their names?"

"Barry and Patricia, so Baz and Pat. But for some reason their friends called them Bat and Pat, and they all found that very amusing."

"And how come you don't see them much now?" she probed.

"I do chat with my mum still but not my dad. We just drifted apart over time. I moved out here. So I only really see them at family events. Even then my old man doesn't often come."

"That's a shame. Are they still together? Were you closer to them when you were younger?"

"Yeah, they're still together and yeah, I guess. They both worked a lot. Me and my dad always talked sports but that's as far as our relationship went. My mum couldn't have any more kids after me, so she would coddle me at times. I guess she was overbearing at times as well. She always tried to force a relationship between my dad and me, that wasn't ever going to be there. I don't think I was the son, my father was hoping for." Cameron was shocked at himself, with how open he was being. Completely not like him. Anna was easy to talk to.

"Do you wish you had a closer relationship with them?"

"I never think about it to be honest." He shrugged, while taking Anna's club from her and dropping them into the basket, at the concierge. "How's things with Wendy anyway?" he asked about her mum.

"Well, that's why I was late this morning. She seemed to have worsened this week and she had an episode. It was quite upsetting really for the both of us. Me and my auntie Maple, we were saying that it might be time we found help." Her tone dropped.

"What, like a carer?"

"Exactly that. She needs full time support. Otherwise I will be more restricted and days like today won't be possible to happen."

"Well, if it'll help you and her it's worth it, isn't it?"

"Yeah, I guess so."

"Come on, let's head home." Anna seemed a little disappointed to be going home. So she suggested they grab some lunch.

"Erm, I can't really. I've got some things I need to do today. Some other time though for sure." They said their goodbyes and headed off home. Cameron didn't have anything on but just thought it was time to head home.

It was a fun date but not as fun as his driving range bets dream. He wondered what was in store for him, in tonight's dream. Action packed adventure he hoped.

16

The Night Bus

"The 407 to Barnum Court Road; next stop is Chisom Street." The synthetic voice called out on the bus. It was late. Cam was on board the 407 bus, a red double-decker that ran 24 hours a day. This was an older model. The seats were worn and a light flickered at the back left corner of the lower deck. Cam was sitting in a priority seat, at the bottom of the stairs and close to the back doors, when an elderly lady got on. He thought it odd a lady of her age out at this late hour. But he offered her his seat all the same, and moved to the back of the bus, under the flickering light. With still several stops before he needed to get off, Cam put his headphones in and leant his head against the window. Even through his music he could hear sounds of thudding coming from the floor upstairs. It seemed a lot of commotion going on up there. There's a TV screen flashing different CCTV views, at the bottom of the stairs. Cam takes his head off the window to watch and see what was going on up there.

A group of teenagers wearing black and grey tracksuits, with scarves rolled up over their mouths and noses. They were all wearing beanie hats, caps or hoodies. They were marching

95

around; using sandpaper to mark the windows with graffiti. The next time the CCTV panned to them upstairs, Cam noticed they were smoking up there too. He just hoped they stayed up there. He rested his head back on the window.

Rain began to patter the glass; just perfect as Cam still had to walk from his stop to his flat. He stared out the window at the ever-increasing rain fall, when a flash of lightning startled him. His head sharply left the window, before he rested his forehead back on the vibrating glass. He watched a rain lash against the window; causing the whole lower deck to steam up. He wiped away the condensation and continued to watch the horrid weather. At least the light had stopped flickering above him. For now, anyway.

There was still a lot of racket coming from the upper deck. At one point it sounded like someone might come through the floor. Cam began to feel a little on edge and took his headphones back out. This way he could hear what was going on better and also one less valuable thing to have out on display. A couple got on the bus eating noodles out of a tall cardboard package. They stumbled down the bus and the woman fell back onto the man, as the driver set off. They were clearly very drunk. They sat in the back right corner of the bus, next to Cam. Cam gave an eyebrow raising smile towards them but they didn't notice. The 'STOP BUS' light flashed up on the destination board but Cam didn't see anyone downstairs press the button. Then he heard banging from the back of the upstairs make its way to the front, soon after on the stairs. "Oi stop the fucking bus bruv!" one of the hooded teenagers shouted as he swung round the hand rail at the bottom of the stairs.

"We're not at the stop yet," the bus driver called back.

"Didn't you hear me, stop this fucking bus now!" the young lad walked down towards the driver with a swagger. "Listen, old man, if you don't stop this bus I will fuck shit up," he threatened before pushing his fist against the glass between him and the driver.

"Fine." The bus came to a gradual stop and the doors began to open, before the halt, half ajar.

"Open the fucking doors!" he demanded with more anger in his voice.

"I'm trying, they're stuck," the driver responded calmly. Then the engine turned off, the bus became very still. They young hoodlums looked around the bus.

"Easy on dear, that's a nice handbag. Got any money in there?" one of the other lads said, as he leant down to the level the elderly lady was sitting. "You don't mind if I have a look, do ya? Sweet!" he went to grab the bag when the guy at the back, eating noodles, called out.

"Why don't you leave her alone? Pick on someone your own size!"

"What? Like you bruv? Maybe you got something I want then? What's in your girl's bag?" he walked away from the elderly lady and down towards the couple. Cam sat quietly trying to avoid any trouble. When the lad locked eyes with him too. "What the fuck you looking at?" he snapped at Cam.

"Nothing. Nothing at all," Cam said, looking back out the window.

"Driver, I give you one last chance the open these doors!" He said with an even angrier tone. Just then the lights turned off.

The bus was in blackout. Cam was frozen. He could hear muffled noise happening around him but he could not turn his head or move his body. He started to panic, he could feel movement to his side, he couldn't make out any words being shouted. A flash of lightning struck and the lights came back on. Cam could move again but everyone on the bus was gone. Everyone except the driver, and they were on the move again. Cam scanned the bus. What had just happened?

Finally it was his stop. Cam pressed the button, thanked the driver and jumped off the bus. The rain had stopped, he looked left and right, but saw no one around, so he popped his headphones back in, and began his walk home. His street was about 30 metres down and on the left, and his house was right down the other end of the road. It was poorly lit by out of date street lamps. Semi-detached houses ran either side before reaching blocks of flats, and then past there, old mansions, now flats where Cam lived. Some of the lamps began to flicker and once again the rain started.

Cam saw shadows moving from behind him, in the lamp lights. He turned around and searched both sides of the street but saw no one still. The lamp above him was now flickering slowly, he looked up at it and the light stayed off for several seconds each time. He reached out and grabbed the post, when he heard someone behind him.

"What's up, bruv? Where are you going, hmm?" Cam was frozen again. His hand fused to the pole, his head facing the wrong direction. But he could tell from the voice it was those lads from the bus. Cam couldn't respond to them, and once again the voices became distorted and he couldn't make out what they were saying. He panicked more as he felt them coming closer, and he even felt a hand reach into his pocket and slide his phone out. Just then a flash of lightning ignited the sky once more and the lamps turned back on. Cam's hand was released from the pole and he swiftly looked round. But again, there was no one there. Just his phone lying on the floor next to him.

He slammed his front door closed and bolted it locked. He leant his back against it and flopped his head back, letting out a huge sigh of relief to be home. He closed his eyes for a second and took a deep breath in, in the darkened hallway.

"Well, well, well. Look who it is." Cam brought his head forward and opened his eyes, flicking the light on and seeing the hooded boy standing before him. "Nowhere to run!" he said with a smirk on his face, knife in hand and slowly walking towards him; the hallway light flicking on and off frantically. Cam was frozen once more. The panic had set in worse than ever. With every flicker of the light, his killer was one step closer. The lad stopped right in front of Cam, lifted the knife high above his head and with his other hand pulled the scarf down from over his nose and mouth, revealing the drunken noodle eating passenger, from the bus. This face quickly turned to the little elderly lady, at the next ignition of the light. Finally as they were just inches away from Cam, the light went off for what seemed an age before revealing Anna's face!

"You don't belong here!" she cried out before lighting flashed through the front door and with it images of the night's events flashed through Cam's mind. He opened his eyes and she was gone. All he could hear now was the sounds of her cries; 'you don't belong here!'

'You don't belong here.' Did this have a hidden meaning? Cameron pondered as he lay awake in his bed. That wasn't the kind of adventure he was looking for, but it was an adventure all the same. As he took his morning shit, on this typically gloomy Sunday morning, he couldn't help but think of the similarities between this nightmare and the one he'd had last week. With being paralysed and the thunder, 'You don't belong here' was the same as well? What did it all mean? Did it mean anything at all? That was the fun of it all though, right?

Cameron contemplated all this while he munched on his morning toast; basically day dreaming the events of last night all over again. He continued his thought process on his slow walk to Maicon's; it had to be slow because it didn't open for another half hour. Even on his walk home he mulled over it, along with other dreams and adventures he'd been on. He couldn't even remember the journey he just took to Maicon's and back; whether he spoke to anyone, what the weather was like or even if he saw anything unusual.

He snapped out of his trance and put the TV on and watched the football highlights, from yesterday's games. There was not much else to do today.

17

Fun Filled Sunday

After a typical week of action-packed dreams and a not so action packed time at work, Cameron reminisced over his favourite dreams, from the last few days. That particular one on Thursday that didn't make any sense, but was still exciting and humorous rolled into one. That really got Cameron thinking. He continued to day dream about these fictional times, while he shovelled sugary cereal into his mouth. He was oblivious to his phone repeatedly vibrating on the arm of his armchair. Anna, Jeffro and his mum had all texted him. But he was in his own little world to notice. They didn't matter at this moment of time. Cameron washed his bowl, leaving his phone over on the chair. He headed to the bathroom and ran the shower, threw his clothes in a pile by the door, checked himself in the mirror, clicked his fingers and pointed at his own reflection before winking. In the shower Cameron could get lost again; detach himself from reality and sing. After exfoliating his body in fruity orange shower gel and foaming his hair, he grabbed the shower head and it was time to perform.

Hundreds of screaming fans sang along with him. Bright UV lights in his shower blinded him as he became one with the music, just as the show lights would. A young lady threw her bra onto the stage; he held the shower puff aka 'the bra' aloft before throwing it back into the crowd. The song was over; breathing heavy after his performance he closed his eyes and he heard the voices chanting his name. He was quickly shocked back to reality as the water turned cold. His eyes are wide open now; he had to wash the shampoo out of his hair with freezing cold water. Well, it was fun while it lasted. He dried and dressed himself at a lethargic pace, before sitting on the edge of his bed and staring out into space. He had chores to do and his fridge needed restocking, but right now he really couldn't be bothered. He mustered up the energy and got himself on the move; shopping first and then the housework. As he strolled to Maicon's, Cameron checked his messages. The first was from his mum.

'Hello darling, how is everything? Have you received the invite for Julie and Carl's wedding? I'm sure they'll be excited to see you. Let me know. Mum xx'

Cameron hadn't seen Julie or Carl for years. Julie was in his year at school and their parents were friends. Her family lived down the road from the Peters; she and Cameron spent a lot of time together as kids. Cameron closed that text down and moved on to the several from his best mate, Jeffro.

'Hey pal, work on my little project going well. Call for an update.'

'Hey Pal, are you around this evening? Project updates.'

'Hey pal, do you still have my Allen keys? Can't find them anywhere.'

Cameron did have his Allen keys at home, but he couldn't remember where. Maybe he would just lie to his best mate and claim he gave them back. Well he wasn't going to reply now anyway. Lastly, he read Anna's message.

'Heeeyyy! Didn't hear from you last night. Hope you're alright. On my way to work. Pop in if you like or we can meet for lunch??? Maicon's are still celebrating their 5 years!'

He closed the messages and locked his phone. He wasn't in the mood for socialising today. He just wanted to get his errands sorted and then chill until he could return to the land of nod this evening. So that's what he did.

The evening whittled down. Cameron watched Harry Potter for the 50th time; The Prisoner of Azkaban, as that was his favourite. He could watch this but not need pay much attention. He had read all the books too but that was too much concentration these days. The films were easier to just have on in the background. He still hadn't replied to any of his messages. That was a worry for another time. Before he knew it, it was bedtime. He prepared himself for another night of action adventure and now the real fun would begin.

18

Let's Meet Again

Monday morning blues hit harder when your only main enjoyment was your hibernation time; having to get through work and the other remaining awake hours is hard work. As he strolled to Maicon's, Cameron felt it only polite he replied to his messages. He let his mum know that he was in fact doing fine- 'same old' and that he had indeed been invited to Julie and Carl's wedding. As he couldn't think of a valid excuse not to go, he asked his mum what her and his dad's plans were for the event. This somehow resulted in Cameron having dinner with his parents, one evening this week. Jeffro's project did seem quite interesting so Cameron sincerely replied asking him to meet up one evening, for an update. His week was starting to look awkwardly full. Lastly, he got back to Anna. He did feel bad about delaying this response, but on the other hand he needed his distance at times. His evenings were packing out this week so he suggested lunch with Anna; Tuesday it was.

"Ah Cameron dear, Mr Kyriakos left this note for you," Jane grinned excessively as she handed a folded A5 sheet of paper to Cameron as he scribbled his name down, on the daily sign-in sheet.

"Thanks. Where is he?" Cameron muttered unfolding the paper.

'2pm meeting tomorrow afternoon. Bring the client folders you've been working on since the summer quarter.'

"He's not in the office today," she replied to Cameron as he turned away, reading the note. What on earth could this be about? More strange behaviour from his boss. This could be a chance for him to find out about any unusual activities. He had watched him all last week, but found nothing. He pondered on this note for 20 minutes. Which was fine. It was only his work, it was distracting him from. He procrastinated the entire morning away until it was time for lunch. He was meeting Anna at Maicon's tomorrow, but for today it was just a meal deal in the break room of the office. That was the plan anyway, but he found Sara and Leah in there gossiping away. Cameron smiled and nodded his head in their direction, before grabbing his chicken mayo sandwiches from the fridge. He scrunched his nose and grinned towards the two girls; miming words that they couldn't make out and pointing towards the door. The girls look confused at one another before shrugging it off, and continuing with their gal pal chat. Cameron grabbed his coat and headed outside to eat his lunch. It was chilly today but thankfully not raining. There was a bench outside the office. He plonked himself down and stared into nothing while chomping on his meal deal. After his food Cameron just sat on that bench and looked out at the on-goings, not really taking anything in. It was dark and cold; his leg was twitching up and down, in an attempt to keep himself warm. Josh wandered past him and called out, "Alright mate?" Cameron didn't register at first that someone was talking to him; rubbed his face and smiled back at Josh- 'Please don't come over. Please don't come over.' He continued walking past and back inside. Thank fuck. Cameron knew he's not a barrel of laughs himself but Josh was so difficult to talk to- a complete wet blanket. He looked down at his watch and realised he'd been sitting on this bench for over an hour. Luckily the boss was out for the day. Although he might have asked Jane to keep an eye on them and she definitely wouldn't hesitate to snitch on Cameron. He did the bare minimum today at work, less pressure while the boss was out of office. He mostly daydreamed, wondered where My Kyriakos was. Up to no good, no doubt.

Cameron was always a good worker back at school. Always hit deadlines, always completed his homework, great attendance, a real model student. Things started to change in college. He became less interested in school. This wasn't due to a flourishing social life or a life chasing girls. He got the work done but he enjoyed it less than when he was at school. Maybe it was the realisation that this was what he'd be doing the rest of his life. Likewise with work at first he was a terrific employee, with great attention to detail and positive effort towards the role. He was showing great signs of a strong future in the company. 4 years down the line and he was still in the same role, at the bottom of the food chain. What happened to that positive go getter? He never got anything in the end.

Tuesday quickly rolled round. A disappointing dream last night; Cam was lost in a foreign country, with nothing to do. He found himself wandering the place, trying to make sense of where he was. His sleep was a little broken and he didn't remember much else happening. Well you win some, you lose some, I guess. His sleep was probably distorted because of his busy schedule today. His 2pm meeting drummed through his mind as he got ready for work. It was straight after his lunch with Anna. Maybe she might help decipher the nature of what he wanted. Also she might have ideas as to what Cameron could say to trigger info regarding his boss' shifty behaviour. A cunning plan was what they need to devise during their limited time together. A little before 1pm Cameron shut down his PC and packed his things away. He watched the clock tick round until his lunch started. That was a long morning to endure. Anna was already at the coffee shop, at the table in the corner, by the window; that was becoming their table, only by coincidence and not by design though. "Have you ordered?" Cameron asked as he approached the table, throwing his jacket over the back of the vacant chair.

"No, I was waiting for you. Shall I go up and order?" she responded, grabbing her purse off the table.

"It's fine, I'll go, while I'm up. What are you having?" Once again they ordered the same meal. What Anna requested sounded good to Cameron and he trusted her judgement already. He sat down, putting a tray down on the table. He took off a plate of food and a coffee mug and slid it over to Anna, before taking everything else off for himself. They exchanged niceties while smiling and holding eye contact with one another. Cameron brought up the daunting note from his boss. Anna being Anna, she tried to put a positive spin on it.

"Like you said, see this as an opportunity to find some stuff out. Probe him about the accounts. Ask open questions. If you really think he's up to something then this is a great chance to do some digging." She assured him that his plan was solid and he felt encouragement through her voice.

"What else is going on anyway? Anything new to report?" she questioned, taking a bite from her sandwich.

"Well I've been invited to this wedding. It's for an old family friend. My mum wants me to go with her and dad," he replied unenthusiastically.

"That's alright isn't it? What's wrong with that? Could be fun."

7 years ago

Putney, Wandsworth, July 16th, 2010

Barry Peters watches himself in the dresser mirror, looping his dress tie round and tugs it tightly round his neck, while his wife was sitting on the bed, as she hooks heels on to her feet. She is wearing a green flowery dress that flows down to her ankles. Barry only ever wore a suit for 1 or 2 reasons. Either he was going to a wedding or he was going to a funeral. 16-year old Cameron walks across the landing in his dress socks, with his suit trousers on and his white shirt open at the neck and un-cuffed at the wrist. He is carrying two silver cufflinks, that he needs his dad to help him with. Their bedroom door is ajar. Cameron reaches out and grabs the handle to open it when he overhears them speaking.

"He's really going through with it? Accounting? At college? With his grades he should be going to university. Not local college," Barry moans to his wife. She stands up off the bed and helps straighten his tie.

"Come on Bat, at least he's doing something. He can make a career out of it too."

"He should be doing something more interesting. Why not sport related? He's always banging on about sport."

"Less and less. To be honest. Hardly at all these days."

"Of course, he is. Always banging on about sport. But going to college to do accounting. It's embarrassing Pat." Cameron lets go of the door knob and flops his hands down by his side. He hangs his head as he walks back to his own room. He sits on the bed motionless and stares down at the carpet.

"Right you ready, darling?" his mum says cheerily as she opens his door. "Nearly time to go. Here let me help you with those cuffs. Your dad'll be downstairs waiting for us."

Present Day

Cameron sipped on the last of his coffee. "That was the last time I went to a wedding with my parents. That wasn't very fun," he said glumly. Anna consoled him and tried to make him feel better about it.

"I think you've made up your mind that you're going to go. Haven't you?" she asked

"Yes probably."

"Well it's no good, reflecting on the past. Just try and think positive and have an open mind. Otherwise you won't enjoy it, if you don't." She reached out and put her hands on top of his that was resting in front of him on the table. He looked up at her and cracked a rise smile. He broke the gaze looking down at his watch. 1:51pm!

"Shit! My meeting! I have to go." Pulled his hands from under hers and got to his feet. Grabbing his coat off the back of the chair and throwing it over his arm.

"Thanks for lunch," she said looking up at him, "next time, my treat."

"Sorry to rush off, I'll text you later." He turned and left in haste before she could say another word.

Anna finished her coffee while watching the world go by, out the shop window. She watched the people in the cafe; eyes glued to their phones. Even some of which are with other people. Some people endlessly scrolling, while others taking selfies or pictures of their fancy coffee. Searching for validation from the world while their friends sit 2 feet away from them. Anna preferred living in the moment with her acquaintances, or getting lost in a good book, while she enjoyed time to herself. This need for social acceptance didn't bother her. As long as she was kind to the people around her, and brought them as much joy as she could, she was happy. She piled the finished plates and empty coffee mugs onto the tray, neatly, before strolling back to work. She had a smile on her face and leap in her step. The world always looked bright to Anna, not much kept her down. But life being life, it finds a way to try. She heard her phone ringing. Her Auntie calling.

"Maple? Everything ok?" she asked as she flicked her hair out the way of her ear, to answer the phone.

"Hello dear, your Mum isn't doing too well again this morning. I just wanted to check on you, I know last night was tough."

"Yes, I'm fine. I'm walking back to work. Do you need me to come home?" it was always worrying for Anna when it came to her mum's health. She noticed a pause in her Auntie's response.

"...No, she is calm now, she seems ok. Listen, Anna, it might be time we start thinking about getting some help. I think she needs constant care now. But I just wanted to check in on you. We can talk about it tonight when you're home?"

"Yes, of course. Thank you, Maple. I'll come straight home tonight. Are you okay?" she asked back.

"I'm fine dear. Enjoy the rest of your day and I'll see you later." Anna lowered the phone and ended the call. She opened a text to Cameron but decided against messaging him. He had enough to worry about today. It was time to put on a brave smile and tackle the rest of the day.

Even with his advanced speed walking back, Cameron didn't make it in time for his 2pm meeting. Mr Kyriakos was in the conference room waiting for him, when he arrived back. Cameron hastily threw his bag and coat onto his desk, while trying to see into the conference room. He looked at his watch; 2:06pm, that's not too bad, he could blame a toilet break. Standing here thinking wasn't making him any quicker getting into the meeting. He scampered over to the meeting room door, took a deep breath and opened the door. "Good afternoon sir. I got your note."

"Cameron boy, come in and sit down." Cameron smiled through gritted teeth and sat down across the table, as his boss instructed. "I'm hoping you know what this is about," he said confidently, pulling several large folders out of a bag on the floor and plonking them down on the desk. Cameron looked over confused and tried to read what was titled on the front of the folders. Through squinted eyes he could make out some of the writing. He read 'Accounts: Whitehalls' and 'Accounts: Saint Clarie's- the accounts Mr Kyriakos had been asking him instead of sending them straight to London. Cameron was even more confused now. "Cameron, we need to talk about these accounts. I recently asked you to send them to me. This was after London reported anomalies in your work, so I've been reviewing your work on our big accounts and I am extremely concerned with what I've found." Mr Kyriakos opened the folders and started to spread sheets out across the table.

"Sir.... are you sure?" Cameron struggled to process all this straight away. He looked across the table and started to look worried.

"Yes, I'm sure. And it isn't just these accounts. I've found mistakes in 7 other smaller accounts. Let's go through them together now." They sat there for 40 minutes while Mr Kyriakos went into detail about Cameron's shoddy work, silly mistakes, and small overlooks. It dawned on Cameron that his boss wasn't fudging the books; he was correcting his. His boss lowered his glasses on his nose and looked deep into Cameron's eyes. Breathing heavy, he cleared his throat.

"This is extremely disappointing, Cameron. Along with your lack of effort, poor attitude and lethargic work rate is very concerning. You sit around a lot of the day, in your own world. I find you day dreaming at your desk constantly. You distance yourself from the rest of the team and don't think I haven't noticed your time keeping. This isn't anything new; I've been concerned about your work for months. What do you have to say for yourself?" His boss asked, with sweat pouring from his brow. He dabbed it with a tissue while wheezing for air.

"I er, I.... I" Cameron didn't know what to say. This whole time he had this vendetta against his boss. He didn't realise his work had slipped. He had just been getting on with it, thinking he couldn't make mistakes. How naïve!

"Cameron, I have given your open projects to Sara and Leah. We're giving you a leave of absence."

"What!?" Cameron snapped genuinely stunned.

"Take the rest of the week."

"Sir, please no. I..."

"You are suspended without pay," Mr Kyriakos said, no longer keeping eye contact with Cameron, and shoving the folders back into the bag on the floor. This meeting was done. He looked up at Cameron once again. "Hopefully you can come back refreshed." Cameron accepted what his boss was telling him but he was still feeling in shock. He nervously looked around the table, trying to gather his emotions. He composed himself and got to his feet. Without saying another word, he gingerly left the conference room. He closed the door behind him and stood motionless for several seconds. The room seemed silent to him, although the usual office hustle and bustle was going on around him. Without breaking his gaze he strolled over to his desk, grabbed his coat and bag and without throwing them over his shoulder, he walked out the office, swinging the coat and bag down beside him.

19

Faceless

The bell called last orders. The crowds started to disperse. Most of the doors were being bolted. The groups in garden were vacated. Some punters were ready to move on to a club, while others ventured to the kebab shops; and some were ready for bed. The music that echoed in the background throughout the night became clearer as numbers of people filtered out, before coming to a complete stop; a classic indication the bar staff was ready for everyone to leave. Along with dimming many of the lights. It was a Friday evening and not everyone was so easily removed. But the pub was technically open for another half an hour. So the staff had to tolerate it for the meantime, while they started to clean around the remaining customers. The pub had 3 entrances; two at the front of the building and 1 at the rear, which led to the beer garden. Only the front left door remained open, with a member of the bar team hovering to ensure no more stragglers came in. If you wanted to go for a smoke that was it, no way back in. There was a collection of tables between each of the 2 front doors before reaching the bar, which was a dominating localpoint, in the middle of the pub. Long gold bars to lean on wrapped round the whole bar, which was a circular shape, with serving points around the entire 360 degrees of the bar. Behind the counter and the bar staff was a tower of spirits, almost as tall as the ceiling. Continuing down, you found the toilets on one side; both men's and women's. The kitchen was opposite, which had a hatch dividing the kitchen and the pub; for easy transport of the food to the tables. Then there were a few more tables before the backdoor leading out the back.

Cam had sunk more pints than he could now count to. He was alone but not ready to go home. He had managed to grab a lager before they stopped serving. He was perched right down the front with a view out the window. It was dark outside; with only the street lights providing any light. The bar staff had already shut off the lamps above the 2 front doors. Rain began the patter against the glass as Cam sipped his beer. His eyes were heavy and his head swayed a little as he tried to focus. He pushed his cheeks up under his eyes to try and keep them open before blinking at a fast rate. The murmur behind him from the other remaining customers got shallower and shallower, until complete silence deafened him. Lightning struck outside igniting the skies, as Cam watched on. The rain poured down now, thundering against the window. Cam turned to see where all the commotion had gone from inside the pub, to find everyone in there motionless. No one was facing him. Not the drunk customers, not the bar staff, and not the staff cleaning. Still there was silence. Cam got to his feet and causeless approached a piss head sitting on the table across from him. He nervously walked around the fellow drinker, but the back of his head followed Cam's gaze. Cam sharply moved his focus to one of the staff, cleaning near-by. He grabbed their shoulder and tried to turn them round but again their head stayed in place. Cam became frantic and tried all different tricks on everyone in the pub. But all he could see was backs of heads. Cam decided to leave the pub so he started to walk towards the only open door. But as he stepped towards it the door never got any closer. Step after step the door remained the same distance away. Cam began to panic, he felt his heart beating outside his chest, when all of a sudden the faceless people began to close in on him. Now Cam was paralysed. He could feel the faceless people moving in on him, but they never seemed to get any closer, just like he could feel the door moving towards him, but never getting any closer.

It was 3:46AM. That dream didn't make Cameron wake up disorientated and he just lay in bed calm and relaxed. He lay awake thinking of nothing. In the back of his mind he was disappointed with what he had just been through, in his subconscious. He was unable to get back to sleep. This wasn't because he had the stresses of yesterday's work on his mind or anything of the sort. He had nothing on his mind. That was until his bladder interrupted his mindless stare. He locked eyes with the wall as he took his piss; he continued to do so for 10 seconds after finishing urinating. He shook the last few droplets of piss out and bumbled his way back to bed. He was awake now. Luckily he didn't have work tomorrow. His brain was waking up now as well, and his thoughts started to creep into his mind. What was he to do with himself this week? He was still struggling to process the whole ordeal from work. He'd had it coming. That much Cameron had decided. He'd brought it on himself. But did he blame himself? He wasn't sure of that.

20

Shock to the System

'Hey thanks again for lunch. Maybe we could grab dinner this week? Would be nice to get out the house. Hope you're meeting went okay xx.'

Anna hadn't heard from Cameron since lunch. But he did tend to be slow with his replies. She headed home after work; worried about her mum and was keen to see how she was doing. She sprang through the door and raced straight through to see her, she was sat watching soaps on the TV. She gave her a hug and her mum in return cracked a smile, before turning her attention back on her afternoon shows. At least she recognised Anna tonight. Anna sat with her mum a while before heading into the kitchen where Maple was making dinner.

"How's she been this afternoon?" Anna asked putting her arm around Maple and squeezing her shoulder.

"Seems fine, she's not really done much. So it's hard to tell. Sometimes you have to keep your eye on her at all times; other times she just sits peacefully in there, minding her own business," she said with a shrug while she peeled carrots over the sink. Anna picked up some potatoes and started to chop them, next to her aunt. "She spoke on the phone with our cousins, up in Hartlepool at lunch. They want to come down at Christmas. It would be great to see them. But I'm not sure it's the best idea. How do you feel about it all, darling?"

"It's hard to process. Her condition has deteriorated so quickly. The doctor thought it might take years to get this bad," Anna said with a soft sadness in her voice.

"I know darling, but these things can escalate. It's impossible to know for sure. But I do think we need a plan; with you working full time then having to deal with her, all evening. It's too much. It'll break you." She expressed her concern while she swiftly peeled carrots.

"I don't mind. I want to help look after her."

"I know darling, but you shouldn't have to. You can't do it all on your own. You have your own life to live. Go out and be young. It's what your mum would want." Maple was stern but fair and behind her hard exterior she had a beautiful heart. They finally agreed that they would seek help; a carer that could come in during the days or evenings and take the load. "I have been researching and there are a few highly rated places locally who have great home services," Maple told Anna, stopping her peeling to grab some leaflets from the kitchen side. "This one here, Raise UK, I've heard good things about, from friends of mine." Anna flicked through the pamphlets. This was a lot to take in. "I will set everything up, and I will meet the companies. You don't need to lift a finger, darling. I know this is a shock to the system but it's for the best."

6 years ago.

Horsham, West Sussex, September 1st, 2011

A mild afternoon, on the back end of a hot summer; Wendy was finishing up with a client, while Anna waited for her at reception, with a basket of snacks. After varied results in her GCSE's Anna was being treated to a day of her choice, by her mum. An A in both English lit. and English language, of course. She had got strong B's in Drama, Geography and Religious studies, and then getting C's in her remaining subjects. This made her mum very happy. She could have done anything, this afternoon, but Anna chose a simple picnic in the park. She just wanted to spend time with her mum. The pair laughed and joked the whole way to the park.

"I'm so proud of you my darling," Wendy expressed lovingly, wrapping an arm around her daughter as they walked.

"Ah thanks, mum. I couldn't have done it without you!" Anna spoke with a ginormous grin on her face. The tight grip around Anna's shoulder loosened. "And yeeesss the book is great. Quite a bit to go but I'm very excited..." Anna slowed her walk. Wendy used Anna for balance as she felt a little unsteady on her feet.

"Everything ok, Mum?" Anna reached her other hand across and grabbed her Mum's hand. "Has your MS been flaring up? We can take a break. Let's sit on this bench." Composing herself Wendy clutched firmly on her daughter's hand. A smile held back the pain, which was still clear in her eyes.

"I'm fine dear, let's carry on walking. You were telling me about your story?"

"Yes, I can't wait for you to read it," Anna said softly.

"And I can't wait to read it!"

Anna never finished that particular book. In fact she had 3 other books which she had started but yet to finish. Her mum would never get to read them now, and even if she did, she wouldn't remember. Some days she didn't even remember her own daughter. Anna and her mum were inseparable. Anna didn't have a very big group of friends and she would often just spend time with her mum. They loved the same shows, books, food, drinks and taste in clothes. Her mum always asked her about boys and Anna had nothing to hide. She would tell her mum everything, like a true best friend.

Present Day

'Hey Jeffro, I can be at yours a little earlier tonight, will you be around?'

Cameron messaged his friend as he strolled to Maicon's; aimlessly attempting to make a plan to occupy his time while he was off from work. Cameron rarely took time off work, as it was the best thing to distract him from his empty boring life; it killed time while he was waiting to return to his dreams, each evening. He only ever took time off when he actually had plans.

'Hey man, yeah come over whenever. I'm here all day. Bring beer.'

Cameron shoved his phone back into his pocket as he took a seat at his and Anna's usual spot; he was dining without her this morning. He indulged in his usual latte and pan au raisin combo, while reading the cup decoration. Time seemed to move in fast forward around him, while he sat motionless, sipping on his hot beverage.

'Ok mate. See you about 4.'

Now all he needed to do was work out what he was going to do for the next 8 hours.

He killed most of the day with cleaning; a good spring clean of his whole flat. No music to assist his work, just so good scrubbing and organising in silence. Cleaning had to be done, and nothing could make it any more fun. He left for Jeffro's in plenty of time. A leisurely walk delayed his arrival; he just had to get out of that flat. Even though it was spotless now. Thinking about work most of the way; could Mr Kyriakos not pay while he was suspended? That didn't seem right. Not that money was a worry for Cameron. He never spent any money really. Other than bills and essentials, what did he have to spend money on? It was still way before 4pm when Cameron got to Jeffro's house. 'I'm sure he wouldn't mind.' When he opened the door to Cameron, Jeffro was wearing a long white doctor's coat and magnifying glasses; he was carrying a clip board.

"Hello mate, come on in," he swung the clipboard across his body, gesturing for Cameron to come in. He looked left and right distrustfully outside before slamming the door shut. "Why are you wearing that?" Cameron asked inquisitively.

"Cause, I'm working," he replied bluntly.

"You're an I.T. technical support agent?"

"Obviously not that job. I mean this!" he pushed the door to his study open and Cameron could see computer parts everywhere, white sheets covering the windows and the Maghurt F4:50 on the desk, with a spot light shining above it. It looked like a low budget surgical suite but for robots. "The work continues; it takes up most of my time now. But there is progress. It works and I have got some small applications working already. I can find deeds to basically every business in this country. Pretty cool huh?" Jeffro turned away from Cameron and switched the small PC on. Cameron walked around the room, picking up parts and taking everything in. "I have just repaired a chip inside it. Let's see what that does. What's new with you anyway, bud?" They both pulled up a chair in front of the machine and Cameron told his mate all about the situation at work. "That totally sucks, man," Jeffro said, eyes fixed on the PC screen. "The worst part is trying to keep myself busy," Cameron replied also staring at the Maghurt F4:50.

"There is plenty you can do. Legos, film marathons, gaming. You could even come and help me with my project." None of these options seemed appealing to Cameron, so he just shrugged it off and awaited the PC to load up. "Did you bring beers?" Jeffro asked turning his attention to Cameron's empty hands.

"Shit! No, I didn't. I completely forgot. Head's not with it right now."

"I get it; this work shit is bound to be a shock to the system. You'll work it out." A loud tune played out from the PC and Jeffro began to click his mouse repeatedly.

"Ah ha!" Jeffro snapped. "Look. Look here is a database that shows me each employee from every small business in England. Their profiles and job roles. The lot."

"Wow. That is actually amazing," Cameron said leaning forward to gain a better view.

"I am telling you man, this PC will be able to do it all."

"What, like personal stuff?"

"Everything!"

"Truly remarkable. Let me run out and get beers. I'll be back."

They worked on the machine into the night, snacking on pizza and beers. This was the first night out Cameron had had in months. He didn't think about his dreams the entire time. It was just him and his best mate hanging out. And that was all that mattered tonight. Eventually Cameron decided it was time to leave. Jeffro looked like he couldn't type another word on the keyboard; they were both shattered. It was 1am. It was way past Cameron's bed time. He strolled home; wishing he'd bought another layer. The autumn wind blew through the air, chilling him right through. Luckily, he was home in no time. He threw his jacket over the arm chair, kicked his trainers off and stumbled to the bathroom. He half- heartedly brushed his teeth before slumping himself into bed. He was out the moment his head hit the pillow.

21

Dr Death

"Excuse me. Can you tell me where we are?" Cam asked as his hand tapped on a man's shoulder. The man crouching down in the corner of a dim room slowly rotated his head to look at Cam. Wearing a surgical mask and a bandana he slowly got to his feet and looked Cam up and down.

"You're late!" He snapped, grabbing Cam by both shoulders. "That'll cost you."

"Late for what? Where are we?" Cam asked, confused and with a slight panic in his voice.

"Come on in and take a seat. How is the back? I hope you're ready for your surgery." The Doctor led Cam to a consultation table in the other corner of the room. A long-necked lamp shone above the desk. The doctor started to aggressively type notes into his computer. As he pounded on the keyboard Cam tried to look around, but everywhere except the desk they were sat at was pitch black.

"Yeees, I see here. You need two vertebrates in your lower back. No problem at all. Walk in the park." Cam looked around again to try and see if he could spot a door, but still nothing in sight. As he turned back to interrogate the doctor he found that he was standing over him, with a large syringe in his hand. "This won't hurt a bit," he assured Cam as he plunged the needle into his arm. "Trust me, I'm a doctor," he said wickedly as Cam's eyes started to slowly shut.

Cam wiped the droll from his lips with the back of his hand, he then ran his fingers across his eye, his head hanging off the side of the bed. He brought his head back up onto the pillow, his body lying dead straight on the table. The room was bright now. He called out but there was no one there to hear him. It was not long before Cam noticed he could not move his body from the chest down. He reached down under his back and felt extensive scarring and heavy duty staples clutching his wounds together.

"Ah you're awake! You've been out for quite some time. Longer than most. Now the surgery was a success; I've managed to put your back, back together. Unfortunately, you'll never walk again," The doctor explained as he scribbled notes down on a clipboard.

"What!? In what world is that a success!?" Cam pleaded with vicious undertones.

"Like I said... Your back is fixed and welded together. There are always side effects to surgeries. I'd take the win if I was you." Cam looked around the room. This was no surgical suite. A long kitchen counter with sink and hob were on the far side of the room. A plasma TV was mounted on the wall to his left and when he looked right there was a basic grey sofa, with one cushion on it and a blanket featuring a herd of horses printed across it.

"I'm thirsty," Cam called out. The doctor was now standing out of eyesight, behind Cam's head, rustling metal tools around. The doctor made his way to the kitchen and poured water from the tap into a paper cup. "I can't really lift my head," Cam informed him as he held the cup of water out for him. So, the doctor dropped a plastic straw into the cup and left it in Cam's hand.

"You'll have to feed yourself, while I prepare," instructed the doctor as he headed back to his table of tools.

"Prepare? Prepare for what?"

"Your next surgery. Seeing as your body is useless to you now. Drink up. It's going to be a long evening."

The doctor scrubbed his hands in the kitchen sink. He pulled on a blood-soaked scrub and ties his bandana tight to his head; all while ignoring Cam's pleas to stop. He stretched yellow marigold gloves over his hands and pinged them into position. "Can you feel that?" he asked Cam as he pinched each toe. "This little piggy went to market. This little piggy stayed home. This little piggy had roast beef but this little piggy had none. But this, this here little piggy was sick. So, let's open him up and see what's going on." He sliced down Cam's little toe opening the small incision he'd made. He proceeded to do this with each toe, exposing the insides of each one. Cam could hear blood dripping to the floor. He was done pleading. He just closed his eyes and tried to think of something else. The doctor worked on Cam for hours, opening and closing different parts of his body.

"I've always wanted to try organ transplant," the doctor murmured as he took the cup of water from Cam's hand, "maybe that could be tomorrow." He stitched up any open wounds and flicked the light off. "Goodnight Cam, see you in the morning." He left through the only door in the room.

Cam lay awake for hours but time moved in fast forward. He started to feel tired and his eyes began to close, when just momentslater the light flashed back on he felt his ankle rotate. He felt movement!

"Good morning, Cam. How are you feeling?" Cam ignored him. "Let's crack on then, shall we?" He gave Cam a fresh cup of water. Another morning of prodding and probing, 'preparing' for surgery this afternoon. "Right, I have a lunch date. I won't be long. Don't go anywhere, will you?" the doctor laughed as he shut off the light on his way out again. In his absence Cam pulled his head up and looked down past his mangled body to his feet. He knew he can make them move. He just knew it.

"Lunch was great. I really like this one. I feel like she can really get me, you know, Cam?" The doctor was very chatty on his return a couple of hours later. Cam remained unmoved and uninterested in what he had to say. "Don't feel like talking? No matter, we can just crack on with work. More water?" He refilled Cam's cup and continued his work. Again, Cam closed his eyes and searched for a happy place. He saw fragments of joy but only small fragments. He dozed off and heard Anna's voice, very softly calling out to him, "Wake up! Cam you have to wake up." His eyes prised open slowly and he saw the doctor leaning over him and slapping his cheek. "You can't die yet! Wake up! That's enough for today. I'll see you in the morrow. After I've had breakfast with my lovely new lady friend."

That evening Cam was sure he felt his knees bending. Was this a weird imaginary sensation? Had he gone delirious? Another night flew by, still no sleep, and then it was morning again. The doctor would be here soon. Cam wasn't sure how much more he could take. He felt anger rush through his body. Then just as the key turned in the door he felt his bum cheeks clench. "Would you like a drink Cam? I have someone downstairs who I'm DYING for you to meet. Sorry poor choice of words." He scurried over to the sink to pour Cam some water when a woman appeared in Cam's eye line. "Ah, here she is now. Anna, meet Cam." He introduced them while he walked over with Cam's drink.

"Anna?" Cam crackled.

"Do, er, you two know each other?"the doctor asked, slipping the cup into Cam's hand.

"What have you done to him?" Anna asked with a sadness in her voice. Cam felt a sense of worth all of a sudden.

"Do you have something stronger, Doc?" Cam asked.

"Why, yes of course, Cam. Whiskey?"

"How about just coffee?"

"Er, sure. Anna? Want one? Anna?" he asked twice after she didn't respond. Her eyes fixed on Cam.

"Yes. Please." He strolled back to the kitchen to fill the kettle.

Anna leans down to whisper in Cam's ear.

"I'll get you out of here. You don't belong here. You don't belong here." She turned her head to see the doctor returning with two hot mugs of coffee.

"No need," Cam responded to Anna as he took the mug from the doctor. "I'll get myself out," he threw the steaming hot contents of the mug back into the doctor's face and jumped off the bed and grabbed Anna by the arm. The doctor flung himself around in agony, bumbling around trying to find the kitchen sink, to relieve himself with cold water. Cam and Anna made a dart for the door but as they reached it Cam's leg began to buckle underneath him. Anna lifted him from the ground and flung his arm around her neck.

"Come on. You can make it," she encouraged him as they limped out the room, "my car is right outside. We just have to make it there before him and we're free." They stumbled down flight after flight of stairs. It wasn't long before they could hear the footsteps of the doctor chasing them.

"Anna, wait. Wait." He dropped to the floor once more. "I can't go on, but you can. Get yourself out."

"I'm not leaving without you." She begged him to get up.

"You must go. But first... kiss me. Kiss me before he gets here." A tear fell down her cheek as she nodded. The sound of the stomping footsteps increased, along with the grunting noise the doctor was making on his way down. Anna locked eyes with Cam and brought her lips close to Cam's. She could feel his breath on hers. They closed their eyes.

He opened his eyes, lips plucked for impact but all he saw was his ceiling fan and he was all alone, in bed. Why did Anna keep appearing in his nightmares? He'd heard her voice and seen her face several times now. And what was with her telling him he didn't belong there. This was messing with his head. But now all he could think about was her pretty freckled face and infectious smile. He liked seeing Anna in his dreams, but he didn't like the dreams he was seeing Anna in.

He grabbed his phone from his bed side table. It was 6am. He stared blankly at his phone with not much going through his head. He found himself staring at the 'games' folder on his phone home page. He'd forgotten what apps were even saved in there. His phone lay out was very basic. He had some apps on the home screen and others hidden away in folders.

He couldn't remember why certain apps were tidily away in folder. He probably just got bored of organising it. His games apps may not have been accessed much recently, but he did used his 'betting' folder more often. Several apps for betting all in one place. He did like to gamble but he mainly used the apps to browse all sorts of different sporting events and categories, from around the world. A great way to kill time. He locked his phone and popped it back on his bedside table. He took himself to the bathroom, placed both hands on the basin and stared into the mirror. So much time to kill today. It was Thursday and Cameron had no plans today. He could text Anna and see if she fancied a coffee before work, he was up now anyway. He hadn't spoken to her since their lunch date on Tuesday. He continued to stare into the mirror longingly. Then it dawned on him. It was Thursday! He let go of the sink and brought his hands up to his face, covering his eyes with the palms of his hands and tilting his head backwards. He had agreed to have dinner at his parents' tonight. What a nightmare! He brushed his teeth and took himself back to bed. He checked train times to London on his phone. He had the entire day to mentally prepare himself for this dinner. He sent Anna a message about morning coffee before work, before rolling over and nodding off back to sleep.

22

Dinner

Cameron sat and waited for Anna, in their usual spot, the table in the corner, by the window. He watched out the window at the people walking by. When like a ray of sunshine beaming through grey cloudy skies he saw Anna appear among the faces, making her way down the road. "Morning," she said softly. Her raspy voice was all too familiar now to Cameron. He got to his feet as Anna sat down. He had a rise smile on his face. He took down her order and headed up to the counter. Anna took off her coat and positioned it on the back of her chair. "Why aren't you dressed for work? Where is your suit?" she asked as Cameron plonked two lattes and two pan au raisins down on the table. He in turn plonked himself down in the chair.

"Yeah, about that. The meeting I had with my boss. Well, it didn't really go that well. He suspended me."

"What!? Oh my god!" she said with genuine surprise. "What happened?" Cameron explained partly. Leaving out some important details about how negligent he'd been; sort of deflecting the blame away from him. Not fully explaining the extent of how bad his performance had been over recent months. "Everyone makes mistakes. I feel like Mr Kyriakos has it in for me."

"But for him to suspend you is a bit drastic. Surely, he went into detail with you. He would have to give you a valid reason?" she asked, biting into her pastry.

"He said, take the time to get my head straight and come back ready for work. So that's what I'm going to do. Work was causing too much stress. So, the break could do me good."

"Well, I still think it's wrong." She continued to console him, as she always did.

"Anyway, I was thinking... Could I borrow that Vampire book from you?" he enquired, sipping on his piping hot latte.

"Cold Fighter? Of course, I have the first book here in my bag," she said reaching under the table into her red leather backpack.

"I had a dream about it recently. But I've never even read it. So thought I'd see what it's actually all about." She handed the book to him across the table.

"It's a great series. I think you'll like it. We can talk it over once you've finished it. It'll keep you occupied while you're not working. Do you have anything else planned?" popping the last bit of pan au raisin in her mouth.

"I've got dinner at my parents' tonight. That'll be fun. We've got to go to a family friend's wedding soon. So, need to organise for that."

"Free dinner isn't too bad though. Hopefully it's more enjoyable than you're expecting. But for now, I need to get to work. Message me and let me know how it goes."

Luckily the train to Putney didn't take too long from Horsham. A quick change at Clapham Common and you're there. Then the walk to Cameron's parent's house was only 15 minutes from the station. Dinner was at 8, to give Cameron plenty of time to get there from work. They weren't aware that he had just been sitting at home reading Cold Fighter all day. Cameron took the book with him on the train. He was half way through it already. The stroll to their house was like a walk down memory lane; nothing had changed. Their street covered in orangey brown leaves that had fallen from the tree. All neatly bushed together on the grass, not a single leaf left on the pavements. 7:38pm. He reached their house; same wooden gate, same front door and same dingy old door bell. He took a deep breath before knocking hard on the door. He heard murmured shouting from inside before his mum swung the door open. Tea towel flung over her shoulder and beaming smile on her face. "Ah Cameron darling, what's the point of us having the fancy doorbell if no one ever uses it!" Fancy? It was about 20 years old. "Come on in. Shoes off!" she frantically shooed him into the house. He kicked his shoes off and took a look around. "Right, go through to the front room. I think your dad's watching football. Dinner won't be long." She scurried off to the kitchen. Cameron headed for the lounge. The TV was indeed playing football in the vast bay window at the front of the room. The room was a substantial size but 2 enormous brown sofas made the room feel small. They had new shag carpets put in a few years ago. To replace the old beige shag carpets they had down before.

"Who's winning?" Cameron asked his dad, as he creeped in silently.

"0-0 it's only 10 minutes in," Barry replied without taking his eyes off the TV. He was sitting on the sofa opposite the TV. Cameron took a seat on the other sofa, behind the door. They sat in silence for around a minute.

"So how's work?" Barry broke the silence but kept his eyes fixed to the TV.

"It's alright. Same old," Cameron replied. His dad nodded and grunted.

"Your mum said dinner won't be long. Gonna miss most of the match' cause she said we have to eat at the table. Even though we eat in here every night when you're not here." He finally looked at his son, but only for a few seconds before his attention returned to the game. They sat again in silence while they both watched the game.

"Their new signing has been impressi.."

"Dinner!" Patricia called before Cameron could finish his sentence. His dad got to his feet, flicked the TV off and walked out, without even acknowledging that his son had tried to speak to him.

The pair took their seats at the dinner table, in the kitchen. It was a small table for 4 people; a green table cloth with petite yellow flowers covered the table. The table needed to be small to fit in the kitchen. The house hadn't changed much since Cameron lived here. The kitchen units were the same wooden ones as when he was a kid; an L shaped fashion on the walls, with a door to the back garden on the other wall. They had a large analog clocks on the 4th wall, on the left as you walked into the room, with the table set up in front of that. The table was neatly laid for the 3 of them. Patricia set herself and Cameron opposite each other with Barry on the edge with his back to the wall. Pie and mash was on the menu tonight.

"I was thinking about doing ham, eggs and chips, but me and your father had that on Tuesday. I know you like pie though. It's steak and kidney." She announced as she placed a gravy train in the middle of the table.

"It looks lovely mum, thanks." Cameron reached out to grab the gravy but his dad snatched it up before he could.

"Yes, yes, very nice Pat." He flooded his plate with gravy before leaning over and gave his wife a kiss on the cheek, still holding the jar of gravy aloft while his son waited patiently.

"How you getting on at work Cameron?" his mum asked as they all tucked into their food.

"Errrr, yeah. It's going well, thanks. How's school?" he replied timidly.

"Hectic! The committee bodies are at each other throats at the moment. Us teachers are just trying to hold things together for the kids at least. The new trust that's taken over don't seem to care about the kids, or us at that. Making endless changes. It's like an office block not a school. Probably run like your offices at Harper's." She rambled on for 5 minutes about the issues within the school set ups now. Cameron just nodded along and agreed with her dismay.

"Any girls, son?" Barry interrupted the conversation to change the subject swiftly. He had wolfed down majority of his food already.

"Erm? No, no girls," Cameron replied as he cut the roof of his pie off, he had hardly touched his food yet.

"Right," his dad muttered with a mouth full of gravy soaked pastry. Cameron could tell his dad was disappointed but acting like he didn't care.

"Well, there is a girl actually. Anna. It's still new but she's really pretty and cool. You'd like her, mum." Getting his mum's attention.

"Ooo that sounds promising. Why don't you bring her to the wedding?"

"Yeah, I'm sure Julie said you had a plus one," Barry said waving his fork around in the air. Cameron sunk into his chair, trying to find his words.

7 years ago

Edmonton, London, July 16th, 2010

Sun was shining on this beautiful wedding. A very merry Barry was standing at the bar with the groom and other male family and friends. 16-year old Cameron stood with his mum and childhood best friend Julie, he kept looking across the room at his dad and his friends. They were drinking lager and loudly exchanging stories.

"CAMERON! CAMERON!" Barry called across the room at his son. "CAMERON! COME HERE SON!" He waved Cameron over to the bar. Cameron made his way over gingerly. "You got a beer, son? Com'on you're old enough now. BAR KEEP! Another lager please, for my son here." Cameron felt a real sense of inclusion. A smile lifted on his face as his dad handed him a pint and throwing an arm round his shoulder. A warm loving feel flowed through Cameron's body. But that feeling didn't last long.

"Have I told you boys about our flight home from Spain, last year?" It dawned on Cameron what was coming.

"Please dad." Barry took another swig of his beer. His arm still around his son's shoulder.

"Shh shh," he muted his son promptly "so we were coming home from Alicante. We're going through security and Cameron's bag gets stopped for search." He bellows, tugging his son around under his arm. "Turns out he had a water pistol in his bag, from the pool. But they unpacked his whole bag." Cameron's head had dropped. "And he holds these boxer shorts in the air with a pen. Cameron had had a wet dream while we were away and the boxers were covered in his cum! The whole queue was crying with laughter!" The group were in hysterics. Barry had gone red with laughter. Cameron was red with embarrassment. He couldn't speak as his dad ruffled his hair. Across the room he could see Julie watching on with a sympathetic look on her face. Cameron wasn't sure she'd heard the story but he could tell she knew they were laughing at him. He felt sick to his stomach with embarrassment; his dad laughing at him. The group quickly moved on with other stories but that feeling sat with Cameron for the rest of the evening.

Present Day

"Nah, we've only known each other a few weeks. I will go to the wedding alone," Cameron shook off the horrid feeling coursing through him and put on a brave face through the rest of dinner. They made plans that the three of them to go to the wedding together. They would get ready at their's and get a cab. Cameron hadn't seen Julie since the wedding his dad told that belittling story, 6 years ago. It should be nice to see her wed though.

Patricia cleared most of the table before taking herself to the loo.

"Do you want a beer, son?" Barry called out while placing dirty dishes in the kitchen sink.

"Yeah, I will thanks, Dad. Actually, Mum might have done dessert?"

"So what? Do you want a beer or not?" he stared at Cameron with the fridge door open in front of him.

"Yes please." His dad nodded and grabbed 2 green beer bottles from the fridge.

"Let's go and watch the rest of the game." They left the dirty dishes in the sink and went back into the front room to watch the football. They sat and drank beer in silence for 15 minutes. The silence was broken by Patricia bringing them a slice of banoffee pie each. Patricia tried to prise some more information out of Cameron regarding Anna, but he was vague and withheld from his mother. It was past 10pm now, Cameron made a move otherwise it'll be the early hours until he got home. And as far as his parents were aware, he had work in the morning. As he walked at a hasty pace to the station Cameron reflected on the evening. It's wasn't as bad as he thought. And it did kill a lot of time. The train from Clapham Common to Horsham clunked along; Cameron could feel his eyes getting heavier. He dozed off for a few minutes. He saw in his mind over exaggerated laughter as he flashed back to the mortifying story his dad told at the last wedding they attended together. Cameron felt small under the laughing faces around him. His eyes opened as another train flashed past in the opposite direction, causing a slight rock to Cameron's carriage. Rain began to patter the windows, which were steaming up slowly from the corners; he would have to walk in this rain. It wasn't long before Cameron was home. Moist and cold; he prepared himself for bed.

23

The Carer

The drain was full but Anna only had a few bits left to wash up. Aunty Maple was drying but an agitated Anna was far too quick for her. Today was the first day that her Mum Wendy would have a carer looking after her, while Maple ran errands and Anna worked. The doorbell rang. Anna opened the door to a short gentleman in a short sleeved light blue nurse's uniform; he was no taller than Anna herself. He had thinning hair, which had started to turn grey. He had a long pointy nose and showed a lot of teeth as he smiled.

"Hello I'm Clive, Clive Johnson. I've been speaking with your Aunt. Maple? You must be Anna?" Anna looked blankly at him. Aunty Maple appeared behind Anna in the doorway.

"Well don't just stand there Anna, invite him in." She laughed under her breath, reaching her hand out past Anna, who remained unmoved. Maple shook the carer's hand and led him into the house past Anna. Anna closed the door behind him. She was clearly not comfortable with this and Maple could tell.

"Just go through there to the kitchen, Mr Johnson. Would you like some tea?" she pointed him down the hall way before turning to Anna. "Come on darling, I know this scares you but it's the right thing to do, for your Mum," she tilted her head as she consoled Anna.

"I know, I know, he's probably great at his job. But what if Mum doesn't like him or this at all?" she pleaded with her aunty.

"I am here all morning with them. I will make sure your mum is totally comfortable before I go out. Trust me darling. You go to work and I'll tell you all about it this evening." Reluctantly Anna left for work. She knew she was over thinking things but he couldn't get his creepy smile and his slender, hairy arms out of her head. She was being silly. She knew she was being silly. She just worried about her mum.

Cameron was already at Maicon's waiting for Anna; a coffee and pastry waiting for her too, at their usual table, in the corner by the window.

"How was dinner then?" she asked after thanking him for the drink. He told her all about his evening, leaving out the flash back he had. He mentioned about them asking about her while Anna slowly zoned out.

"Are you okay? You don't seem fully with it this morning?"

"Sorry, it's the first day my mum will have a carer. I'm worried about her. Maple is there this morning and I'll be there tomorrow, so we can get used to it as well."

"Did you meet the carer?"

"Yes, only briefly though."

"What's he like?"

"Not at all what I expected. But then again, I'm not really sure what I expected."

"It will take some getting used to, that's for sure. But ultimately it's the best thing for your mum, right?"

"Yeah."

"Then you're going to have to give it a go." Cameron checked his watch. "It's 10 to. You should get to work." Anna gulped down the last bit of her latte; Cameron watched her with a warm feeling inside him. She was so pretty, he thought, as the lowering cup exposed her freckled face.

"Thanks Cam, I'll text you later." She was on her feet grabbing her coat from the back of the chair

"Anna! Wait." He got to his feet hastily as she turned back to look at him, and before she could speak he grabbed her arms tightly and landed a kiss on her lips; his eyes closed. She kissed him back instantly closing her eyes gently. Their lips unlocked just a few seconds later and their eyes widen and lock each other. Cameron smirked as their stare was broken.

"Now I really must go. Text ya later," and off to work she went. She didn't look back as he watched her leave. He let out a long breath before sitting back down at the table. He grabbed Cold Fighter out of his bag and cracked on with his reading. He had the rest of the day to kill, before heading to Jeffro's again tonight.

In her lunch break Anna called her Aunty Maple to see how things went with the carer but annoyingly she got her answer machine; she anxiously texted her.

'Helllooo. Just checking in to see how this morning went. Please get back to me if you see this message. Love you lots xx.'

She sat staring at her phone for the rest of her break. But she had nothing from anyone. She texts Cameron just before heading back to work.

'Heyyy. How are you getting on with Cold Fighter? I should have brought it to read in my lunch break to try and distract me from thinking about my mum. Haven't heard from Maple all day. I hope everything went ok. Can't wait to get home later! Hope you're having a better Friday than I am! Xx'

5pm felt like an age to come. Anna had left work on the dot and was charging home. She still had no correspondence from Maple. She wasn't the greatest with technology though. Cameron had however got back to her.

'I'm sure everything is fine. No news is good news. That's what my mum always used to say. Let me know everything later though. Cold Fighter is almost finished! We can chat about it over coffee tomorrow? How about after the carer leaves?'

It wasn't long before she was home. Maple and Wendy were sat watching TV together. "Maple!? Why didn't you reply to my message?" Anna snapped immediately; her hands out in disappointment.

"Oh, sorry darling, I left my phone at home all day. I haven't even checked it," she replied without even taking her eyes off the TV.

"What the point of you even having that phone?" Again no reaction from Maple or Wendy. "Well? What happened?"

"What do you mean what happened?"

"In the show you're watching," Anna hinted sarcastically. "With the carer!?"

"He was lovely, darling. Very helpful and funny too."

"Funny? He was funny?"

"Yes, and your mum liked him, didn't you Wend?"

"Who?" Wendy asked snapping her gaze from the screen to her sister.

"Mr Johnson," she reminded her

"Yes, he was lovely. Very funny."

"There you are see, darling. I'm sure you'll like him too."

"He made a cracking cuppa too," Wendy added. "Not as good as yours though, Anna," she said with a cheeky look at Maple. A slight weight fell from Anna's shoulders. She took a chair with her Mum and Aunty. "Right, now then. What is happening in this show!?" The three laughed together. Anna looked longingly at her mum. Maybe she was going to get better. Maybe Maple was right about everything and having a carer was going to help her mum feel bett

24

Progress

It was dark now on these autumn evenings in West Sussex. Cam could feel eyes on him. He stopped walking and scanned his surroundings. He felt safe on these streets and the roads were well lit by the street lamps. A cold breeze tickled his neck as he restarted his journey to Jeffro's. He felt a heavy weight strike him on the side of the head. In a panic Cam decided to run but his legs didn't seem to take him anywhere. He lifted his fist in front of him preparing himself to fight. Punches were thrown in his direction but he managed not to get hit. He saw 4 maybe 5 guys trying to attack him. His arms were heavy now; his fist still up in front of him, but any attempt to throw a punch back resulted in his hands dropping swiftly downwards. He swivelled in place, trying to avoid a beating; his arms were still not working. He couldn't defend himself. His phone appeared in his hand. Anna's name was flashing on the screen. He felt the presence of his attacker lighten, soon he couldn't see or hear them anywhere. He answered the phone. "YOU DON'T BELONG HERE," Anna's voice calls down the line. "What does that mean!? Anna? Hello?"

These afternoon naps were becoming all too common. Cameron had to stop dozing off, especially when he went back to work next week. He looked down at his phone. Anna's name lit up on the screen. A text.

'Heyyy, good news, mum seemed to love the new carer. How's your day been? I would love coffee tomorrow. Lunch at Maicon's? It's nice knowing you're around Cam. Thanks xx.'

Cam replied simply.

'It's a date.'

"How's the progress?" Cameron asked Jeffro, handing him some beers at the front door.

"Progress is very good my old friend, come in and take a look for yourself," Jeffro replied leading Cameron to the office.

"Can't do anything about the loud annoying jingle when we turn it on?" Cameron asked as the PC fired up.

"Yes, but to be honest… I kind of like it," Jeffro opened two beer bottles and took a seat next to Cameron. "Now check this out. I have managed to work out how to get into company records, and not just small businesses but big corporate companies. Also look at this…. Different security settings for social media. I can see the encryptions to Facebook's firewall. No way of changing them… yet, but pretty cool." He used the keyboard to navigate the screen, rarely using the mouse. Cameron watched on in amazement. Jeffro really was a wizard. This was crazy.

"So, I kissed Anna," Cameron said casually as they worked on the PC.

"I'm sorry what? When did this happen?" Jeffro inquired whilst continuing the focus on the monitor.

"Earlier today. At Maicon's."

"That's a long time coming. You talk about her constantly when we work on this machine!" Jeffro finally took his eyes of the screen and looked suggestively at Cameron.

"Shut up! No, I don't," Cameron chuckled at Jeffro.

"But yeah, I was just watching her and I have felt like it was overdue.

"Good man. What happened then? After the kiss?"

"Well, not much really. She went to work."

"Have you not spoken to her since?"

"Yeah. I have texted her. But we haven't mentioned the kiss. Do you think I should have?" Cameron sought advice from his trusted friend.

"Yeah! But then what do I know. Been many moons since I kissed a girl."

"Good point. But maybe I'm seeing her tomorrow. I'll talk to her then."

"So you like her then?" Jeffro's attention turned back to the PC work.

"I do yeah. She's great. She's funny and so friendly."

"Not to mention she's hot, am I right?" Jeffro nudged Cameron's arm with his elbow. Cameron laughed and smiled fiercely.

"Yeah yeah, she's hot! Anyway let's crack on shall we?" The two of them continued to work on the computer; sipping on beer. "Jeff? Do you ever think we were made for more than this?" Jeffro looked back to his friend with a confused look on his face.

"More than what?"

"Just all this? When were at school did you think life would be different when we were older? Like we'd be rich or famous?"

"I don't know. I've not thought about it. To be honest I've got no interest in being famous. And with the help of this bad boy I will be rich!" Jeffro tapped the Maghurt F4:50 and winked at Cameron, "Why do you ask? Do you wish you were famous?" Cameron paused and thought hard about his response.

"I just thought life would be more fun when we grew up. Full of adventure."

"We're working on a Maghurt F4:50 here; doesn't get more fun that this?" Jeffro eagerly typed on the keyboard.

"I guess so," Cameron stared at the monitor and zoned out briefly, while he let Jeffro work.

Once again the two best friends worked late into the night. Unlocking new advanced levels on the Maghurt F4:50. Cameron did not hesitate to walk home, even after his nightmare earlier that afternoon. He thought about Anna the whole way home. He couldn't wait to see her again tomorrow. He fantasised about her soft lips; his lips gently brushing against them; feeling her supple skin on his finger tips and the warmth of her body against his. He was home before his mind could wander any further.

25

The Date

Thick brown hair everywhere except his head which was turning grey and thinning, Anna asked herself why that happened to men, as she watched Clive Johnson clearing up the breakfast bowls. Even his fingers were hairy; she bet his toes were too. She studied him a while. He was an odd looking man; his upper teeth over lapped his bottom lip when he smiled and his pointy nose seemed to lengthen at the same time. He was short and thin, some might assume he was sick too, although he was very capable of looking after Wendy according to his CV and his impressive first day on the job.

"Right sweetheart, I'm off shopping," Maple let Anna know as she threw her long shiny purple coat on over her hunched back. "Please make an effort and talk to Clive. I'll be back in a couple of hours." She hooked her tiny handbag over her arm and made her exit. Anna heard commotion coming from the lounge.

"Who are you?! I asked for coffee not tea!" Wendy was yelling at Clive as Anna came into the room.

"Everything ok? Mum?" Clive turned to look at Anna.

"She asked for tea," he said confidently.

"Yes, I know she did," Anna made her way over to her mum. "Mum you did ask for tea, silly. I can make you a coffee if you like?" She shook her head and grabbed the mug of tea.

"This will do."

"How about you, Clive? Tea?" she turned her attention to the carer.

"I'll make them. You sit with your mum," he grinned.

"Mum, that's Clive. He's here to help us. All of us."

"Yes, I know. He's lovely," her mum replied, watching her morning chat shows. Anna put her hand on her mum and watched her a moment. In the adjoining kitchen Clive made tea. Anna went to see if he needed a hand.

"She gets confused," Anna consoled Clive.

"I know. I've seen it before. It is harder at the beginning though, with a new family. I just want to make a good impression. I know I can really help you guys. Sugar?" he stirred the tea.

"No sugar for me, thanks. So how long have you been doing this job?" Anna already knew this from reading his CV 20 times, before they hired him, but she wanted to make conversation.

"4 years although I was an NHS nurse for 15 years before that. Your mum told me you're a writer, that's pretty, cool."

"She told you that?" Anna looked out of the kitchen to her mum.

"Yes, yesterday. She beamed with joy." Anna's face fell a little with disappointment.

"No, I'm not a writer. She's getting confused again." Clive handed Anna a mug, before grabbing his own from the side and taking a sip, inhaling an unnecessary slurp from the piping hot drink.

"Ahhh," he expressed before walking past Anna and sitting down with Wendy. Looks like that conversation was done. The three sat and watched TV; not much interaction happening. Anna noticed a graze and some cuts on Clive's left wrist.

"What happened to your arm?" Anna questioned Clive.

"I do a lot gardening at home and for my patients actually. I had a fight with a rose bush and lost," he bellowed a short exaggerated laugh before his attention turned back to the TV.

"Shall we play a board game?" Wendy asked out of nowhere. Anna and Clive glanced at one another.

"We sure can," Clive responded, "as long as Anna is happy to?"

"Yes, fine with me. Let's play something," Clive took the mug from Wendy and Anna.

"What do you want to play?" he asked, carrying the dirty mugs to the kitchen.

"How was this morning, Anna?" Maple called out taking her coat off. "It's freezing out today. Do you have any plans?" kicking her shiny red kitten heels off and walking into the front room. "Where's she?" she asked her sister, who was watching TV with Ludo the board game, sat on the side table, next to her.

"Where is who?" she replied turning her attention away from the TV to Maple.

"Anna. Where is Anna?"

"She's upstairs in her room, getting ready. She's going out for lunch. With a boy I think." Wendy sharply turned her attention back to the TV. Maple swiftly makes her way to the kitchen. "Not sure where Mark is though," Wendy said. Maple immediately turned back to look at her sister.

"What did you just say?" she rushed over while she awaited a reply.

"Mark. Not sure where he's got to." Maple looked confused. Mark was their older brother. But he died over 10 years ago. "We played Cluedo. I won. Colonel Mustard. Candle stick. Dining room."

"Don't you mean Ludo?" Maple mentioned, lifting the box up to show her.

"Noooo. Cludeo! Mark always hates it when I win," Wendy smirked, not taking her eyes off the TV.

"You're right. He does," Maple replied taking the Ludo box away and putting it on the shelf. "Tea?" she called out.

"No thanks dear," Wendy called back, again watching on the TV.

"Where are you off to?" Maple asked Anna as she joined her in the kitchen. "You look nice. Love the jacket." She complimented her on the pink denim jacket she was wearing. "Thanks. Just off to lunch," she replied in a rush.

"Oh yeah? Who with?"

"Just a friend. Going to Maicon's."

"Just a friend, hmm?"

"Yep, just a friend." She looked at her Aunty as if to imply the question 'is there anything else' to which Maple raised her eyebrows and looked back at her niece suggestively. "You know your mum said you, her and Uncle Mark all played Cludeo this morning."

"Cludeo? Uncle Mark? We played Ludo with Clive the carer," she replied while searching the kitchen counter for her key.

"I know that. But she said Cluedo with Uncle Mark. Like you used to, when you were younger." Anna stopped searching and looked at Maple.

"It's not the first time either. She called me D the other day. You remember D? She was our Aunty, me and your Mum's. Everyone said I took after her." Anna slowly nodded, with a worried look across her face. "I don't mean to worry you, darling. But we need to keep a closer eye on things for a while." Anna's nodding became more exaggerated.

"You go and have fun and I'll watch your Mum." Anna kissed her Aunty on the cheek and called out to her mum as she left. Wendy oblivious to her daughter's goodbye was uninterrupted as she watched the TV.

Cameron had pissed the morning away watching sports news channel. Info was going in but not much was being retained. So he was prompt to his lunch date with Anna. It looked like he had put an effort in, in his chequered shirt and chinos. But that was his go to outfit. He was sitting at their usual table by the window, with a latte waiting, when Anna arrived. She looked around for him, at the door, knowing full well where he'd be sitting. Maybe she was a little nervous. To Cameron it looked as though she was moving in slow motion as she searched the cafe. She smiled at him from across the room. All of a sudden Cameron was a little nervous too.

"That was delicious," Cameron expressed as he polished off his sandwich. "Could do with something sweet though. Did you see they've got millionaire shortbread on the menu now?"

"I did," she said with a rise smile, "although I'm not a huge fan of caramel. I'll get the brownie, I think."

"Good choice as well, I'll go grab them."

"No, I'll go. You got the coffees. Let me just finish my sandwich."

"No probs. So you like the new carer?" Cameron continued their conversation, taking a gulp of his latte.

"He seems nice. He seems professional."

"But?" Cameron interjected as she paused.

"But I don't know. Something feels off with him. Maple says I'm just looking for something to be wrong."

"Maybe Maple is right?"

"Maybe." She seemed disheartened but got up to grab their sweet treats.

"Are you free this afternoon?" Cameron enquired, his eyes on Anna over the edge of the mug, as he finished off his coffee, while she took another big bite of her brownie.

"Free as a bird. Why?"

"Funny you should say that. I have a surprise planned for you."

"Cam, where are we going?" he loved when she said his name in her raspy voice. He smiled at her as she stepped off the bus. "Not far now and you'll find out. Come on this way," he took her hand instinctively and led her down the road.

The sign read 'HUXLEY'S – Birds of Prey Centre and Garden' with a silhouette of an owl's eyes and beak. A large car park to the right and hut like building on the left, enclosed a range of birds of prey to explore with lush gardens and footpaths. It was cold today so there were many people around.

"£10 each please," an admissions cashier said. Cameron took his wallet out of his coat, while Anna eagerly looked around.

"Wow, this is really cool," Anna expressed, taking it all in.

"Yeah?" Cameron watched her as she watched her surroundings.

"Yeeaah! I didn't even know this place was here. Have you been before?" She continued to explore.

"No, but my Dad took me to one similar in London, when I was a kid." Her attention turned to him.

"That's cool. Does he like this sort of thing?" she asked.

"My dad? No. He thinks it's boring. But somehow enjoys fishing. No, my granddad loved his birds. He and I both did. He was meant to take me but he was ill. Sooo my Mum made my Dad take me."

"Well birds fascinate me!" Anna added.

"Well the show starts soon, so let's have a look around quickly first." They saw a range of different owls dotted around the grounds, including some rare breeds, such as the spectacled owl known as the panda owl, with its big black eyes, it resembled a panda. Anna pointed out it also looked like a furry penguin. That owl was her favourite. Cameron was rather impressed by the eagles, especially the male bateleur eagle, with his shiny smooth black feathers and illuminous orange beak. He looked fierce and ready to hunt. Anna captured most of it on her phone, taking selfies with Cameron and some of the birds along the way.

The show was on a beautiful grass lawn; a variety of red, yellow and purple flowers surrounded the field along with green bushy trees. The barn owl came out first and flew around, before guests got to meet a tawny owl. The tawny owl was beautifully soft, with a mixture of white and light brown feathers and narrow beady eyes. Cameron volunteered Anna take part in the finale of the show, where a falcon flew from guest to guest. The bird landed on the leather glove Anna held out. She got a moment to take in the detail of the majestic animal close up. The bird locked eyes with her as he turned his head 180 degrees; his body stayed dead still.

They finished off the afternoon with a coffee at the tea room in the centre.

"I had an amazing time today, Cam. Thank you for a great date." Cameron blushed as he sipped on his coffee. "Are you ready to go back to work on Monday?" Cameron's face dropped from trying to fight a smile off to a genuine frown.

"I had forgotten about it to be honest. It's been so nice being off. Had a chance to clear my head and see my friends and family." Cameron had an unfamiliar feeling of warmth inside of him, as he contemplated on his time off. He had enjoyed himself for the first time in years. A dark feeling then came over him as he reflected on his recent dreams; how mundane they were. No thrills. No adventure. He shook it off. He just wanted to enjoy the rest of his date with Anna. "I finally finished Cold Fighter. It wasn't what I expected at all."

"Oh no way! What did you think?" Anna excited.

"Well, I had a dream about it before I read it. Needless to say it was very different." Cameron chuckled. "He killed vampires because he wanted to protect human life; they can't defend themselves. But the way I see it let the strongest reign that's the circle of life. What gives us any more right on this planet than any other species? Right?" he eagerly awaited Anna's response.

"Yes and no. He recognises that if the vampires continue to kill the humans at the rate they were then the vampires will eventually starve, without them; he believes there are no good vampires, including himself. He does however spare vampires with similar views as him, to try and live with the humans. Like everyone, he is just doing what he thinks is right. Not everyone will agree."

"Yes, you're totally right. I can't wait to read the next one. Do you have it?"

"Of course. I'll bring it when I see you next. We should think about getting back though; I don't like to leave Mum for this long on my day off. But this has been fantastic. Thank you Cam." She leaned in and placed her hand on Cameron's arm; leaning in and softly kissing him. She smiled as the connection was broken.

Cameron made it back home in time to catch the football. He cracked a beer open and kicked his feet up. If his side won, it would top off a pretty great day. He texted Anna.

'Hope you got home safe. Great to see you today. Just watching the football. We're 1-0 at half time x.'

The afternoon with Cameron had given Anna the opportunity to take her mind off things at home. However, she was brought back to reality when she did arrive home.

26

Nightmares

Leaning on the kitchen side, Anna pushed soggy cereal around a pool of milk as she had breakfast. She dropped her spoon into the bowl and looked out into the front room at her mum watching TV, in her chair. Maple is storing away utensils from the drain.

"Tell me again. What did she say?" Anna said quietly.

"I told you last night, dear. She kept bringing up Mark over and over," Maple replied while closing the kitchen drawer, "and then she freaked, she ran up into your room and panicked you weren't in bed. She kept shouting at me. Saying Uncle Mark had taken you out while you should have been in bed asleep." Anna turned to watch her Mum again, from the kitchen.

"Her episodes are getting worse. She's not just confused anymore. She's confusing reality. Is Clive here today? I hope he's ok with her, while I'm at work. How long will you be out?" Maple could hear the concern in Anna's questions.

"Clive will be fine. He's a professional. I will only be out a few hours. Besides your mum seems a lot calmer this morning; go and sit with her a while. Tell her about your date." Anna did just that and at least for now her Mum knew who she was and was living in the present. Anna texted Cameron back on her walk to work.

'Morning, sorry I didn't get back to you last night. Hope your team won in the end. I'm on the way to work. Let me know if you're around for coffee today. Be good to chat xx.'

Cameron sat in his arm chair lethargically scooping cereal into his mouth, while staring aimlessly at his blank TV screen; reflecting on another shit night sleep. His recurring nightmare was back. He lay in a dim lit room, paralysed. He heard movement around him and began to panic. He heard voices but could not make out the words. He told himself while asleep that he was dreaming all this and told himself to remain calm, but his panic only heightened. He attempted to call out for help, but no one was listening. He thought he could wake himself up by shouting but he didn't. He was locked in a deep sleep with no way of getting out. He was awoken again by Anna's voice whispering in his head, "You don't belong here."

His phone buzzed beside him but he was unfazed and unmoved.

Screeching tyres followed by a bellowing thud snapped Cameron from his trance, the sound was so loud and clear it felt like something had come crashing through the side of the building. Cameron rushed to the window to find an old mini wrapped round a tree outside. The car was cream in colour with black racing stripes on the hood and a union jack flag on the roof. The car must have been moving at some speed; the engine had somehow removed itself from the front of the car and was now smoking in the middle of the road. Many passersby rushed to help. Cameron contemplated going out to help, but what could he do really? Someone else had surely called for help. He spectated from his first floor window; a man had managed to prise the driver's door open and was yelling instructions. But from where Cameron was standing it didn't look like the driver could hear him, he wasn't moving at all. Maybe that was the instruction. Cameron cracked his window to see if he could hear anything but the ongoing alarm from the car played out over everything else. As he stood there and watched, Cameron felt a sense of nostalgia from when he would sit at his bedroom window and nosy at passers-by; creating lives and stories for each of them. Cameron's conscious mind no longer hauled the imagination capacity for that. Leaving his phone sitting on the arm of his chair he quickly changed into some warmer clothes and headed for Maicon's. He could get a better look at the wreckage outside, this way.

Cameron crossed paths with Anna; she was just leaving Maicon's as Cameron arrived. They exchanged pleasantries but Anna had to get to work. Cameron failed to even mention the horrific car crash outside his flat. She could sense from his demeanour that something was off with him, and why didn't he text back this morning? Cameron had no such thoughts; he grabbed his coffee to go and made his way home. All he could think about was the terrible dream he had last night. He needed some adventures soon. Maybe an afternoon nap would bring some excitement later? In a world of his own, he walked by the wreckage, outside his home, oblivious. Anna sent another text before starting work.

'Is everything ok? Xx.'

She wanted to mention something about her mum but was also worried about Cameron. She thought maybe he was tired and had a bad night's sleep. But not in the way he actually had.

Cameron knew he needed to mentally prepare himself for going back to work tomorrow. But this morning he didn't want to think about it. He looked out his flat window out on the carnage outside, sipping his coffee. Policemen were putting up tape around the crime scene and blue lights flickered against the window. Screeching tyres rang through his head. As he stared down the police tape evaporated in his mind, the policemen returned to their cars and drove away in reverse and he pictured the speeding mini detach from the tree and bolt backwards down the road swerving around a fox in the road. There were foxes everywhere around here. Cameron saw a pack of them just last night, looked like they were holding a monthly meeting. Was that the cause of this accident? A hard eye closing blink shook off these thoughts and the policemen with their tape reappeared in his view. He finished off his coffee and distracted himself with housework; the only time he cleaned was to kill time.

A hard morning cleaning had worn Cameron out. He slumped in his arm chair as the kettle began to boil; his heavy eyes were hard to keep open. He would just rest them for a minute.

Darkness echoed in the room as he opened his eyes. His body so heavy, he was being forced into the chair. He heard murmuring behind him, he could turn his head on its axis but could not see anyone behind him; his body still set deep into the chair. His fingers gripped the arms of the chair, his nails scratching the fabric. As he turned his head back to front centre he saw Anna's face inches from his!

"You don't belong here!" she snapped. And her face faded away at the click of the kettle. Cameron's body was released from the chair and he looked left and right; taking a deep breath in and out when he realised he was dreaming again.

Anna hadn't heard from Cameron all morning, she didn't see him at Maicon's during her break. She typed out another text to check in but deleted it before sending.

"Anna, I am nipping out for the afternoon, will you be ok closing up the shop?"

"Yes, no problem." Anna called back Leone. Although it was busy this morning, Anna found it odd her manager leaving early. Anna felt comfortable on her own. She could really chat to the customers and offer her recommendations. Leone always moaned at Anna when she took too long with customers, even though they usually ended up buying more. The afternoon was dragging and there was no stock to fill up or tidying to do. Anna just sat and waited.

"Hi Anna," a regular customer chirped as the bell above the door rang out. "I loved those two books you recommended last week."

"Hi Carol!" Anna leaped to her feet to greet her. "How are you?"

"I'm great, apart from the weather out there. The temperature has definitely dropped this weekend. Winter is officially here."

"It certainly is. And how is Josie?" Anna beamed with enthusiasm as always.

"Yeah she's good; with her dad today, which means I can come and grab some more books! What would you recommend?

I'm looking for dark and twisted." Anna laughed and gave a suggestive eye brow raising face; leading her across the shop.

"I read this one last week. Very dark. Had me completely locked in the entire time."

"Men Amongst Men," the customer read out the title.

"What's it about?"

"Life isn't all it seems to these men. Is what they see and hear, what is really there? That you will have to work out."

"Ooo, that sounds interesting. And if you recommend it then I trust that it is! I'll take it."

"We also have these new book markers in; ultrathin but strong. So it's not too bulking inside the book. Not to mention the gorgeous pattern!" Anna handed one over to the customer.

"Oh yeah! They are nice. I'll take one too." Carol handed it back for Anna to put in the bag. Another satisfied customer.

At home Anna relieved Clive of his duty. Aunty Maple still wasn't home.

"How's she been?" Anna asked Clive.

"Really good actually, we went for a walk and she has been helping with housework. She did drop a plate in the kitchen but I quickly cleaned that up, no bother. And now she's in the front room watching TV," a cheesy grin sprawled across his face. Anna still found him creepy but she couldn't deny he was doing a good job with her mum.

"Well thanks, Clive. You can head off now."

"Right you are. Say goodbye to her from me." He grabbed his coat and left. The grin smacked across his face the whole time.

"You alright mum? Tea?"

"Yes, thanks Maple."

"It me mum." No response. Anna brought the tea in and left a mug next to her mum's chair. "What happened to your arm?" Anna noticed red marks on the top half of her mum's right arm. She took hold of the arm as she sat down next to her.

"Mum? What happened here?" Wendy shrugged her shoulder.

"I'm not sure."

"Does it hurt?"

"No, I'm fine," she assured her daughter.

"Hmm ok. How was your day?"

"Yeah the usual, me and Mark went shopping then did some house work. Then I've been waiting for you to get home from school. Do you have homework? I'm sure Mark will help you if you ask nicely."

"No, no homework today, Mum." A sense of disappointment sat in Anna's voice. "I'll put dinner on when Maple gets home." Anna looked longingly at her mum.

"Ok darling, be nice to see Maple again. Don't see her much these days."

"Maple is living with us now mum, remember?"

"Don't be silly darling, I love my sister but I wouldn't want to live with her again!" Wendy chuckled and watched on at her shows. Anna had her attention fixed on her. She squeezed her hand tightly. "I love you, mum," she whispered with a sadness in her voice.

"I love you too, darling," her mum replied.

27

Work Work Work

The time had come for Cameron to return to work. His hopes of action-packed adventure during his last sleep of his time off eluded him, which hadn't put him in the best mood. His time keeping this morning was all over the place and he was running late. Brushing his teeth as he piled papers and snacks into his work satchel, he dribbled toothpaste down his shirt. He noticed in the mirror as he spit and rinsed. He stared himself down in the bathroom mirror. Should he change or should he just leave it? He had no time for such meaningless decisions. He threw the satchel on to the bathroom floor and frantically unbuttoned his chequered shirt on his way to his bedroom. Off came navy blue chequered shirt and on went red and black chequered shirt. He finished buttoning it as he swung his front door shut. It was only when he got to Maicon's that he realised he had left his satchel at home, inside which was his notebook with all his work passwords inside. He really needed this morning coffee. "Large latte please.. Extra strong." He impatiently waited at the end of the counter for his coffee. He had 5 minutes to get to work. He shuffled his music and 'Rihanna – Work' played through his headphones. How fitting. He walked in time with the lyrics as he paced to the office. Work, work, work, work, work, work; step, step, step, step, step, step.

"Good morning, Jane," Cameron panted as he gasped for air, looking up at the clock on the wall and seeing it was 9:02.

"Welcome back Cameron, cutting it fine for time, aren't you? Mr Kyriakos is in his office. He said for you to go straight in when you got here."

"Right, ok thank you, Jane." Jane nodded her head in a diagonal direction and carried on with her work. Cameron threw his coat on his desk and headed for his boss' office. One deep breath and opened the door.

That wasn't so bad. Cameron was clear on what was expected of him and had his task for the day lined up. All he had to do now was get his head down and get it all done. Simple.

"Welcome back Cameron, are you well rested?" this smug little prick Josh. *Thinks he's special now does he? Probably after Cameron's job now, is he?* Cameron thought to himself as he smiled back at him through gritted teeth.

"Thank you, Josh," Cameron immediately turned his attention back to his work.

"Good morning Cameron!"

"Yes, thank you, Leah." She was on her way over of course. Needed her gossip.

"Get up to much while you were off?" She probed, plonking her coffee mug on Cameron's desk.

"Not really; lots to do today though. If you don't mind..."

"No, I don't mind. Was weird you not being around. I was telling Sara on Friday how it felt weird. Was it weird not being here?"

"Not really. But I do need to get this work done." This went on for another 5 minutes. Leah didn't get the hint. She just got bored of chatting with him. And of course, the rest of the office took their opportunities to welcome him back. He felt like a bereaved the way everyone patronised him. Before he knew it, it was 10 o'clock and no work was done; already behind schedule. Right... coffee, then he can crack on. Off to the kitchen he goes. He ended up making tea and coffee for the entire office and passed biscuits around. A quick toilet break, then he could crack on with his work.

"Sorry to bother you, Cameron but could you quickly take a look at this account? It's one of the accounts I've been looking after." Sara dropped a file onto his desk. Cameron shed light on what she needed which wasted more time. Sara finally retreated back to her desk across the office and Cameron could start his daily tasks. He checked his phone. He had completely forgotten about Anna! He should really text her back. Ok, just as quickly as he can.

'Hellooo. Sorry I didn't get back to you yesterday. Back to work today got lots to do. And not much time to do it. Everyone is being nice tho. Feels weird being back. Haven't had time off in a reeaally long time. I have so much annual leave left. I am really sorry about not getting back to you. Been so busy and mega tired. How was work yesterday? Anyway, I should get on with things here. Chat to you later.'

Once more look up at the clock, his eyes widened and his pupils dilated. Already gone 10:30. No more distractions. He loaded his computer and instantly his email started popping off. He was only off a few days. He had better sieve through them and make sure he hadn't missed anything important.

Cameron looked around his neatly presented desk. Where did he put the jobs list that Mr Kyriakos had assigned to him? He looked under the keyboard and his paper tray; couldn't see it. Great! He must have left it somewhere. After 10 minutes of searching he found it in the kitchen. He read through the long list and felt a little overwhelmed. He grabbed another biscuit and a glass of water and headed back to his desk. He opened a folder on his PC and started typing '10 minutes until lunch, Cameron. How are you getting on?' Cameron could feel the body heat radiating over his shoulder. He swivelled on his chair and looked up at his boss.

"Erm.. Yeah, not bad. Getting back in the swing of it."

"Good. I expect everything done by 5 this afternoon." Cameron looked up at the clock on the wall. It was 12:23. He may as well head out for lunch and start again in an hour.

Anna was un-boxing books when her phone twinkled in her purse. She hoped it was Cameron but she hadn't heard from him since their date; which she felt went really well. So why hadn't he called or text since? Maybe Cameron didn't enjoy himself as much as Anna did. She daydreamed about their kiss. Cameron certainly didn't come across as someone who would rush Anna. But maybe that was his mind? She got lost in her thoughts until interrupted by Leone. "When you're done with the delivery could you dust the windows?"

"Yes, no problem... Leone can I ask you something?"

"Sure," she encouraged with a friendly tone.

"Well I'm sort of seeing this boy. He is great. But only when we're together. When we're not he seems distant and I feel like he has something else on his mind."

"What? Sex? Most men do." Anna blushed at her boss' question.

"No. I just feel like he's keeping something back. Not just from me. From everyone." Anna felt it hard to explain.

"He seems a little strange," Leone said.

"I'm probably making him sound strange but he's not. He's lovely."

"Sooo?" Leone insinuated.

"So what?" Anna looked on confused.

"Have you? You know? S.E.X?" she spelled it out for her.

"Nooooo," Anna dismissed blushing more and more "we have kissed though," she added as she fought back a smile, "but I need to know him more before I take things any further. Find out if or what he's holding back. Do you think I'll scare him off not taking things further?"

"If you do, then he's not worth it, babe. Now get back to work."

The hours ticked by. Cameron found it tough all day to stay focused on his work; he had checked his weekend bets and placed some more, for the upcoming games. Mindless social media scrolling snuck into his work time as well. Around 3pm he could over hear Leah and Sara gossiping. Cameron recognised one of the names in the conversation; Leah's ex-boyfriend. He was up to no good again. Cameron had managed to get some work done. But only parts of every job on the list, nothing completed. Well that was a job for another day. A good but slow start as he got back into the swing of things. As the clock stuck 5pm Cameron grabbed his things and bolted for the exit, before Mr Kyriakos grabbed him for a chat. With his headphones in, he braved the cold and charged straight home from work. A text from Anna pinged through as he got to the bottom of the stairs to his flat.

'Hii, that's ok. I'm used to your slow replies now. Hope your first day was good. Any plans tonight? I've just finished and heading home to mum. Are we doing Maicon's this week? Xx.'

Ready meal slung in the microwave for dinner and a bit of tele to get him through the evening. He arranged lunch with Anna tomorrow and didn't look at his phone again this evening.

"Mum your arms!" Anna noticed when she got home that Wendy's arms had begun to bruise. "You really need to be careful. These are looking nasty." Anna examined her wounds, the previous marks on her arms were now bruising and she seemed to have many more today. "Have you fallen today?" she insisted.

"Not that I know of, it's fine. Any homework today, darling?" Anna's concern lifted and her response was dejected.

"No mum, no homework."

28

Electric

A warm sensation rushed through Cam's body. It felt like power and confidence. A sense of purpose coursed through his veins. Nothing was impossible for him. He was faster, strong, smarter, maybe the fastest, strongest and smartest. He could do anything. He looked around the street he was in, pavements turned to grass, cars passing by turned to footballers and houses turned to huge crowds. The ball came to his feet, he took one touch and pinged a 30 yard pass straight to the striker's feet, who was brought down on the edge of the box, by a defending player. Cam lined up the free kick before curling it over the wall and past the keeper! He sprinted off in celebration and the grass beneath him turned to orange rubber track, he looked left and right and he had huge stocky men, in tiny shorts running beside him. He pulled out ahead of the rest with ease; didn't even duck his head at the finish line. He snatched the union jack flag and threw it up behind his head and roared out loud to the crowd. Who started to aggressively charge down towards him; one by one he fought them off, damming right and left hand jabs to each attacker; every blow accurate and destructive. The track was full of wasted bodies. He looked down at his feet as they start to sink into the ground; the rubber was now sand. He felt heat from a beaming sun hit his face and the oncoming threat turned into beautiful women; each one more beautiful than the last. They all wanted a piece of Cam as he strolled down the beach. He would snog each one before choosing which to take on a date. The sun turned to moon and a light breeze replaced the warmth. He was no longer walking on hot sand but a dimly lit side street, with wind instruments playing in the background and his stunning date on his arm; he intook the smell of garlic and herbs, in a traditional Italian restaurant. He charmed ever so impressively - his date, the waiters and the other guests couldn't get enough of him.

He felt electric.

His alarm echoed the room and woke Cameron from his slumber. He lay awhile looking up at his motionless ceiling fan, taking a moment to appreciate a much-needed captivating dream. Being mindful of the time, he reflected on his adventure whilst absorbing his reflection in his bathroom mirror. Simultaneously preparing himself for another day at work. He felt like he'd been back for weeks, when in reality it had only been one day. He struggled to stimulate his mind at work all morning; easily distracted again, meant little work was being completed. He tried to focus and put his mind to finishing at least one task before lunch. This he almost did, but he couldn't work into his lunch as he was meeting Anna at Maicon's.

Anna was already there waiting for Cameron at their usual table by the window. She had a coffee waiting for him so he bought lunch. He placed 2 sandwiches down on the table and threw his coat on the back of the chair. He walked round and gave Anna a peck on the lips, before taking his seat across the table. He felt like he had known her for so long, it was comfortable being with her. Anna on the other hand wanted to know more. "How have the first days been back at, work?" she asked.

"Hard work, got lots to do." Which was partly true; he did have lots to do but it hadn't been hard work.

"What made you choose accounting?" she continued with genuine interest.

"I'm not sure to be honest. It seemed like a secure job. It felt like a grown-up job. Something I could make a career from."

"That makes sense. What did you want to be when you were little?"

"A footballer like most kids! But that wasn't really a possibility."

"Why's that?" she asked, washing down some sandwich with coffee.

"Well, I wasn't very good. Even my super coach dad couldn't make me any better. But I was always good with other parts of the game."

"Maybe you could have coached like your dad?"

"Not like him. He was so confident. When he spoke, people listened."

"Well, what is your dream job now? Do you have one?" she inquired.

"I'm not too sure to be honest. I don't really think about it." He thought in his head the only dream worth chasing was the ones he had in his sleep at night. "I guess it would have to be something sport related. I thought about journalism when I left school."

"Why didn't you follow that up? You're smart enough for sure." He paused and finished off his coffee before replying.

"I guess it was unrealistic. I had to do something serious and get a job to start earning money. I wanted to leave my parents' home and I did just that once I finished college. Did you go to university?" Anna in turn finished her coffee before answering. "I did. Can you guess what I studied?" she smirked across the table.

"Don't tell me? English Lit?" he smirked back at her. "Bingo. That obvious is it?"

"Yep, that obvious!" they both laughed.

At the cafe door Anna lingered as she looked out at the grey sky. Cameron was throwing his coat on next her. Rain started to fall.

"I had a lovely time," she uttered, still looking up at the skies. Cameron grabbed her arm and turned her to face him; without saying a word, landed a strong kiss on her lips. Rain spattered their faces as they kissed for several seconds.

"Me too," he replied.

He felt electric.

Sunday evening and another week had passed; boring mundane work, fun with Jeffro and Anna and a mixture of exciting and dull dreams. Next weekend was the wedding of Julie and Carl. Cameron hadn't seen Julie since the last family wedding. They were so close growing up, but like everyone else in his life, Cameron pushed her away, everyone except Jeffro. He was ever present for Cameron. He was a constant.

His weekend winded down and Cameron was mooching around his flat. His phone buzzed on the kitchen unit. His mum.

'Do you have a suit to wear for the wedding? Do you want to get ready with us and all head together? Let me know xx.'

Of course, he had a suit. Why did she speak to him like he was 12 years old? He wore the same suit for every occasion, just swapping the tie each time. Smart.

29

Friday Night Dinner

After a long week of tedious work, stale dreams and a vacant social life Cameron had Anna coming over for dinner. He hadn't seen her all week but they had been texting continuously. He felt like he needed to impress her but yet his cooking skills had much left to be desired. He lived off ready meals and yogurts. He decided on a pasta bolognaise; the only dish he remembered his mum teaching him and she was an expert at spag bol. He popped into the Budget-Mark on his way home from work; he planned on making it all from scratch but to avoid any fuck ups he thought it best to buy the sauce in a jar. He bought a stick of garlic bread to go with it too.

He had no candles at home or anything romantic at that matter. His front room light however did dim. That set the mood a little. His flat was always clean though. Cleaning helped kill time for Cameron and he had a lot of time to kill.

"This is a lovely building," Anna said as Cameron let her in.

"It's an old mansion that has been adapted into flats."

"Very nice! I bought some red wine. I didn't know what you liked or what we were eating!" Anna was wearing red tights with a red skirt that had handles that went up over her shoulders; with a yellow and red hooped t-shirt, under her warm winter coat.

"Oh, that's great; we can have it after the meal. I won't drink with dinner. Come in. Let me take your coat." He looked around for a place to put her coat. He decided to just throw it on the kitchen counter. "Make yourself at home. Dinner will be about 10 minutes. Oh, do you want a drink?" he asked as he nervously fumbled around. Anna sat in Cameron's armchair. It was the only seat in the front room although it was wide enough for 2 people to sit. Closely.

"That reclines." Cameron instructed as he plonked 2 plates of pasta on to the table. Anna made her way over to the table. Thankfully this had 2 chairs. "Aaand garlic bread. Bon appetite." He proudly said as he placed a stick of garlic bread, sitting on a chopping board, in to the middle of the table.

"Do you speak French?"

"Err, no!"

"Well this looks lovely. Do you have any parmesan?"

"Oh, shit no!" He was annoyed at himself for not thinking of cheese.

He washed up everything straight after eating. Anna was in charge of picking the film to watch. She struggled in her mind to work out what Cameron would like. She would watch anything. She was hoping that not much watching would be happening. She elected for a comedy. She loved Adam Sandler.

Cameron dimmed the lights even lower after he finished clearing up. He put 2 glasses of wine on the side table and took a seat on the arm chair next to Anna, just as the opening credits were playing. The pair edged nearer to one another naturally as the film played on. Cameron slyly put his arm around Anna so her head slid comfortable on his chest. "Pass me some wine please." Anna reached over and handed him a glass, resting her hand on his leg after. She ran her hand up his leg and placed her it on his lap. Cameron's heart began to race inside his chest, he clutched the wine glass tightly in his hand. She slowly unzipped his flies and sneaked her hand inside. She felt him grow harder inside her grasp. She looked up at him and leant up for a kiss. They locked lips for several minutes but Cameron didn't initiate anything further. She dropped her head back on to his chest, took her hand out of his trousers and rested it on his stomach. They watched the rest of the film. Cameron felt dejected. He cowarded out and offered Anna another glass of wine.

"That was good," Cameron said as the movie ended.

"Yes, I enjoyed that. Very funny. Wow it's late. I should head off. We still grabbing coffee in the morning?" she asked as she threw her coat on. Cameron tried to work out if he'd upset her. She seemed her normal self.

"For sure, 8 o'clock?"

"Perfect. I'll see you then." She gave him an extended peck on the lips before heading out. Cameron hung his head after he closed the door shut. What happened there? He asked himself. Disappointed he didn't make a move. His confidence was shot. He thought about this as he washed the wine glasses. He thought about it as he brushed his teeth. He thought about it as he lay in bed, unable to fall asleep.

His eyes closed and in his mind he saw Anna, standing naked, just out of reach. She turned away and sauntered away from him. He followed in pursuit but she began to vanish. Cam became cemented in his place; his feet locked in position.

"You don't belong here." Anna's voice echoed around him. Oh god! What was that? It felt so good. Was that Anna? He looked down and saw a jelly fish cloaking his manhood. Cam felt disgusted but was powerless to it. He looked up but a force pushed his gaze back downwards. Now his lower body was submerged under water. Different horrid creatures festered on him. He screamed out in horror.

"Make it stop! Make it stop!" A naked Anna swam towards him. A naked Anna swam straight past him. His eyes opened. A hypnagogic hallucination. A waking dream before he fell into his sleep. He felt inside his boxers. He had messed. What a weird passage of time! He took himself to the bathroom to clean up; replacing his sticky underwear for a fresh pair and tucking himself back into bed.

Let's try this again, shall we? He closed his eyes.

30

The Wedding

Every window in Cameron's flat was dripping condensation. Winter was certainly on its way. He was cocooned under his duvet; he didn't want to leave the warmth of his bed. Alas he only had a few hours before he needed to be at his parents' in Putney. He looked up at his ceiling fan thinking how it was the only part of his flat he didn't clean; he could see dust and cobwebs collecting up there. Why is it even here? To cool the room for the 3 days of heat that come each summer in the UK? His alarm released him from these mindless thoughts of his useless bedroom ceiling fan. His alarm was sounding to remind him that he had scheduled coffee with Anna this morning before she started work. He struggled to recall his dream from last night. Maybe that was for the best.

Cameron felt disgusting on his walk to Maicon's as he had forgotten to brush his teeth. But oh well, minty fresh teeth didn't mix well with coffee. He cupped his hands over his mouth and breathed into them, then instantly sniffed the air trapped in his grasp. Everything seemed fine but Cameron pondered on this method and questioned its accuracy and effectiveness of one smelling one's own oral odours. Whilst captivated in this thought Cameron failed to realise he had just walked across 3 drains. He halted his strides and froze. He didn't need this today. Not on the day of the wedding. Maybe if he told Anna when he saw her, that it is bad luck and it happened to him, which would cancel out the bad luck; by recognising the potential for bad luck to strike. A double bluff on fate if you like. He raced to the cafe and found Anna waiting patiently for him, as usual, at the table by the window, as usual.

"It's a shame you couldn't bring a plus one today. I would have loved to come with you," Anna expressed to Cameron.

"That would have been nice. But I guess Julie didn't expect me to have anyone to bring." Anna wasn't being weird. Which was good. Cameron was desperate for there to be no awkwardness after last night.

"It would have been weird meeting your parents for the first time at such a big occasion," Anna humoured as she reached across the table to hold Cameron's hand. Cameron's face turned from subtle happy to slight confusion as he processed what Anna had said. Why was she talking about meeting his parents all of a sudden, that was a little out of the blue. "Are you looking forward to it?" she asked.

"Not really. Just want today to be over to be honest. I hate the same small talk with all the family. Same old shit over and over. I haven't spoken to Julie in years. I don't think she'd even invite me if our families weren't close. We were best friends when I was younger but I've only met Carl a couple of times. Are you looking forward to work?" The pair still had one hand joined across the table; leaving one hand accessible for coffee drinking, of course.

"Yes, Saturdays are great; lots of regular customers. The day goes quickly as I'm busy most of the shift. What time are you leaving?"

"I've got to be at my Mum and Dad's for midday. So I'll probably head off just before 11." Anna could tell form Cameron's voice that he had no excitement or interest in this at all. "The worst part is it will finish so late, I will have to stay at my parents' tonight."

"Well you can text me if you need an escape!" She said with a cheesy grin spread across her face. Cameron lifted a rise smile, from one side of his mouth before moving on. "You up to anything tonight?"

"I'll probs just get a takeaway and read a book indoors. One of my regulars has gifted me a hand me down book. I'm excited to read it. Nice when the customers give me recommendations for a change." They carried on chatting for 10 minutes until Anna had to head to work. "Text me and let me know how it goes today." Anna leant down and kissed Cameron as she threw her handbag over her shoulder. "Oh don't get up," she said, placing her hand on his shoulder.

"I'll walk you out. I'm going to grab another coffee before I go anyway." They shared a slightly longer kiss at the door before Anna rushed off. Cameron needed one more coffee to ready himself for the day ahead.

He got to his parents a little after 12. But why he bothered he did not know. His dad was sitting watching football build up in the front room, in his vest and pants, while his mum was still in her nighty. "Blimey Mum! Put some clothes on!" Cameron shielded the view of his half naked mother with his hands.

"Wow, don't you look handsome," she said as she ignored his comment and grabbing him for a hug instead. "Go through and sit with your dad. My make-up is nearly done." Cameron was wearing his only suit. A grey two piece; not light, not dark, just grey. He had opted for a maroon wool tie for this event with little grey and white specks found hidden in the texture. His hair was pushed to the side with clay. He didn't often put anything in his hair.

"Alright, Dad?" he groaned as he plonked himself on the sofa across from where his Dad was sitting.

"Yeah, morning son. Beer?" He tilted his half-drunk bottle in Cameron's direction.

"Erm... Nah it's a little early for me. And not the morning either." His dad just grunted in reply. "Shame we'll miss the game today. They'll kick off just as the ceremony will be."

"I didn't know you were still following them." Bat said forcefully as his swigged his lager.

"Yep, same as always." Barry Peters looked at his son with his bottom lip over lapping his top one, impressed.

"You look good, son. Nice tie." He necked the remainder of the beer and got himself to his feet, letting out a massive sigh, "Bloody back. Work has killed me! Best get ready before your Mum starts nagging. Sure you don't want a beer?" Cameron just shook his head. He put some bets on while he waited.

"Cars here!" Patricia Peters called out from the top of the stairs. "Can you let them know we'll be right out, Cameron?"

Cameron listened to his Dad bang on about football the entire journey. Until they pulled up to golf course 45 minutes later. A long stone covered drive way led to a big red brick coloured building. The drive way split into a loop for an in/

out service. A grand ornate porte-cochere led to the entrance. Everything else you could see was green; green grass, green trees and a lake that reflect the greenery. Guests had begun to arrive and were filtering through inside the building. Carl and his best man were inside greeting people; both wearing similar grey suits to Cameron, only smarter and three-piece. Carl's tie was white while in compadre's was sage green. There was a towering staircase opposite the front door which led up and either left or right. Shiny wooden handrails ran the entire routes. Carl explained the ceremony was upstairs to the right, the wedding breakfast would be hosted in the room to the left upstairs, while the party and bar were situated downstairs round the back of the stair case. Pat commented several times to Cameron how beautiful everything was. Cameron couldn't deny it though. It looked phenomenal. Baz in turn continuously commented on how much money they must have spent *'on a do this fancy'*.

Cameron cracked a genuine smile as he saw his childhood friend appear at the back of the room in her fabulous slick wedding dress. She had the perfect body shape for a wedding dress. Her hour glass figure looked perfectly at home in the rustic off white gown. She had classy, flower patterned lace sleeves that ran all the way down her arms and over the backs of her hand; an elastic hoop secured them to her finger; she had a veil sprouting from her dark hair, that matched this pattern which masked her face as she strode down the aisle solo and clutching gorgeous sage, blush and white bouquet in her hands. Cameron remembered that she always said she wanted to walk down the aisle herself. One because then it would all be about her, which she joked, but Cameron was sure she really meant. And two because she believed that it was a silly tradition. It had nothing to do with the credibility of her father, whom she loved very much and he was always there for her. Julie's dad was always a father figure in Cameron's life. He believed in Cameron, always making Cameron feel valued.

"She looks tall today," Pat whispered to her son.

"She does! Tall, proud and confident- must be those louboutin stilettos on her feet!" Cameron laughed just as he made an endearing eye contact with Julie, who blushed at his gaze.

Baz made a B line for the bar as soon as the happy couple were back down the aisle and out of sight. He brought Pat and Cameron drinks back, as they mingled with other guests. Cameron was starving but didn't remember what was on the menu. "Mum I don't remember picking what I wanted for dinner?"

"That's 'cause we didn't get a choice. Everyone is getting the same." Cameron prayed he liked it; he hadn't eaten since 9 o'clock this morning.

Finally everyone was sat for the wedding breakfast as the couple paraded through the circular tables to the head table, which was long and rectangular. Everything in here looked on point as well. Cameron said to his mum how Julie had always been a perfectionist and it had paid off now.

Caesar salad to start but it was so fresh no one complained. Bottles of wine on the table were restocked straightaway- no questions asked. Cameron enjoyed a nice glass or 5 with food. They heard from Julie's father as he gave an awkward but loving speech. Then the main course came out- a full blown roast dinner. Chicken, veggies, roast potatoes, parsnips, Yorkshire puddings and the piece de resistance, pigs in blankets. All cooked to perfection and smothered in gravy. Cameron was starting to enjoy himself. After the dinner the groom gave an extremely long but profoundly emotional speech, thanking lost loved ones along the way. Hopes were high for dessert after an impressive display throughout the meal; but hopes were crushed as tiramisu hit everyone's place mats. Disappointment echoed through the hall. The best man, Chris, had the crowd in stitches as he stitched up his best mate, in his speech. Full bellies didn't stop laughter rumble through the room. He left everyone stunned with a story revealing how he and Carl were bonded for life; explaining how Carl lost his virginity behind some bins on a holiday to Greece, to the same girl, Chris had lost his virginity to, just a few hours earlier. Carl's grandmother, who was sitting just 10 feet from them, could not believe her ears.

"It's so great to see you, Cam." Julie said as she sat down with the Peters. She had always called him Cam. Julie pointed out the he had drunk eyes already. He expressed that he was a fan of the wine! They caught up briefly before Bat plonked a pint down in front of Cameron, which she took this break in conversation as good chance to move on. "Catch you guys in a bit, got lots of people to see. Love the hat, Pat." That put a beaming smile on Cameron's Mum's face.

"So what's going on with Hendricks this season?" Julie's cousin, who was on their table, asked Cameron. "Only 1 goal and 2 assists so far this season. Way off his tally from this time last season," Barry interrupted before Cameron got a chance to reply.

"He's not interested is he, he's expecting one of the big clubs to come in for him in January. They won't though, not with his poor performances. He needs to get his head up and start taking players on like he did last season; just lazy if you asked me." He glugged on his pint, smug with himself. Cameron interjected.

"Problem is everyone is doubling up on him now. As soon as he got the ball a central midfielder comes across and closes him out with the full back. I think he's playing smart." Cameron started to explain. "He moved the ball into space and opened up the game. Franco on the other wing gets more of the ball now 'cause he's allowed a lot more time and space. That's why we've not suffered from Hendricks' lack of numbers. We've just found other ways. He is still a classy player."

"I've noticed that," Julie's dad Tony put his hand on Cameron's shoulder. "Especially last week against City! They had 3 on him. Left loads of holes in the middle and we still won comfortably." Tony confidently backed up Cameron's point.

"I wouldn't listen to him. My son. Thinks he knows it all. You could just about mark the names on the team sheet, let alone any of the players on the actual pitch. Fucking useless he was." An onslaught of abuse was followed by an evil cackle of laughter. Cameron grabbed his pint and excused himself from the table.

"Oh Baz why you gotta say these things for?" Pat huffed at her husband.

"What!?" he snarled. "He's too sensitive."

"Always good to see you, Bat." He raised his glass towards Cameron's folks.

"Tony." Barry Peters respectfully tilted his glass on the table, in Tony's direction.

Cameron had taken himself out on to a balcony off from the hallway to get some air. It was dark out now; a crisp autumn evening. The moon ignited the golf course as Cameron looked out across the horizon. He sunk his beer down as he took in the night skies; he was feeling wavy now. He had a blank text message to Anna, open on his unlocked phone, in his hand.

"Cam?" a soft voice spoke behind him.

"Nat?" The realisation came to him as he turned to see Julie's younger sister standing there "Wow, you're all grown up." She looked a lot different to Julie, although they had some similar facial features. Natalie had piercing green eyes and golden blonde hair, while Julie's was jet black. Natalie was stunningly beautiful; she always has been. She was shorter than her sister and had more natural curves. Cameron couldn't help but notice her cleavage exposed from her bridesmaid dress, as she made her way over to him.

"What you doing out here? It's freezing." They looked out on the open field together.

"Just needed to get some air. Was a lovely ceremony."

"Yeah. So beautiful. Carl's speech had me in tears; had to reapply my make-up. How do I look!?" she turned to him with a cheesy grin and her hands nestled under her chin in a lily pad shape. Cameron chuckled as he looked back at her. He didn't know what to say as he took in her beauty.

"You look," he paused, "you look great!"

"You know it must have been almost 10 years since we last spoke." She worked it out in her head as she said it. "I saw you at Jack's wedding. But couldn't buck up the nerve to speak to you."

"Why would you need to buckle up the nerve?"

"Well, I had a huge crush on you when we were little; Julie's cool sexy best friend." Cameron was taken back; no one had ever described him as cool or sexy before.

"Wow, I had no idea. You were just Julie's annoying little sister." He raised his eyebrows at her. "I'm only kidding." He wrapped his jacket over her bare shoulders, as she shivered.

"Do you remember me, you and Julie all climbed that tree out in our garden. You both went down before me and I got stuck up there. You had to climb back up and get me." She reminisced.

"Oh yeah! Your parents wouldn't be home for hours; couldn't leave you up there, all day."

"Ahh, my hero!" she joked. "Shall we go inside and get a drink?" He nodded and she took his hand and led him back inside.

Cameron avoided his father for the remainder of the night, spending most of his time chatting with Julie and Nat. He even engaged in some light one, two step dancing, after a few rum and cokes. Cameron slumped down at their table as the night winded down. He watched his Mum and Dad locked together; swaying from side to side as they slow danced together. He pulled his phone out and unlocked the screen. A blank message addressed to Anna was still waiting.

"It was really great seeing you tonight Cam." Nat's voice slurred from behind him. He leant his head back and caught her eye over his shoulder. A smirk formed from one side of his mouth.

"You really need to stop sneaking up behind me."

"We should get together again soon," she stated.

"Are you still living over Putney way?"

"Yeah, I'm still at Mum and Dad's; milking the free ride for as long as possible." She sat down next to Cameron. He hated coming back this way. Seeing his mum and dad was a chore.

"How's things with your Mum and Dad?" he asked.

"You heard then. Things aren't the same but they still love each other. Dad is just too wrapped up with work and it drives my Mum insane."

"Is he still at the paper?" Cameron rested his hand on hers, which was resting on her knee.

"Yep, he'll have been editor for 10 years, this year." She didn't sound ecstatic by this. She sandwiched his hand in both of hers.

"It would be good to see you again," he admitted.

"Give me your phone then." Cameron took a few seconds to take her in, as she typed her number in to his phone. She really was stunning. He broke his luring stare as she passed the phone back to him. She leant in and kissed him right on the corner of his mouth; noticeably closer to his lip than his cheek. "I think your parents are ready to go, but text me yeah?" she stroked his leg and got to her feet.

"Yeah." His voice croaked as he replied with a nervous smirk on his face.

"Bye Pat. Bye Bat," she chirped as she skipped past Cameron's mum and dad. She took one more glance back at Cameron after passing his parents and he watched her glide away.

"Ready son? The cars outside waiting."

"Yeah, let's go."

He stared at Nat's number in his phone book the majority of the ride home. The night was a bit of a blur now. He couldn't really believe what had happened. He closed his contacts and opened his messages; there was the unwritten text to Anna. He pondered a moment, looking out the window. He looked back at his phone, about to type, when he clicked the lock button and shoved his phone back in his pocket. He rested his head back and closed his eyes. The car ride was beginning to make him nauseous. He burped and a small amount of sick flowed up his throat and lingered in the back of his mouth. He swallowed it back down and opened his eyes again. He unwinded the window and let the cold air leave his stomach. He recognised streets and buildings, thankfully they were nearly home.

Pat placed a washing up bowl next to Cameron's bed, just in case he needed it. Cameron removed his suit trousers but fell to the bed and passed out, before he had time to remove his shirt. His mum pulled the duvet over him and left him be. He never did send that message to Anna.

31

Jeffro's

The room spun as Cameron's eyes adjust to the light. It felt strange waking up in his childhood bed. He glanced down at the washing up bowl to find no vomit. He sat up and rubbed his eyes, taking a second or two to judge if he was feeling rough; it would seem he had narrowly avoided the hangover, for now at least. His belly started to rumble, he hadn't eaten since the wedding meal yesterday afternoon; he smelt bacon wafting from the kitchen, through the landing and into his bedroom. He shuffled his feet into an old pair of his dad's slippers and threw his teenage self's dressing gown around him. He released a lengthy fart as he took his morning piss, in the family bathroom, before making his way down stairs.

"What's the time?" he asked as he entered the kitchen and realising he had left his phone upstairs.

"Almost 10," his mum replied as she slaved away over the hob. "I'm surprised you're awake. I was about to send your father up to wake you." Bat was sat, hidden behind the Sunday papers. "Yeah, but luckily you're here," he muttered from behind the sports section. "How you feeling son? You didn't look too healthy when we got home." He folded the top right corner of the paper and peered round at Cameron.

"Surprisingly I feel fine, just tired," he said with a spring in his voice.

"Take a seat and food will be ready in a minute." Pat instructed. Cameron and his dad sat in silence as they waited for their breakfast. "There you go. Two full English. Tea, Cameron?"

"Yes please, mum."

"What time you heading off?" Pat asked as she set two mugs of tea down along with her own food; scrambled eggs on toast.

"I'll probably go straight after breakfast if that's alright; I'm meeting Jeffro this afternoon." Which was a lie, but he didn't want to hang around.

"Yes, that's fine dear. How is Jeffrey these days?" To which Cameron replied in his usual fashion.

"Same old."

Funnily enough Cameron noticed that Jeffro had in fact texted him. And funnily enough he did want to meet later tonight. Cameron replied agreeing to meet. If anything it was just a good way of passing the time tonight.

On the train Cameron messaged Anna.

'Good morning. Yesterday wasn't as awful as I thought it would be. Good to see some old friends. Sorry I didn't message you. Are you at work already? What are you doing tonight?'

But it was Natalie who consumed his mind for the rest of the journey home. Absent of headphones to listen to music or watch anything on his phone, he day dreamed of Natalie;

reminiscing about yesterday. The ticket inspector passed through the carriage and brought him out of his reverie. He headed to Maicon's for coffee before heading home. Even with the boost of caffeine he felt weary as he relaxed in his arm chair; he fought to keep his eyes open. A light sparked in his mind and a nap would be beneficial to help him get through the evening with Jeffro. He gave in to his heavy eye lids and drifted off to sleep.

In his psyche he was confronted with a vision of Natalie, she was in sun kissed wheat field, skipping along and running her arms through the wheat tips; her illuminating smile constant as she looked back at Cam. The hot sun reflected off her blonde locks that bounced gracefully with each stride. Her smile slowly turned to a frown; she was no longer running, her arms were by her side and the sun set rapidly behind her. The moon filled the sky now and Cam heard someone calling out, "You don't belong here" behind him. It was Anna, 20 metres away. She was calling him towards her with her arms. Cam turned back to find Natalie standing inches from him; her eyes were blood shot. Her head tilted to left 45 degrees as her jaw unhinged, her mouth widened to the size of a watermelon and her legs extended, so she was towering over Cam. He felt a presence behind him. It was Anna; also red eyed, also looming over him. He pinched his eyes closed and felt a surge of heat strike his face. He opened his eyes and they were both gone; the sun had returned, however he heard a clunking sound, getting louder and louder. A colossal combine harvester was nearing closer and closer to him; he ran for it, as fast as his legs would take him, but he felt gravity defying him. His footsteps were feather light on the ground and the churning sound from the advancing tractor grew more menacing with every pace.

Just as the panic set in Cameron was awake again. Fixed in his chair his confused mind tried to process the proceedings that just unfolded inside his musings. Street lamps outside were lit and darkness filled his front room. What time was it? He checked his phone. It was 5:16PM. And a text from Anna, received at 2:55PM.

'Heyyy, I'm glad you had fun. I was lonely all evening. I read a book while Mum watched TV then had an early night. Work has been mega busy today and up to nothing tonight! Why, did you want to do something? Xx."

He was meant to be at Jeffro's in 45 minutes, therefore didn't have time to see Anna. Then he had a thought.

'I'm going to my mate Jeffro's house tonight. Why don't you come?'

He replied to her before getting himself up out the arm chair and into the shower.

'Yeah sure, as long as he doesn't mind me crashing your night xx.'

Cameron sat on his bed in his towel.

'Meet at mine and we'll walk there together.'

Which is exactly what Anna did; she had the tights and skirt combo on again this evening, but in purple and black, not yellow like Friday.

Cameron gave Anna a step by step explanation of the wedding yesterday. He did however fail to mention that Natalie had given him her number; he skipped over Natalie complete actually. He stopped for beers on their way and got a bottle of wine for Anna. She didn't work Mondays so a few drinks tonight wouldn't hurt.

"Who is this?" Jeffro bluntly asked, his arm out, stopping them from entering the building.

"This is Anna. The girl I told you about?" Cameron replied putting his arm around her.

"Arghh, you been telling people about me?" she joked. Jeffro then proceeded to interrogate her, on his door step.

"Can she be trusted? Do you or any of your family work for the government? Or in the public sector?" he quizzed.

"Errr, no? I don't think so," she stuttered.

"You don't think!"

"Don't be stupid mate," Cameron interjected. "Let us in; it's freezing out here."

"Hmm, ok in you come," he said frantically pulling them inside. A quick look left and right down the street before he followed them in. "Go through to the kitchen, Anna, I need to speak to Cameron." He smirked and showed her down the corridor. "Why did you bring her here!?"

"She's alright. What you worried about?" Cameron shrugged off his line of questioning.

"I'll tell you what I'm worried about." He looked over Cameron's shoulder to see Anna snooping around in the kitchen. "Come on I'll show you." He grabbed Cameron by the scruff of the neck and led him into the office. "It's complete. Look. I've finished." He unveiled the Maghurt F4.50. "It does it all. Everything we've read about. It's all true." Cameron took it in amazement.

"It's amazing." He wandered to the computer with his eyes fixated on it.

"What's that?" Cameron and Jeffro's gaze snapped to the office door, where they see Anna standing. Jeffro raced over leads Anna away and slammed the door shut. Cameron swiftly opened the door again and joined them in the hallway.

"Just show her Jeff." Jeffro looked at Cameron, and then at Anna, his mind was searching for guidance.

"Ok, swear what you see here will go no further than these 4 walls." Anna chuckled at Jeffro's unfazed glare. "Swear it!"

"Just swear it Anna," Cameron decisively instructed.

"I swear." Jeffro took a moment and then led them both back into the office. A noise similar to an old clunky printer sounded as he fired up the Maghurt F4:50. 'Maghurt' shone brightly in white Italic writing across the screen. The home page was a black screen with a blinking orange line in the bottom left corner.

"Simple but mighty this machine. If I escape this search engine system I can browse the web as normal et cetera. But this search bar is where the magic happens. Right, give me a year."

"A year?" Anna replied, confused and intrigued. Jeffro turned and grinned, looking through his thick set glasses with an evil look.

"Yes. A year. And let's say... a profession..." Anna looked at Cameron for guidance but he perched his lower lip over his top and shrugged his left shoulder at her.

"Hmm... 1979," she said with confidence. "Policemen."

"So random," Cameron commented.

"Right you are! 1979 coming up." He eagerly tapped away on the keyboard and a programming noise sounded from within the machine. It didn't sound healthy. "What police force?" he pressed. "Errr... The Met..." She stuttered in response. A few seconds passed as Jeffro typed again.

"Here we are. The entire Met police force roster from 1979-1980. Case files. Some are classified, which means even the top dogs in the police can't see them."

"Fucking hell Jeff!" Cameron interrupted "This is illegal!"

"I know, it's great isn't it?" Jeffro laughed as he pushed his glasses tight to his face and returned to the screen.

"What next?" He showed them both the full power of the Maghurt F4:50.

"This is so cool; you two are such nerds." Anna was impressed. Something she found Cameron continuing to do.

"So Cameron? How was the wedding then? Any goss?" Jeffro prised himself way from the computer for just a moment to pester Cameron with some questions.

"No, no gossip; was all a little boring to be honest," Cameron replied awkwardly and unconvincingly.

"Egh- fair enough." Jeffro's attention was drawn back to the monitor, his focus glaring through his thick glasses.

"Oh, why don't you tell Anna about that game we used to play at school? You know." He tried to catch the right words to describe what he meant, but he was only bumbling. "Where you would say do this or that, when this happened or you had to do that. You know!" Cameron looked awfully confused as he tried to process what Jeffro was trying to say. Anna looked intrigued but they were going to lose her interest any moment. "Would you rather?" Cameron questioned Jeffro.

"Would you rather!" Jeffro confirmed.

"I'm not sure Anna wants to play that," Cameron presumed.

"I do want to play," Anna snapped excitedly.

"She does want to play!" Jeffro reiterated. Cameron resisted briefly but the pair goaded him into playing.

"Basically someone gives 2 scenarios and you have to choose which you'd rather. It's pretty simple."

"You do one," Jeffro asked promptly, "yours were always so good." Cameron looked unforgivingly at his best friend and gave a sarcastic smile. He turned his attention to Anna as he begrudgingly thought of an example.

"Erghhhhh. Ok, What would you rather... Your calves cramp up every time you laugh or your back spasms every time you cry?"

"I'm sorry what?" Anna laughed and held her arms out in confusion.

"Yep. Yep. That's the game. You have to answer. Try and think logically; if that's at all possible here."

Anna stood and thought, still slightly bewildered by this game.

"Well I guess I laugh more than I cry, but back spasms are worse than calf cramps. Ooo this is actually hard."

"Yep, that's how it gets you," Jeffro jumped in. "It's complete nonsense, but you don't want to get it wrong." They all laughed.

"I'll go back spasms," she said assertively.

"Ooooo," Jeff and Cameron sounded suggestively.

"What? What? What would you choose?" Anna asked in a panic. The boys just looked at one another laughing.

"That was your question, not for us to answer," Cameron interjected. Now you'll never know our thoughts on it and it's reeeeally annoying!" Anna shunned her little button nose in disapproval.

"No fair! Ok my god!" She took a moment to think; tapping her fingers on her chin.

"Would youuu rather... Shout 'I FEEL NICE, LIKE SUGAR AND SPICE' after every time you sneeze ooor fart every time you sit down in public transport?" She raised her eyebrows as she impressed the boys.

"That is a good one," Jeffro approved while Cameron was deep in consideration. Laughing already as he begins to answer.

"As much as it would be mental to shout that every time I sneezed! I'd have to shout I feel nice like sugar and spice. As I take the bus so much!" Anna's eyes filled with tears of joy. Cameron couldn't contain his laughter.

"Imagine you had both and you sneezed as you sat down on the bus next to a little old lady. Fart and shout 'I FEEEEL NI'," Jeffro was laughing too hard to even finish his sentence. Suddenly Cameron's face dropped, while he watched Anna. He zoned out from the laughter, as he had flash backs to his nightmare where she was haunting him; only for a few seconds and then he was back in the room. Anna had picked up on it nonetheless.

They all spent the night chatting and drinking. Jeffro told Anna all about Cameron as a teenager, which made him feel uncomfortable but Anna loved it.

"I'm starving. Shall we grab some food on our way back?" Cameron asked Anna as he gathered his phone and wallet from the office desk.

"Sounds good."

She got to her feet as well. "It was great to meet you Jeff." She leant down and gave him a hug.

"Likewise." Cameron in turn shook Jeffro's hand on his way out.

"Don't get up, we'll see ourselves out."

They picked up a kebab on their way home, both feeling a little wavy from the booze tonight. Anna grabbed his hand as they strolled with a sway back to Cameron's flat.

"So you and Jeff are real close huh?" Anna gazed up at him with a rise smile.

"We've been best mates forever," he replied confidently, looking out at the fog gathering on the roads. "He is my closest confidant."

"Did he always live with his Grandma? Did they live in London before?"

"No, he lived near me growing up. With his Mum; sadly, she died when we were in college."

"That's awful." She squeezed his hand a little tighter.

"Yeah, she lost a long battle with cancer. She was sick for years. So Jeff was sort of ready for it. So that's when he and his little brother moved here to live with his Grandma; he would commute every day back to London for college. He just got on with it. To be completely honest..." Cameron looked down at Anna, feeling a warm sense of trust. "To be completely honest, he is the reason I moved here. I wanted to get away from London so bad, that when Jeff told me about a job here, I jumped at it." Anna wrapped her whole arm around his and leant her head into him. "I've never told anyone that," Cameron said resting his cheek down on the top of her head.

Cameron invited Anna in to his flat to eat the food, which they immediately threw on the kitchen side and grabbed each other for a snog. Still locked in the kiss they fumbled their way into the bedroom. They broke away from one another as Anna took herself to the bathroom.

"1 minute, I'll be back." Cameron got into bed, still with his tracksuit on. A few moments later Anna joined him. She scooched under the covers and pulled herself close to him, reaching down his trousers; he was already hard. She took her hand out of his jogging bottoms and Cameron pulled them down to his feet. Anna took her tights off and climbed on top of him, grabbing his manhood and guiding it inside her; she let out a moan of relief and slowly started to push herself down on him. He grabbed her lower back and rolled her round, so now he was on top. He looked longingly into her eyes.

"Go slow," she whispered.

32

Reality on the Rise

Laid on his front Cameron reached out an arm across the sheets, patting around for Anna. She was not there. He rolled himself on to his back and reached out again to caress where she had slept. He could still smell her perfume in the air. He closed his eyes and reached down into his boxers as he cast his mind back to last night. He rubbed himself harder as he recalled scratching along her soft buttocks and down her leg, as he was deep inside her; he envisioned her perfectly perked bosoms flowing in motion with each stroke. He was panting heavily when he heard a flush coming from the en suite bathroom. Anna was still in the house. He snapped his hand out of his underwear and flopped himself back on to his front.

"Good morning!" Anna called out softly. Her raspy voice was more croaky in the mornings. Cameron turned to face her, acting as though he had just woken up. "I wanted to get out of your hair before you head to work. Last night was amazing." She threw her long- sleeved shirt on the edge of the bed next to him.

"Really was," he said, stretching arms and chest out.

"Well, text me later. It's 7:45 by the way." She leaned down and gave him a kiss before seeing herself out. Cameron exhaled hard as he heard the front door close. That was close.

Anna was fully expecting a roasting when she got home. But fortunately, Maple was already out and Clive was with her mum; she took herself straight upstairs. She lay on her bed with a joyful smile on her face.

Cameron had to get up now for work, he couldn't afford to be late. He checked his phone for the time before rushing out the door; he still had time for coffee from Maicon's, before work.

Anna came downstairs to the call from Clive that he was heading out for groceries. She made tea for her and her mum before sitting down next to her.

"So, are you going to tell me what happened last night?" Wendy said as she turned to look at her daughter, eyebrows aloft. Anna paused; taken aback that her mum remembered last night for one, and also knew that Anna was her adult daughter and not a teenager, as she had been of late. "Don't think I didn't hear you sneaking in this morning." Anna prepared to lie to her Mum; they hadn't had a relationship like this for years, as so she wanted to cherish it. She told her all about Cameron and that she spent the night with him, leaving out the gory details. "As long as you're being safe and you're happy, then I'm happy." This left Anna with a smirk she couldn't shake off; water gathered at the bottom of her eyes. She knew it was unlikely to stay this way but just this moment meant so much to her. "Do you mind getting me a pillow? My back is aching."

"Yes, of course." Anna jumped up and grabbed a cushion from the rarely used sofa. "Need a blanket too? You must be freezing in that vest top." Wendy leant forward so that Anna could stuff the cushion in behind her. This exposed her upper back; Anna noticed red marks. "Mum? What is this?" she pulled her top down and noticed marks on neck and across her back. She examined them closely; it looked like something heavy had been on her neck. "Looks painful. Mum? What is this? Has someone been grabbing your neck?" Anna knew this wasn't from falling. Someone or something had done this to her.

"I... I don't know." Confusion fogged over Wendy.

"I'll ask Clive when he gets back. He might know what happened."

Cameron was dealing with a Monday morning meeting; the whole team crammed into this meeting room, where he struggled to focus. His mind characteristically wandered. He was thinking that this was the room he got suspended in. There was no window in this room and the lights were blinding. He was sure that Leah was hitting on him one Christmas party; she was extremely drunk at the time. He couldn't make out Jane's handwriting as she took notes frantically. Why did she need to note take at every meaningless meeting? Mr Kyriakos had a rip in his shirt. He started the meeting on his feet so Cameron didn't notice. But he couldn't stand for long and the rip showed itself, after he sat down.

"Cameron?" Oh shit. What was the question? Cameron panicked as everyone sat there staring at him.

"Yes?" he stuttered.

"Where are you with the weekly numbers?" Mr Kyriakos repeated.

"Basically done. Will be done today," Cameron answered unconvincingly.

"Make it this morning. Before Lunch. It should have been finished last week." Cameron nodded as his boss turned his attention elsewhere and in turn Cameron's attention turned to other things. He wondered what Anna was up to, on her day off. What would he do if he won the lottery? His phone buzzed in his pocket. Eyes fixed on his boss; he slid it out of his pocket and without moving his head, only his eyes, he peered down at his phone. It was Anna.

"Morning Clive," Anna rushed out to the hallway as soon as Clive got back from the shops. He took his jacket off and hung it up by the front door. Anna helped him to carry bags of shopping through to the kitchen. "I noticed red marks and bruising around the back of mum's neck. Do you know how that happened?" Clive had his back to Anna as he stacked food into the cupboards. He answered after a brief pause.

"Yes, I gave her some neck and back exercises to do. You know to help with her posture. She sits in front of that TV for 8 hours a day. I think the stretches and weights have been a little too much. But it has helped her. Her body is just not used to it. The bruising should go down and her neck will be stronger than ever. Here let me show you the sort of exercises we've been doing." He demonstrated a range of weight assisted stretches and explained in detail their purpose. It all made perfect sense to Anna. "Well that's a relief," she said. "A weight off my shoulders," she joked and laughed with him.

"Tea?" he said as Anna tapped away on her phone.

"Huh?" She looked up at Clive shaking a tea bag in the air. "Oh no. Thanks."

'Lunch? Maicon's? Xx.'

In which Cameron replied,

'Yep. 1 o'clock.'

Their usual table by the windows was occupied by someone else as Cameron got to Maicon's; it was particularly busy today. He grabbed 2 coffees and found a seat by the back wall. He found himself watching the bustling people in the coffee shop, while he waited for Anna; something he hadn't done for many years. He noticed himself this old trait returning. He felt content for the first time in years. But the life in his non-mortal world was unfulfilling and distant at the moment. The lust for adventure eluded him. The thought of this damped his mood and his attention to detail of his surroundings left. A darkness hanging over him was brief; once again lifted with the arrival of Anna; a colour bundle of joy approaching.

"Hey Cam! I'm gonna grab a pastry. Want one?" She hurriedly placed her coat over the chair and gestured towards the counter. "Busy huh!?"

"Err... Yeah, pan au raisin please."

"No probs," Cameron's mind was taken back to the world beyond being awake; the strange events troubled him. And again, Anna became a buffer between conscious and unconscious thoughts, with the delivery of sweet treats.

"So how's work?" Cameron pulled himself together to try and hold a conversation.

"This morning was tedious; a meeting around small things that could have been covered in an email." Cameron trailed off his sentence as he thought to himself that he couldn't remember what was covered in the meeting. Maybe it was more important than he suspected. "Anyway, how's your morning?"

"Well I was in great mood this morning, for some reason." She insinuated in Cameron's direction and he blushed and nervously looked around. "But I found these bruises around Mum's neck. Really worried me."

"Oh my god. What happened?" Anna explained plainly what Clive had gone through with her. Cameron looked confused in response. In his expert sports opinion something didn't sound right. "Anna, that doesn't make any sense. Even with excessive weight, the neck and back shouldn't bruise from those exercises. You'd have to be doing a full-blown work out for bruising like that to appear." Anna in turn began to look confused.

"You don't think?"

"No way."

"Well Clive is an expert. He knows what he's doing. He said a little bruising is normal."

"And was it a little bruising? Or a lot of bruising like you described?"

"Well it did look very sore."

"I would ask him to avoid these exercises if I was you. Something doesn't seem right to me."

Anna was dead quiet through the rest of lunch. She wanted Cameron to put her mind at ease but he had done the opposite. She toyed with herself about what she should do. She had to talk to Auntie Maple.

Cameron kept himself to himself the rest of the afternoon at work and actually performed quite constructively. He got plenty of tasks ticked off his list; including the forbidden numbers report, his boss demanded from him. An early night was on the cards tonight. He watched the football with a ready meal.

He was asleep the moment his eyes closed

Darkness all around him, cold breeze chilled his arms, the sound of thunder echoed in the distance, a sense of fear rattled through his mind. He didn't like this. He told himself, 'It's just a dream. Just wake up and try again.' Maybe next time he'll find himself submerged somewhere better; somewhere fun. He tilted his head up and cried out "WAKE UP! WAKE UP!" He felt confident that would do the trick. It was a strong bellow, yet still nothing. He was still here. He called out again, that felt even louder; a deep booming shout "CAM! WAKE UP!" It wasn't working. Cam's mind was telling him that he was shouting out in his sleep. When in reality his motionless body just lay there, quiet as a mouse, in bed. He tried flinging out his arms, maybe the motion would wake him, but again, his body was lifeless out in the real world. Panic started to set in again, as his mind was telling him that maybe he was stuck here; stuck in the darkness. He took a deep breath and felt his body weight build. His head was hard to hold up, his legs pulled him down the ground; his hands were keeping him from lying vertical on the floor. But soon these gave in too. Noises started to heighten around him as he lay paralysed on the ground. Gushes of wind clipped past him, rain started to spike him in the face; it was cold and wet and Cam was powerless to defend himself. He closed his eyes and accepted his fate, sense of pressure was released and his surroundings became more bearable. He opened his eyes and the sight of Anna startled him. She screamed in his face, "YOU DON'T BELONG HERE!"

Tears ran down Cam's face as he clamped his eyes shut once more. Everything was still again, the heavy wind was a light breeze again and light started to pierce through the blackness above him. A thin opening in the darkness beamed through on Cam's face. The light through his curtains had finally woken him.

Another evening had passed. When will the good dreams return? Life was so much better when dreams were fulfilling; or was it?

33

Reality Sucks

20 minutes of aimless staring up at his ceiling fan had made him late; even so he didn't rush through his morning routine. He eyeballed himself in the mirror as his electric toothbrush ran out of battery; he finished his clean manually, not losing eye contact with himself for a moment. He then grasped the basin with both hands and leered closer to his reflection, contemplating life and rueing the missed adventures in his dreams. At long last he tore himself away from the bathroom mirror and trundled into the shower; hot water rinsed his hanging head as he now focused on a small corner of the shower where black mould was forming. The morning was slow going but eventually he was dressed and ready for work, it was obvious the lack of attention he had paid getting ready, his black and yellow polka dot tie looked hideous with his black and blue chequered shirt. He watched his feet hit the cracks on the pavement, with no thought or care. His face was lifted to the sky at the touch of rain against his face, which got heavier with each passing second; of course, he had left his umbrella at home. Dripping water dribbled from his hair and down his face as he waited in line at Maicon's; the queue

was much longer than usually due to the late time. One foot in front of the other as each customer was served, Cameron was clearly in no rush and he showed no attention to the hustle and bustle around him; a giraffe could have served him his coffee, and he would have been none the wiser.

Not by design but Mr Kyriakos was out of office today; only a glaring look from Jane was there to greet Cameron's late arrival. A smile and a compliment may have bought her silence on the matter, but Cameron was clearly unbothered, whether she grassed him up or not, as he strolled directly past her to his desk. Bubbly as ever Josh tried to engage in fruitful chit chat; it took him 10 minutes to realise the grunting Cameron wasn't taking anything he was saying in. Josh being Josh still made and brought coffee to Cameron, at his desk. The clock on the wall seemed to tick slower and slower the more Cameron watched it. Lunchtime eventually came round; sandwiches from home were squashed in his satchel. He just ate there at his desk, not even bothering to take himself to the kitchen; in there he may have to socialise. Emptiness filled his mind as he suppressed the idea of piecing together what was happening of late, the nightmares and fucked up dreams that were haunting him. He felt a grey cloud hanging over him, as another working day passed.

Slumped in his arm chair with an unopened, warm beer in his hand, Cameron fixated on a black TV screen in his front room. A buzz at the door snapped him out of his trance. Who the hell could that be? He lifted the telecom phone off its hook and buzzed the door open, without checking who it was. He then unlatched his door, returned to his armchair and his idle TV. "Cameron?" a voice said from the half-opened door. Cameron had completely forgotten that he had invited Jeffro round. Not to be rude and knowing that Jeffro rarely left his own house; he got up and invited him in.

"Beer?" he held out and offered up his own unopened beer.

"Sure. We going pub?" Jeffro asked, trying to work out Cameron's mood.

"Sure," Cameron half-heartedly replied.

Still in the clothes he wore to work Cameron sat at the pub table waiting for Jeffro to return with drinks. The pub was heaving, business must be good. They recently started doing food and now got lots of families in during the week, Jeffro explained as he plonked two pints of lager down on the table.

"Oh yeah? How'd you know that?" Cameron asked as he took his first sip.

"Read it online." Jeffro took a large glug of his drink.

"Oh right." They both took another mouthful, Jeffro watching Cameron as he did so. Cameron's eyes were somewhere else.

"What's going on with you, bad day at work?"

"Not really," was Cameron's lifeless response. "You?"

"Ha ha, very funny." Finally a bit of humour from Cameron. Jeffro was spending all of his spare time on the Maghurt F4:50, but they weren't allowed to talk about that out in public like this. Out of nowhere Cameron started to open up to Jeffro. "Work is draining to be honest. I'm not too sure what I'm doing with myself lately. And my dreams.." he stopped his train of thought.

"What do you mean your dreams? What dreams?"

"Just forget it," Cameron insisted.

"No, what do you mean? Like aspirations?" Cameron sighed and looked down into his beer.

"My dreams Jeff; when I'm asleep."

"You're having a tough time sleeping? What's going on? I thought things were going good for you?"

"They are. They are," Cameron tried to shrug it off.

"So what's this about dreams?"

"It's nothing Jeff, another drink?" Jeffro finally dropped it. They engaged in broken conversation throughout their second beer and Cameron cut the evening short, shortly after.

At home he had a quiz show playing in the background; he checked his phone for the first time today. Texts from his Mum and Anna; he read and closed with no reply.

"How was your day, Maple?" Anna asked as she sat down with her Auntie and Mum, to eat the dinner she had prepared.

"Productive. I've been looking for work. This food looks lovely dear."

"Yes, it does, darling. Thank you," Wendy added.

"Why are you looking for a job?" Anna asked.

"Well, to keep me busy, bring some extra money in. And now we have help with your Mum, I can."

"You know you don't have to," Anna said assertively.

"I know. But I want to."

"While I remember, we need to talk to Clive on his next shift."

"Why's that, dear?"

"Have you seen Mum's neck? He said it's from stretches and exercise. Cameron says that shouldn't be happening."

"Ooo Cameron aye?" Maple cheekily grinned across the table.

"Ooo who's Cameron?" Wendy interjected.

"I've told you about Cameron! Anyway... He knows about these things and I think we should ask Clive to stop with the exercises, and just focus on catering for Mum and what not." Anna's serious tone hit through to Maple.

"Ok, dear we'll talk to him."

"Thank you, other than that, I think he's doing a great job with Mum." There was a moment of silence as they tucked into their food. Anna checked her phone after dinner; nothing from Cameron all day.

It was the next day and Cameron had met Jeffro for lunch, at a cafe round the corner from his work. A little concerning that Jeff was leaving his house twice in as many days. A chat was needed; Jeffro was clearly concerned about him. Cameron bought them both hot sandwiches.

"Tell me more about these dreams. So I don't mistake your meaning," Jeffro interrogated Cameron early.

"I thought we were leaving this?" Cameron said dejected.

"I'm not leaving anything. I want to know what you meant. It's clearly bothering you." Jeffro was very insistent.

"They were my escape ok? My dreams were always fun. They brought excitement to my life. But now that's gone." Jeffro was shocked by what he was hearing but tried to be supportive as ever.

"Ok... But why is it important? It's only dreams. It's not real."

"It's important because it was better than real life. I could be anything. Who knows what adventure I would go on each night?"

"I want to be supportive mate, but I think you should talk to someone about this. It sounds like you have a problem."

"I knew you wouldn't understand. That's why I haven't told anyone."

"Maybe you haven't told anyone 'cause you know it's a problem?"

"I don't have a problem. Everything was fine. Then it changed."

"This isn't normal mate." Jeffro seemed to patronise although being genuinely serious. Cameron grabbed his coat from the back of his chair. "I'll see you later, 'mate.'" He stormed off, leaving his half-eaten sausage sandwich behind. Jeffro sighed but let him leave, he felt it best to let him cool down by himself.

Cameron walked right past his office and headed straight home. Tears nestled in his eyes; a strong blink released a trickle down his cheek. He rushed up the stairs of his building and slammed his front door shut; leaning his back on it in the process. He threw his head back twice smacking it on the wooden door. He couldn't settle the rest of the afternoon; found himself anxiously pacing and processing everything he was thinking, but his head seemed to scramble even more. He stopped pacing and stared at a faint reflection in his window. It was getting dark out there; and gloomy clouds gathered in the sky. Cameron's breathing was rapid and heavy, his hands were shaking; locked firmly in a fist. His legs began to tremble as he felt his heart rate increase more and more. He started to feel dizzy; he stumbled back and collapsed in his arm chair. He tried to control his breathing, closing his eyes; unrhythmic inhales and premature exhales were increasing his stress levels. Finally he pulled himself together, his legs and arms loosened and his breathing felt more structured. He sat there and pestered his own thoughts the rest of the afternoon.

34

Into the Darkness

Alone for the third night in a row, Cameron pushed spaghetti bolognaise around the plastic container that it had been cooked in. He lethargically took another bite. He hadn't been to work since Monday morning. He hadn't spoken to another human being since lunchtime that day either. Countless unanswered messages clogged his phone; his Mum, Anna and Jeffro all trying to reach him. Even his Dad had messaged him, asking if he wanted to watch the game at theirs tonight. Cameron was sure this was an indirect attempt from his mum to get through to him, and not actually his Dad wanting to spend quality time with his son. Cameron was reading each message he received but had no will to reply. His life beyond all this wasn't much better; two nights' sleep full of wasted potential. With a blanket wrapped round him he shivered as he finished his dinner. He turned the heating on and nestled himself in his armchair for the evening. In complete darkness; flickers from the TV ignited his face as he watched a film, he'd seen hundreds of times as kid; just as he did yesterday evening, and the evening before that. He sat there, emotionless, watching his film and chugging downing a bottle of beer. He grasped the empty bottle and rested it on his stomach as he slouched deep in his chair; his head tilted back and to the right slightly as his eyes began to sting; he fought to keep them open. The bottle fell from his hand on to the floor as his eyes locked closed. Drool formed in the corner of his mouth and a sharp grunt from the back of his nose woke him; but only for a moment. His eyes promptly closed again as he drifted off into a deeper sleep.

Even in his dream Cam was just sitting in his arm chair, the only light relief was from the flickers on the TV screen. He looked around him, everything was the same. Maybe he was not asleep? Maybe he was already asleep? Maybe he'd been asleep the entire evening. His upper lip was hooked on the left side, his eyebrow followed suit; causing his right eyebrow to cover the top half of his right eye. A dark feeling coursed through his body; a croaky chuckle sounded from the back of his throat, which turned into bold, evil laughter. His eyes glued to the screen he sat there and sneered at the TV. He lifted his right arm up in front of him, turning his head at an angle to focus his stare on it. He pressed his thumb to his middle finger, as the other fingers closed. Tension built between his thumb and middle finger before they split either side of each other, letting out a high pitch click.

The end credits of the film woke him; he listened to the bellowing music and watched the names run up the screen. Why were the credits so much louder than the actual film? He clicked the TV off and threw the remote on the chair side table. He kicked the empty bottle on the floor as he stood up, looked down at it and decided to leave it there until morning. He looked around his apartment, it was uncharacteristically untidy. He had let the mess get out of hand. But that was a worry for another day. He trundled through the bedroom to the bathroom and sat down to take a piss. His chin perched in his hand, which was held up on his leg. He sat there for another minute after finishing his piss, forgetting to flush as he headed straight for his bed. He'd decide in the morning whether he would go to work or not. Play each day as it came.

The morning was crisp and fresh, even the sun was trying to crack its way through the silver sky. Anna was up bright and early. Today was all about family; she had taken the day off. Along with Maple and Clive, she was taking her Mum out. It was Clive's idea; a way of getting Wendy more active, trying to stimulate her mind. Clive and Anna were packing picnic style food into a blue and white cooler, in the kitchen. Although he was technically on duty, he wore his own clothes today; much more casual. Assembled with creased blue jeans, a brown woollen fleece and brown leather lace up shoes; very different look to Anna's colourful wardrobe, but she didn't judge.

"I'm just popping to Maicon's, do you want anything?" Anna asked Clive as she threw her coat on.

"Go on then. I'll have one of those fancy coffees, you're always drinking. Get a hot choccy for your Mum." Clive zipped up the cool bag and beamed a smile at Anna.

"Great idea! I'll get Maple one too!" She beamed a smile back at him. As she made her way to Maicon's, Anna checked her phone, still nothing from Cameron. She was starting to worry about him. The condensation and steam on the Cafe windows indicated a vibrant crowd in the coffee shop this morning. Anna squeezed through the crowd to join the queue, she hummed nursery rhymes in her head as she waited.

"Anna." A voice from behind Anna in the queue sounded. Her face lit up when she turned round to see who it was.

"Jeffro! How are you?" They let others pass them in the queue as they chatted. Jeffro's hair was as scruffy as ever, tucked behind his ears. Anna thought that he must have owned the bootleg jeans he was wearing for years; they were faded in all the bend places, mainly the knees.

"I'm really good, to be honest I don't come in here much, I was hoping to bump into Cameron. You haven't spoken to him yet, have you?" Jeffro asked.

"No, I haven't actually. But he does take a while to reply sometimes."

"Yes, he does," a wayward eye from Jeffro indicated that he was withholding some information.

"But?" Anna pressed.

"It's just something he said last time we spoke, weirded me out. Has he ever mentioned his dreams to you?"

"What do you mean his dreams? Like his goals and aspirations?" This prompted a rise smile from Jeffro.

"That's exactly what I said. But no, he actually dreams. Like nighty night birdy I'm going on an adventure dreams." Jeffro went swiftly back to looking stressed.

"No?" Anna said back.

"Arghhh! Don't worry then."

"Yeah, it's weird, we spent the night together after we came to yours on Sunday..." Jeffro taken by surprise looked even more uncomfortable upon hearing this news, "but I've not seen him since. Part of me wants to just turn up at his and check on him, but I don't want to look like a stalker." She laughed nervously.

"Yeah, play it cool. I get ya, I get ya." He awkwardly nodded his head in approval, pushing his glasses up his nose and firmly against his face. She could tell the unease in his posture.

"He has however never taken this long to reply. Has he always been that way?" her sad demeanour was hard to miss. Jeff knew what Cameron could be like. He felt her pain.

"Did Cameron tell you I had a brother? I don't suppose he would." Anna looked puzzled, deep through his thick glasses and into his eyes. "That's probably because he's dead." Jeffro struggled to keep eye contact with Anna, but she couldn't take her eyes off him. "He was younger than me, 5 years actually. Our dad left shortly after he was born... And then after my mum died, he found things very difficult... We moved here to live with our Grandma and he didn't have any friends here. He moved to a school locally, whereas I was travelling back to college in London every day."

"Yes, Cameron did tell me that." He locked eyes with Anna.

"I probably could have done more. But one day after college, I got home late and I found him." Jeff paused for a moment and composed himself. "He had hung himself from the loft beams." The eye contact was broken as his head fell.

"Oh my god Jeff, that's terrible." She tried to console him, a tear formed in the corner of her eye. "That must have been really tough."

"It was. But you know who was there for me, really there for me, helped me through it? Was Cameron. I don't know what I would have done without him." This brought on a slight smile as a tear ran down Anna's cheek. "I know what he can be like Anna. I know he can be distant and selfish. But he has always been there for me. Through it all; he would do the same for you. I know it. It's just who he is."

"Thank you for sharing that with me. I can tell it's difficult even now." She rested her hand on his arm and squeezed it tight. "Are you going to go see Cameron?" she asked.

"Yes, I might do tonight, I assume he's at work right now. It sounds silly, but he's the only family I have now." He shrugged. "How come, you're not at work?"

"It doesn't sound silly at all. We're taking my Mum to the park. Get her out of the house." Anna wanted to ask about Jeff's family but didn't want to pry at this time. He was clearly on edge and she didn't really know him that well yet.

"Sounds good, well I'll catch you later then." Jeffro held Anna's arm briefly.

"Good luck with Cam," she said softly.

"Thanks, I'll get him to text you. Rude git." She sniggered and he smiled, leaving hastily.

35

Sniper

Pinpoint red laser glowed from the glass eye piece; up high in a concrete building, a warm breeze swayed through the open side of the room where brickwork was missing. Cam laid legs akimbo, leaning on his elbows and an elongated rifle nestled in his hands. He was in a small windowless room at the top of the building. An old frail curtain slowly flowed above him. Clusters of dust swarmed down on the streets; echoes of laughter and music came from the street level buildings. He hadn't missed a target all evening. He searched for his next victim; he didn't know how he was choosing them. His fingers hovered on the trigger before squeezing it tightly- HIT! Another fatality perfectly executed. As he peered around through the telescope again, he noticed a man, with a strong moustache, seemingly staring at him. That was impossible, he was miles away; another man joined the moustached man, and stared with him. Cam swiftly moved his focus to somewhere else and again he saw a woman holding a baby, looking directly at him. Everywhere he looked was met by someone looking back. They knew. They knew where he was. Cam prised his eye away from the lens and dropped his head. He had to pack up. He had to leave. He took one last glance through the gun but there were no people at all out there. Cam heard footsteps. They'd found him. There was only one way out of here and that route was now blocked by the oncoming threat. Jeers from the stairwell became louder. Cam had no choice, he'd have to fight; his weapon was no use to him in such small quarters. He could hear the angry voices shouting, he couldn't work out the language. He closed his eyes and accepted his fate. The door rockets open to the cries of angry enemies, he opened his eyes and there was no one there. Gravel from the floor started to circulate into a dust devil, which formed in the doorway. Collecting dust and swirling at an increased speed, it tore its way towards Cam, consuming him. Dust and rubble tornadoed around him a voice called out, "YOU DON'T BELONG HERE", as he gasped for air!

Cameron downed water from the glass on his bedside table. He couldn't complain that wasn't an adventure. Maybe not what he was looking for, but it was still something none the less. The night before dream had cheered him up a little which prompted an early morning clean-up of the flat. He still had hours before he needed to leave for work, whether he would go or not was yet to be decided. He did however decide to check his phone. Missed call from his boss was not a good sign; he'd been AWOL for 2 days now; 2 days of moping around. His absence couldn't have gone down well at all. Today he decided to call in sick, seeing as it was Friday. Even Jane wasn't in yet but a quick apologetic voicemail would do the trick; he can think of a good excuse over the weekend. Several unanswered messages on his phone were still unbearable, although today he would be a bit more productive. He threw his grey jogging bottoms on paired with a trademark chequered shirt and headed to Maicon's. It was still so early, even they were just opening up when he arrived. Maybe he didn't need coffee. Don't be ridiculous he told himself. Always needed coffee. "Large latte please." Cameron ordered; his attention easily moving on to pamphlets on the counter.

"No problem, in or out?" the barista asked.

"Huh?" Cameron flattered his eyes in a panic, looking up at the waiter.

"Are you drinking in or taking it to go?" Cameron thought for just a split second.

"In... Please." Not another soul in sight as he watched on at his and Anna's table, across the shop by the window. The gentle call of his name, from the barista behind him echoed 3 times before he snapped out of his gaze and grabbed his coffee. He wandered over and took a seat at their table, just in time for the arrival of the second customer of the day. The cafe got busier and busier, people sat around Cameron with their morning drinks. Others passed by the window, in big winter coats. Cameron just sat aimlessly watching out the window, sipping his coffee.

Anna wanted to text and tell Cameron about her wonderful day at the park yesterday. But with no response from him in days, she left it for now. The perfect day it was. They had such a laugh. Her Mum was present and not confused with who they were. Clive was right, the day out did her the world of good. Clive was in nice and early today.

"How's she doing?" he asked Anna as he kicked off his shoes. In his usual nurse's uniform.

"I don't think she remembers much, if any, of yesterday. She's just sat in front of the TV again." Anna seemed dejected.

"Oh that is a shame; she seemed to really enjoy the day. What time are you off to work?" Clive clutched Anna's right shoulder in an attempt to console her. His grip was firm. It reminded her of when her uncle Mark would squeeze just above her knee. Boy that used to hurt.

"I'm leaving in 10." She put on a brave smile.

"I'll put the kettle on." He released her shoulder and headed to the kitchen. "Morning Wendy!" He shouted out on his way. Anna watched on with a glimmering smile as Clive and Wendy sat watching TV this morning and sharing a pot of tea; she grabbed her rain mac from the banister, noticing a faded coffee stain that never did wash out. Reminding her of the day she met Cameron.

"I'm off too. See you later." Anna called from the front door. A raised hand from her mum could be seen reaching up from behind the back of the sofa. A quick pit stop at Maicon was needed this morning.

The queue was enormous by the time Anna made it. She looked down at her green dinosaur watch; she had to rush. She noticed Cameron sitting at their usual table as she searched around the busy shop. She leant out of the queue and waved her arms around but he was still sat motionless staring into space.

"Caaaam!" Eventually she got his attention by calling his name. He looked awkwardly back at her. She gestured her hand towards him to come and join her. Reluctantly he did get to his feet and make his way over, gingerly. He hadn't had a conversation with another human being for 3 days.

"I saw your glass was empty, do you want another one?" she broke the ice. He struggled to maintain eye contact with her.

"No thanks. How are you?" he asked. Keen to tell him all about her day yesterday, she took a moment and resisted. Clearly, he wasn't himself; she didn't want her story to fall on deaf ears and she was eager to ensure he was ok.

"I'm fine, in a real rush to get to work." This news was a light release for Cameron. He wouldn't have to chat for too long.

"I'm sorry about not replying these last few days. Things have been a bit manic." He looked down as he told his lie.

"Oh, well, that's alright." She said disappointed. Finally, she was at the front of the line. "2 secs Cam, let me just order."

"You go ahead, I'll leave you to it. See ya later." He rushed off before Anna could say much, as she tried to order at the same time.

"Oh... ok" she said as he was already a few steps away. With a dampened mood Anna carried on with her day; it saddened her to see Cameron this way, she only hoped it was nothing to do with her.

Jeffro was waiting at the bottom of the stone stairs at Cameron's flat as he arrived home with coffee. He saw him down the road, looking uneasy and anxious. Anyone else acting this way would be alarming, but for Jeffro this was the norm.

"Jeff? What are you doing here?" Cameron shimmied his keys out of his coat pocket.

"Been worried about you man. You're not replying to my texts. I haven't heard from you since we last spoke at the cafe." Jeffro couldn't stay still; Cameron could see the paranoia coursing through him. Reluctantly Cameron invited him in. "So what's been going on?" Immediately Jeffro seemed more relaxed upon entry into the flat. He sat down at Cameron's dining table.

"Nothing much, I've just taken some personal days from work," Cameron said, taking the seat opposite him across the table.

"Personal days? You've only been back a few days. What's really going on?" Cameron took a long drag of his coffee, avoiding eye contact with Jeff. His eyes fixed on his cup as he set it down on the table, without moving his head he looked up across the table at Jeffro. He had been bottling everything up inside all week, it had consumed him. It was time. Time to lean on his friend.

"Jeff I'm struggling." His eyes rolled back down to the table. "Mate. Just tell me. Maybe I can help." Cameron's eyes glazed over as he felt sick to his stomach with apprehension; small movements with his sealed mouth made it obvious he was holding back. Hesitant he focused on the table to restrain any tears, his eyes moved back to Jeffro.

"I'm not sure anyone can help. Arghhhh, I don't know how to explain this. You'll think I'm mad."

"You've been flirting with that for a while already." Jeffro tried to lighten the mood.

"You won't understand," Cameron whispered under his breath. "But I need to tell someone. It's eating me alive." One more swig of his coffee. "Here goes. I feel like I am living two lives."

"Go on...." Jeffro encouraged.

"My conscious and unconscious lives; my dreams have been my escape, where life was full of fun and adventure; something I could look forward to, to get me through my boring life." Jeffro's brows frowned as he tried to take this information in.

"But that's exactly what they are... Dreams. It's not real life."

"You're right. They're better. It felt real. And for a time I was happy. But then when anything good happened in my life, my dreams would be affected. They would be cruel or scary. Like you with your Maghurt, the wedding and Anna. Anna..." Cameron gripped his cup firmly. He didn't expect anyone to understand.

"So that's why you've been blocking us out?"

"I didn't realise I was. Everything has just happened."

"If things are going well in your real life surely that's a good thing?"

"In a way yes, but I couldn't get away anymore. I lost my adventures. It's like I have this monkey on my back. Carrying it around, in fear. Dragging me towards the darkness and away from the light. And with it, it brings, crippling anxiety and constant trepidations." Jeffro leaned in on the table and took a moment.

"Is the monkey there when you're with Anna?"

"The monkey is always there. Reminding me of what I'm losing. Anna brings me back to the light and the monkey becomes lighter to carry." Cameron flumped his head into his hands.

"Losing what though, mate?" Jeffro spread his hands and fingers out evenly on the table.

"I'm scared of losing my dreams, and being stuck in this mediocre life."

"It sounds to me like you need to take some responsibility and change your life. Don't lock yourself away and rely on make believe to make you happy. Grow some balls man. You're in a dead-end job, where you hate your boss. You came here, 'cause you hate your dad. But the whole world isn't against you. Your self-loathing is on you, you have a chance to be happy, but it's up to you. Stop using the way others treat you as an excuse to be miserable." He leant back in his chair. He slowly got up and wandered over to Cameron's side. He put his hand on his shoulder. "I'm going to make a tea, and then we're going out. I won't take no for an answer."

"Where are we going?" Cameron said softly, looking over his shoulder at Jeffro in the kitchen.

"My house. But first we're going shopping. The Maghurt is finished. I want some cool accessories." Cameron turned away from his friend and looked out across the room and out the window. A warm but brief sense of content flowed through him. "Go pack a bag, you're crashing at mine. Don't want you being alone. Let's see what you dream of."

36

Seeing Red

The autumn weather only allowed a small amount of natural light, through the kitchen window, at this early hour, as Jeff poured freshly brewed coffee into two very retro looking mugs. "How long have you had these?" Cameron asked smirking; holding one of the mugs out in front of him, as he joined Jeff. "These have to be at least 20 years old. My Nan used to collect them. From Easter eggs. Every year she did. Most of them have broken over the years. A few have survived though." He handed and snatched it back off Cameron and filled it with coffee. "Are you going to text Anna today?" Cameron grabbed the mug back and made his way down the hallway to Jeff's office; Jeff followed.

"I want to. But I'm not sure she'll want to talk to me. I've avoided her all week. Life was simpler before she came along."

"I've got a feeling she would want you to. Remember. Your real life matters." Cameron blowed on his piping hot mug of coffee.

"Yeah, yeah, I know, I know."

"So text her! Trust me. But first you want a go on the Maghurt?" Jeffro set his coffee down on an old CD box and swung into his office chair. The Maghurt F4:50 was now fully accessorised and looked less like a piece of junk, ready to be recycled. A spanking new state of the art keyboard had twice as many buttons as a standard QWERTY keyboard; a short cut for everything. Jeffro had very little interest in flair unless it was PC related. He had decorated the monitor with retro cartoon stickers and keyboard, mouse place mats to match. Classic 90's was the theme with Spongebob, Fairly Odd parents and The Simpsons, amongst many others. Splashes of X-Men and other super heroes, made appearances as well. Batman batarangs on each clicker of the mouse.

"This way if anything ever happens and someone finds this machine, it looks more like a geek's normal PC. Don't you think?" Cameron laughed at the question.

"Oh yeah, definitely," Cameron replied sarcastically.

"Plus it looks super cool." Cameron just smiled and nodded. They both knew that was the only reason they decorated it.

"As much as I love your coffee, I'm going to head to Maicon's and grab a proper one. You want anything?" Cameron asked.

"What day is it?" Jeffro was thinking out loud.

"Saturday! Grab me a selection of the daily newspapers." With his back to Jeff, Cameron rolled his eyes. He grabbed his coat from the sofa across the room. "Yes, no problem." Cameron knew he was going to rummage through those papers and find a conspiracy somewhere. He'd been doing that since they were teenagers.

"And text Anna, you might be able to meet her in Maicon's!" Jeff called out a split second before the front door slammed closed. Cameron had heard him and stopped at the end of the drive way to contemplate messaging her. He pulled his phone out of this jacket pocket and opened up his conversation with Anna. He looked down at his phone for another few seconds, locked his phone and stuffed it back in his pocket. As he strolled down the street he looked up at the bare trees, swaying in the light breeze; he thought about Anna. What would he say to her? It was pretty awkward when he saw her in Maicon's yesterday. He'd have to face up to it at some point. Texting her would be a simple way to ease his way back into conversation with her. He had a plan. Message her when he is close to Maicon's to show that he did want to see her, but not leaving her enough time to see it and make her way there. Therefore, she would just text back and Cameron will have more time to prepare to see her again; the perfect plan. Only round the corner from Maicon's now he opened up his messages and started to type.

"Cameron," he heard, as his eyes were glued down on his phone. "Anna," he replied as he looked up from his screen "What are you doing here?"

"Just getting my coffee before work," she said holding up her coffee mug.

"Ahh of course," he was blank. He could feel how awkward he was coming across; just standing there with his phone still in his hands. He stuffed it away in his jeans pocket, along with it his hands. He pushed his lips tightly together and raised the corners, along with his eyebrows. He tapped his fingers nervously inside his jean pockets. His eyebrows lowered and his facial expression changed; as if he was deep in thought. In reality his mind was blank. His forced smile shone even more fake now.

"Right, well I best head to work." She broke the excruciating awkwardness and headed off. Cameron let out a big breath and relaxed his shoulders. She looked back and caught him miming "what the fuck was that" and gesturing his hands in annoyance. He went bright red when he noticed her looking back at him. He wanted the ground to swallow him up; instead he made haste and headed into the coffee shop. He couldn't text her now. He had to give it some time.

Anna has to shrug off that weird encounter, after mulling it over for the rest of her walk to work. She couldn't believe how awkward things had got with Cameron. One minute they were good, the next they were like strangers. Today had already gotten off to a rocky start as her Mum panicked this morning after she got confused who Anna was first thing, but seemed much calmer by the time Anna had left. She seemed to calm down, once Clive had arrived. Anna had lunch plans with Maple, before she headed home to take over from Clive. Anna was finding it harder to not think about it, while she was at work all day. She wanted to text Cameron. She wanted to sort things out. Things were just easier when he was around. But she was starting to feel like she couldn't just text him. So for now, she left it.

"Jeff!" Cameron called out upon his arrival back. "Jeffro!?" Cameron called again with no response. He stood silently in place and could hear the shower running upstairs; Cameron took his coffee into the office. Bored of waiting he powered up the Maghurt and sipped his coffee while it loaded. He cracked the blinds, knowing it would annoy Jeffro, he did it anyway. Smugly he typed in the password, smugly because Jeffro trusted him and him alone with that encrypted piece of information. The system was ready; an orange flashing courser flickered in the corner of the black screen. He linked his fingers together and cracked his fingers out in front of him, took another hefty glug of his coffee and contemplated what to search. He typed -

/Roger Booker//::.....

Waiting a few seconds and a list of matches filtered down the screen; slowly scrolling down, there were too many to go through individually. He needed more info. He felt like a novice; Jeffro made it all look so easy. He pondered again. He needed key words or people to link with who he was searching for. He typed.

/Roger Booker//::......

/England, UK//.....

There were still too many to go through one by one.

/Roger Booker//::......

[England, UK]//::

[Mary Booker]//::

This didn't change the list. Cameron deliberated once again. Then it dawned on him, Mary and Roger were never married. Cameron couldn't remember her last name. Anyway. He typed.

/Roger Booker//::......

[England, UK]//::

[Mary Booker]//::

[Jeffrey Booker]//::

Surely not even Jeffro could hide from the Maghurt F4:50. And hey presto, there he was. One name listed as Roger Booker. Cameron clicked the name and began to read the personal details. There was a lot there; Roger had been on the wrong side of the law on several occasions. Cameron's eyes were glued to the screen.

"Blimey! He's back in Putney!" he said aloud.

"Who is?" Jeffro said from the doorway of the office, spooking Cameron, who frantically tried to close down the info on the screen.

"Oh no one," he struggled to clear the screen as on this computer you didn't have to click a little X in the corner, you had to retrace your steps to return to the beginning. Jeffro made his way over before Cameron could delete anything.

"Come on, show me!" He laughed as he grabbed hold the back of the chair Cameron was sitting on, jolting him away from the PC. His face dropped when he saw the content on the screen. "What the fuck are you looking him up for?" Jeffro spun Cameron round completely so he was facing him. "My fucking Dad, are you mad?"

"Whey... That rhymed!" Cameron instantly regretted trying to make a joke of it. Jeffro was clearly not amused.

"I've put up with your shit for weeks and you do this?"

"Come on mate. Aren't you even a little bit curious about him?" Cameron pleaded with him.

"No, I'm fucking not. I try not to ever think about him. My mum died twice. The day he left and the day the cancer won!"

"I'm sorry mate. I don't know what to say."

"There's nothing to say. I think it's best you go home." Cameron accepted this request immediately and got up from the office chair. Jeffro in turn slumped himself into the chair. Cameron looked back at his best mate as he grabbed his jacket and headed straight out.

Lunch came around and Anna was waiting for Maple in a cute sandwich shop wedged between a dry cleaners' and a chemist. A long narrow room; one set of table and chairs outside and a long lunch bar with stalls against the right hand wall, which was fixed with a corner to corner mirror. The serving counter was tucked into the back right corner; a gigantic coffee maker situated behind the servers, dwarfed everything else inside the restaurant. A range of sandwich fillers arranged neatly inside the glass counter; sweet treats along a shelf above. A pink and lilac floral wall paper plastered along the left hand wall completed the decadent decor. Two coffees were set down in front of Anna, a black Americano for Maple and a latte for herself; just then her Auntie walked through the cafe door; a tiny bell above the opening door got Anna's attention.

"Hello dear, have you ordered food?" Maple asked, throwing her long leathery red coat over the chair and plonking her little box handbag on the side.

"No, I was waiting for you."

"What do you want? I'll go up and order."

"Thanks, I'll just have a tuna sandwich," she said with a cheery smile.

"Tuna sandwich, right you are."

"And some crisps," Anna snapped as Maple headed for the counter.

"Crisps. Got it. What flavour?"

"Cheese and onion."

"Anything else?"

"And a cake. Something chocolaty. Surprise me." Maple smirked and waiting a moment, to ensure there were no more requests. "You've got a big appetite today," Maple said as she took her seat next to Anna. "Hungry?"

"No, I think I'm stress eating."

"What's got you stressed?" Maple pressed, taking a slurp of her piping hot coffee.

"Well, Cameron I guess. Something is up with him; I'm not quite sure what. I'm not sure if it's something I've done." Maple looked down her glasses at Anna.

"A boy huh? What's happened?"

"It could just be me over thinking but things were going really well, but lately I've barely heard from him. It's like he's gone off grid. We've gone from texting every day to awkward meeting outside Maicon's."

"Men are tricky to work out my dear. I'm sure it's nothing you've done. He'll come around. And if he doesn't it is his loss."

"I guess you're right."

"Just talk to the boy," Maple said assertively. "I'm sure he'll appreciate that." Anna's attention drifted off as she thought about it a while "I'm heading to York, to meet my cousins from Hartlepool straight after lunch. I'll be back the same time tomorrow afternoon." Maple gave Anna the run down, Anna in turn nodded as she processed the information.

"How was Mum this morning?" A question that lingered on Anna's mind a lot of late.

"Yes, fine dear. Clive was there with her when I left. She will be on her own this afternoon, which will be a good test for her. Are you home normal time from work?"

"Yes, around 5:30. What time is Clive clocking off?" Anna asked anxiously.

"He'll head off around 3. She'll be fine for a couple of hours dear. Don't threat."

Cameron twiddled his thumbs as he stared aimlessly out of his front room window. His phone was resting face down on the window sill. There were many passers by going about their day, down in the street, although none drew Cameron's attention. He found himself getting lost in his own mind, just as Jeffro had helped drag him out. He had to make amends. He just had to. He snapped out of his self-pity state briefly. He didn't want to drift off to sleep. He didn't want to face his subconscious mind. He needed to avoid his dreams at all costs right now. A distraction, looking around he couldn't help but notice the state of his flat, he knew that cleaning would distract him. He needed his flat to be clean. His flat was always clean; the whole time oblivious to his phone pinging over on the window sill.

Anna texted Cameron in her lunch break. She took a deep breath before sending. She didn't want to give up on him.

'Hey! That was kinda awkward this morning. How have we come to this? I miss you. I can be here for you, if you'd let me. Hopefully you get back to me xx.'

She left the conversation between them open while she ate her sandwich. A reply never came.

Anna was desperate to get home and see her mum. Work was a nightmare all afternoon and she needed to vent. As soon as the clock hit 5, the shop door was locked and she was on her way. She walked with a spring in her step to get home sharpish. It didn't take her long; 10 minutes at this pace.

"Mum! I'm home." She called out as she kicked off her shoes and hung her rain coat on the banister. "Mum?" She popped her head in the front room. Wendy wasn't in her arm chair watching TV. The TV however was on. She headed to the downstairs loo across the hallway. "Mum? You in there?" Drumming her knuckles on the door. The door was unlocked. No sign of her. She headed back to the front room, when she heard sobbing coming from the kitchen. Anna looked through the hollow alcove in the front room. "Mum!" She yelled and ran towards the kitchen. Wendy was covered in blood, her hands shaking out in front of her. She was gasping for breath.

"Mum? What happened?" Anna asked frantically. She noticed a chef knife on the floor by her Mum's feet. Her arms were bleeding. The blood was everywhere, even matting her hair into blood filled clumps. Anna trying to stay composed sat her mum down on a kitchen chair; picking up the knife and throwing it in the sink. She grabbed a tea towel and ran it under the sink. "I'm coming Mum." She squatted down and grabbed her mum's arms, dabbing the wet towel on them before wrapping it round. Wendy couldn't focus her eyes on anything as her pupils searched the room. "Mum, look at me. Look at me! I'm going to grab the first aid kit. Don't move. Okay? Mum... look at me. I'll be right back." Her mum still shaking nodded her head. Anna sprinted up the stairs and grabbed the first aid box from the bathroom cupboard, slipping down the stairs in her rush to get back down. "What happened?" She demanded firmly.

"I... I don't know." She was crying; she looked frightened. Anna grabbed her phone from her pocket; her hands caked in her mum's blood. She typed 999; hesitating to press call. They would take her mum away. They would lock her up. Take her away. Anna didn't want that. She threw her phone on the kitchen counter and tended to her mum's wounds.

"Mum I need to you think hard, what happened?" Sobbing, Wendy replied,

"Darling, I don't know."

"Did you do this to yourself?" Anna locked eyes with her Mum. Wendy in turn stopped crying, held the eye contact with her daughter and composed herself.

"No." She seemed confident. "Him. It was him." She muttered under her breath. "Mark."

"Who mum? Who?" Anna didn't get another response, the bleeding had stopped. The cuts weren't deep. "I'm going to wipe them with these disinfectant wipes and wrap these bandages around them. Okay?" Wendy nodded repeatedly. "This might sting a little."

Anna leaned on the wall of the alcove between the kitchen and front room, watching her Mum as she watched TV.

"You need anything Mum?" Without taking her eyes off the screen Wendy shook her head. "Ok, let me know if you do. I'm right here." Anna turned her back on her mum and looked at her phone. Her thumb hovered over Cameron's name. She didn't know what to do. She needed someone. She pressed his name.

'Calling... Cameron'

It rang.

And rang.

And rang.

"Hello?"

37

Imposter

Sloped in his armchair, Cameron clutched his phone and stared at Anna's name flashing on the screen. Only the flickering from the TV gave the room any light. The damage was done. Could he face her? Conversations with Jeffro raced through his thoughts; the tether of that relationship was wearing thin. He had to make amends with his best mate. But right now Anna was waiting. He couldn't bear to desecrate another friendship. He clicked answer and slowly brought the phone up to his ear. There was a paused moment of silence before Cameron croaked, "Hello?"

"Cam? Oh hi. It's Anna." She winced her eyes closed and gritted her teeth. Obviously, he knew it was her.

"Yes, hi Anna." He was as equally awkward. "What can I do for you?" There was another pause in conversation, while Anna gathered her thoughts.

"Cam, it's Mum she…" yet another pause "she… well she's not doing too well and erm…" Cameron felt the anguish in her raspy tones. "When I got home from work today she was bleeding. Bleeding bad. I don't know if she did this to herself. She doesn't know what's going on. Maple isn't back until tomorrow. I am scared to leave her." She was listing things more and more frantically. She took a final pause and composed herself once more. "Cam, I need you." Cameron's mouth slowly moved up and down, but no words came out. He didn't know what to say. "Do you think I should call Maple? Do you think I should call an ambulance? I don't want to leave her side tonight. I'm scared to sleep. Cam I need you... now." Cameron took a breath.

"Ok."

This was more than the motivation Cameron needed to get his back side up and moving. He turned the TV off and threw the remote on his arm chair. He trundled in the dark to his bedroom, waving his arms out in front of him, as to avoid bumping into anything. He wandered into his en suite, still in darkness; clicking on the mirror light to aid his vision to pee. Back to darkness as he flicked that light off again after flushing. He finally turned the big bedroom light on and turned out some clean clothes from his wardrobe; throwing a chequered shirt and some black jogging bottoms on the bed. He looked down at the outfit. He knew these clothes didn't go, but at this point he really didn't care. Flicking his bathroom mirror on once again he flattened his hair down to, in his opinion, a reasonable look. He headed for Anna's.

This was the first time Cameron had been to Anna's house. This was the first time Anna had ever brought a boy round. Not the circumstances either of them would have thought this moment happening, for the first time. Anna was elated at the arrival of Cameron. She scurried him into the house.

"Come in, come in. Come and meet my Mum." She leads the way into the front room. Wendy was sitting watching TV.

"Mum?" Wendy uncharacteristically turned around in her chair to face the door. She could sense a boy was here. She took a deep and meaningful look at Cameron standing in the doorway of the room. "Mum, this is Cam, my friend. Cam, this is my mum, Wendy."

"It's a pleasure to meet you." Cameron said nervously, noticing the heavy bandages on her arms.

"Likewise." Wendy said assertively, before turning her attention back on the TV.

"Well... I think she likes you. Tea?" Anna was at ease now Cam was there with her. They all sat and watched TV for some time, while all got comfortable with each other. Wendy hadn't long started a film. Not much conversing needed to learn a lot about one another.

"Do you mind staying with her a while? I need to shower and get out of these clothes. Do you mind?" she said hopefully to Cameron.

"No not at all," he said without a second thought. She rested her hand on his and smiled, taking herself off upstairs. Cameron didn't flinch, just sat and watched the film in peace.

"Everything ok?" Cameron turned towards the door to find Anna stood in the doorway in petite white pyjama shorts, decorated with little pink flowers and a vest top; her auburn hair, much darker when wet; long, straight and sticking to her chest. Her nipples were erect from cold droplets of her freshly washed hair, and piercing through the grey vest top. He gulped profusely and nodded; he couldn't take his eyes off her.

"Everything's fine darling," Wendy called back, slowly turning her head and smirking at Cameron. "Isn't it, Cam?" He nodded slowly and replied through a lump in his throat, "Yep."

"Good!" Anna smiled and took herself to the kitchen.

Anna woke Cam as she crawled under the covers. Disorientated he felt her warm, wet mouth bear down on his cock.

His eyes shot open, he was awake now! He looked under the duvet but no Anna, just a piercing bulge in his underwear. She was unlikely to come in and surprise him as she shared downstairs with her Mum. Cameron lay in her bed and nosily scanned the room; it was rather plain which surprised him, being Anna's room. No shoe rack but a ceiling tall book shelf covered the main wall. A pale light from the street lamp outside ignited the bed which was located under the only window in the room. The weak curtains were definitely not going to keep any light out in the morning; Cameron remembered Anna saying how she loved the light in the mornings. He lay a while longer thinking of various things, each thought circled him back to Jeffro. He needed to sort things with his friend. Jeffro was his last passing thought as his eyes closed shut again, as he drifted off to sleep.

"Morning," Cameron said softly, catching the attention of Anna who was staring into space, in the kitchen, as the kettle boiled.

"Oh morning, how did you sleep?"

"Very well actually," he said convincingly as he nodded in approval.

"Good, I was in and out. Mum is still asleep in there. Tea?" The kettle clicked.

"Aghh... Yeah please. Hey, how come you love coffee so much but here all you drink is tea?" Cameron asked.

"Mum loves tea..." She replied with little hesitation. Cameron pulled his bottom lip out, tucking his top lip in under and nodded in appreciation.

"Listen I was thinking last night." He had Anna's attention as she poured the tea. "We need to go and see Jeffro. This carer, how much do you know about him?" Anna looked confused.

"Clive? What's that got to do with Jeff?" She handed him a mug which he instantly put down on the counter.

"Yeah, maybe he knows what happened to your mum?" His brain was racking, his gestures were more rapid than they should be at this time of the morning. "You said he left early, what if she was acting differently before he left, what if he had something to do with it."

"Well.. Yes, it's possible I suppose. She did say something about a 'him' but she mentioned Mark... my uncle." She was beginning to get on a level with Cameron. Cameron edged towards her.

"And didn't you say your Mum always calls him Mark?"

"Yes, she does, but what's that got to do with Jeff!?" They were both in the middle of the kitchen as they tried and pieced it together. Cameron grabbed her by the wrists.

"I just know he can help. The Maghurt..." it clicked in his brain "the Maghurt is the key!" He pulled her close to his body, their eyes locked on each other. After a moment's pause they threw themselves into a kiss, just as Wendy walked into the room.

"Morning kids," she chirped. The kiss was halted immediately and Cameron pushed Anna to arm's length.

"Oh, morning Mrs Davenport," Cameron's cheeks blushed with embarrassment.

"Morning Mum, tea on the side," Anna blushed too with a smile.

"Thank you darling. And Cam... it's Ms Davenport." She raised her mug in respect to Cameron before taking herself off to the front room.

"Trust me. Jeffro can help." He focused back to the situation at hand. "Only problem is... He's sort of not talking to me right now." He lowered his voice.

"What do you mean, sort of?" Before he could answer Wendy called out.

"Stop whispering in there you two. I've just caught you snogging my daughter, no secrets in this house." Anna grabbed Cameron by the hand and led him through. Cameron told them all about what happened between him and Jeffro and they in turn gave him some advice. "Your friend won't stay mad forever, just go and speak with him." Wendy closed out the conversation. "Now off you go, let me watch my morning shows."

"Maicon's?"

"Do you even have to ask? Maple will be home soon. We'll go then." They had to wait for the café's Sunday opening hours anyway.

They devised a plan. What they were going to say, the apology for Cameron to give and how they were going to win Jeffro over. The plan went out the window the moment Jeff slammed his front door in their face before Cameron could say 'hi mate'.

"Let me try." Anna said, softly clutching Cameron's hand. Cameron looked defeated already. Cameron took a few steps back and began to pace. Anna knocked again on the door. "Jeff! It's me. Anna. Just me. Can you let me in please? I need a wee." There was a few seconds' pause before a crack appeared in the door. A flicker reflected the sun off Jeffro's glasses, in the gap in the door. He then opened it full and allowed Anna in, staring down Cameron as he closed the door again.

"You know where the loo is." He brushed past her and back into his office.

"We need your help Jeff," Anna pleaded with him as she returned from the bathroom.

"Not interested." He clicked continuously on his computer mouse.

"He's really sorry Jeff," she wandered over and leaned on his desk. He took his eyes off the screen and looked up at her. His eyes were huge through his glasses. "Did he tell you what he done?"

"He did."

"Oh wow. At least he's man enough to tell you. If you knew what he done to our family, Anna."

"I don't want to act like I know what you've been through. But I can relate." She made her way round the desk and sat beside him on a green plastic chair. She looked intensely into his eyes. "My dad left when I was very young. I never even knew him. And Cameron sure as hell doesn't know how you feel, but he can relate too. His dad has been absent in plain sight, his whole life." Jeffro got what she was saying.

"Right... how can I help?"

"We need the Maghurt." His attention was well and truly hers. "And we need an expert who can use it!" She smiled at him and he smiled back.

"Go and let that numpty in and tell me everything!"

Jeffro was poised and ready to search; Cameron sat alongside him on the plastic chair. Anna was pacing the open room on the other side of the desk, her arms hanging low beside her.

"His name is Clive Johnson. He works for Raise UK nursing home," Anna said sternly.

"Yep, found him."

"Already!?" Anna stopped pacing and turned to the boys.

"Yep," Jeffro said confidently, rotating the screen to face Anna. "Hold up there's a photo of him here, let me print it." Anna rushed round the table and watched an old printer, which sounded like a 1950's type writer chunk out an A4 piece of paper, a man's body printed, the face yet to follow. A tall man with dark stubble. "Wait... he's from Scotland?" Anna watched the paper closely, briefly distracted by Jeffro's comment.

"Huh?" she snarled, scrunching the freckles on her nose up.

"Scotland... born and raised. Says he still lives there now. Says he left his last job whilst up there, 2 months ago. A nursing home called Brad Beacon House... Before joining Raise UK but he has no address down here."

"This is not him." Anna held the picture aloft. "This is not Clive," she stated, sharply looking at Jeffro, "he most certainly does NOT have a Scottish accent."

"It has to be. Look... Clive Johnson, Raise UK nursing home... Do you have a picture of him?"

"No." She sighed, slumping her arms down beside him again.

"Yes, you do..." Cameron interjected. "On the website. You showed me when he started working for you..."

"Oh yes! They have pictures of all the staff on the website." She rapidly unlocked her phone and started to scour the internet. "Here! Here." She flipped the phone to show Cameron, he took the phone from her and zoomed into his face. He analysed the picture for a few second before getting to his feet and hastily walked around the table; tapping wires that sprung out Maghurt. He grabbed a grey spiral lead in his hand and with a look and a nod to Jeff he plugged it into the bottom of the phone. Leaning forward with intent Jeffro proceeded to type away on the perplexing keyboard.

"This is not Clive Johnson." His voice echoed an eerie tone. Cameron and Anna huddled around him as he read from the screen. "Billy Crimley, 42, several sex offense cases, no convictions." Jeffro clicked a link to print. "And look, he lives right here in Horsham- 18 Acre Drive." Cameron grabbed that print out. Cameron handed Jeffro the paper from the printer. "It's a new article. Billy Crimley stalked a 13-year old girl, in 2011, waiting for her outside school and trying to lure her back to his house with money. The case was thrown out due to lack of evidence."

"How come we have never heard of this?" Cameron asked.

"Look at the paper's name..." Jeffro flipped hold the page up for them to see.

"Glasgow Evening News. Scotland!?" Cameron said, baffled.

"Yes, it all happened in Scotland."

"What's his address?" Anna demanded.

"Should we call the police?" Jeffro asked, as he hid the screen from her.

"The address Jeff..." she said more firmly.

"Let's talk about this," he insisted. "Cameron?"

"No Jeff, let's pay this guy a visit." Jeffro taken back by this showed them the screen.

"Cameron? You sure about this?"

"Yes! Let's go on an adventure. Find out what happened to Wendy!"

"I'm with you Cam." Anna couldn't control her smile.

"Jeffro?" Stress written all over his face, however, without a second thought he was in.

The 3 of them tried to unravel this whole thing on their walk to the carer's house. Who was Clive Johnson? Did he know Billy Crimley? Was the carer really Billy Crimley? As they turned off Hurst Road, Acre Drive bowed up and round, to Albion Way. Every house on Acre Drive looked basically identical; big bungalows that had an upwards extension. Bushy shrubs in every front garden. No parking restrictions or permit rules. A peaceful road, wedged between two busy main roads, either end. Jeffro was counting the door numbers, as they strolled up the road.

"10, 12, 14, 16 aaaand 18." Anna grabbed his arm and tugged him back.

"You 2 go and knock. He knows me. Will definitely spook him." Cameron was clearly nervous. He nodded, although it was obvious he wasn't taking in any of the directions, Anna was trying to map out for them. She and Jeffro devised a plan of action. "Got it Cam?" she asked.

"Egh... Yeah!" All the windows at the house had white, patterned, netted curtains hanging inside, which made it impossible to see anything from out here. There was however a long, thin, textured glass window, running either side of the heavy looking wooden front door, which itself had frosted glass windows in an oval shape.

"Good luck guys. Just like we spoke about. You'll be fine." She shooed them away and hid herself behind a neighbour's bush. Cameron and Jeffro both took a deep breath before gingerly approaching the front door. Cameron stepped in front of Jeffro and rapped his knuckles on the door, three times. The door creaked open, leaving Jeff and Cameron stunned by who was standing there.

Clive Johnson, the real Clive Johnson held the door ajar with a strong straight arm. "Can I help you?" A thick Scottish voice questioned. Jeff and Cameron paused. Cameron composed himself.

"We're looking for Billy Crimley..." Jeffro looked briefly at Cameron, who was standing confidently next to him, then sharply turned his attention to Clive, who in contrast had a sickening look of worry on his face. "Does he live here?"

"Never heard of him." Clive replied pumping his impressive chest out and shrugging his broad shoulders. "Anything else..." before Jeffro or Cameron could respond, what sounded like pots and pans clanging sounded from inside the house, panicking Clive Johnson. "Well goodbye then." He slammed the door closed; pulling a curtain across behind it.

"What was that sound?" Jeffro asked Cameron, grabbing his arm. "Come on let's go. This is freaking me out."

"Why the hell is Clive here!?" Cameron swiped his arm away from Jeffro's grasp. "Come with me." Cameron started to circle the house.

"Cam, what are you doing? This is dangerous." Anna sneakily jogged over as Cameron analysed the garden fence and what lay the other side. "Tell him Anna. We need to go." Her eyes fixed on Cameron as she rested her hands on her knees, crouching down. Jeffro did the same. Cameron in turn joined them in the huddle.

"What's the plan here, Cam? Jeffro's right, this is dangerous."

"I saw someone jumping the other fence, down the side of the house. He's made a runner." Cameron looked over Jeffro's shoulder, giving him a view of one exit of the road. "I can't see anything. He must be long gone. Let..." he gestures his thumb upwards to indicate jumping over the fence.

"You are mad?" Jeffro straightened up.

"Come on... He's gone. Now's our chance, let's just peer through the window. See if we can see anything in there."

"Why wouldn't he use the door?" Anna mutters under her breath "Why would he jump over the fence?" She says louder. "Cam?" He shrugged.

"S'pose we spooked him." Jeffro and Cameron boosted Anna over the fence into the garden; Cameron gave Jeffro a boost and Cameron jumped the fence. They reconvened on the other side, composed themselves then tip toed their way over to a window. When they peered inside they just saw an ordinary kitchen; the back door led to that kitchen. Jeffro cupped his hands around his face and leant against the door's frosted glass. The door swung open under his weight. He looked over at Cameron and hissed. Cameron made his way over; pushing the door completely open with his arm. The three stood in the doorway. Who will move first?

Cameron made an over exaggerated step into the door step, as if the entrance was booby trapped. A sigh of relief from everyone when his leg was still intact. He proceeded to enter the house.

"Cameron! What are you doing?" Jeffro hissed in a spiteful whisper. Cameron pressed his finger against his lips at Jeffro and whispered back, "Be quiet!" He continued to advance into the house. The kitchen was dated, worn out brown cupboards and rustic white tiled floor. Two tall fridge freezers, sat either side of the kitchen doorway, boxing the door in. He made his way over to the door, peering his head round the corner. The glass from the front door, lit a hallway well. The walls were a pale peach above a flowered orange border; coral beneath. He turned back to the others and pointed at a closed bedroom door, mouthing 'I can hear someone in here.'

The sound of the bedroom door opening prompted Cameron to shoot back into the kitchen, hiding himself behind fridge. Anna and Jeffro jolted down outside, under the window.

"Shut up moaning," a voice instructed. Clive Johnson wandered into the kitchen and dropped a bloodied knife into the sink; Cameron still hidden from view, by the enormous fridge. He looked at the door, he was trying to calm his breathing, as to not make a sound. He considered making a run for the back door; he didn't want to alert Clive of Anna and Jeffro's whereabouts. For now, he was unaware anyone was there. Clive swiftly left, mumbling under his breath; Cameron heard the slamming of a bathroom door, down the end of the hallway, by the front door. Jeffro and Anna pleaded with Cameron to come back outside. Cameron with his back pressed firmly up against this fridge closed his eyes, took a deep breath before taking one last look at Anna's face, as she peered round the back door. He made a rash decision and headed for the bedroom. Cameron could not believe what he saw.

A human shaped ball, under a duvet, on the bed. An elderly weary face emerged. "Can you help me?" the man's weak voice called out. "Where are we?" he continued. Cameron was left stunned silent. The voice requested again, "Can you help me?"

"Can I help you?" A much deeper and stronger voice echoed from behind Cameron's frozen posterior. Unwillingly and gradually, Cameron turned his head. Clive Johnson towered over him, grabbing Cameron by the arm. "What are you doing in here!?" Saliva thrashed from his mouth. "You're not meant to be in..." His shout cut short by a blow to the head; Anna stood over him, with a shattered china plate in hand, as he hit the deck. He was still conscious. Cameron put his body between Anna, in the door way, and Clive Johnson. Clive's victim was still wallowing in the bed. Clive dazed, shook his head. He noticed blood coming from his face as he dabbed his hand against it. He stumbled as he attempted to get to his feet; Cameron pushed him back to the ground with his foot. Now Cameron was towering over him. Jeffro backed him up with a large kitchen knife in hand. All three distracted by a moan from the bed, Clive got to his feet and barged his way through them. He headed for the front door; falling short and holding his side. Jeffro looked at the knife that was hanging beside him in his hand. Blood dripped off the end.

"Anna, check the guy in the bed," Cameron instructed. "Jeffro, call the police... and an ambulance. Clive, you stay right there." Anna swiftly side stepped past the blood stains on the carpet.

"He seems ok, a few bruises. That's all I can tell." Anna unfolded the duvet. A fragile, grey haired man was displayed, confused. "He doesn't know where he is."

"Better make that two ambulances, Jeff."

Clive didn't say a word until the police whisked him away in the ambulance. The wound wasn't deep and they assured Cameron that he would live. They thanked them for all they had done, the trio may have well prevented many more elderly victims at the hands of Clive Johnson. But not everything was still adding up for them. Where was Billy Crimley, why was he claiming to be Clive Johnson and why was Clive Johnson in Billy Crimley's residence? Where was the link? Anna gave everything they knew to the police, leaving out HOW they knew a lot of it. The police assured them, they'd do everything they could to get to the bottom of this. But as far as their concerned, they had their man.

"Mum!" Anna called out, "we're home." There was no answer. "Maple?" she waited a second but no answer there either. "They must be out. Tea?" She asked Cameron. Jeffro had gone home by this point. Cameron nodded but grabbed Anna's arm as she headed for the kitchen, landing an almighty kiss on her. She beamed with delight. "Tea it is."

"Hello Anna," someone welcomed Anna as she swung the kitchen door open, she knew from the croaky voice who it was. Billy Crimley stood behind Wendy, whom he had tied to a chair. A knife held against her throat. "So, you know my little secret." Anna looked panicked, Cameron grabbed her arms and pulled her back, close to his body. Any sudden movement could spell the end for Wendy. "I'll tell you what. You let me go. You don't tell anyone. And I won't kill your Mum. Hmm? How does that sound." Anna froze before splattering out her response, "Yes, yes whatever just don't hurt her."

"We all know Wendy won't remember a thing," he said smugly. "What about you, boyfriend. You won't say anything will you, hummm?" Cameron shook his head.

"Don't be scared darling, Clive is going to bring me back. He promised." Anna could tell by her mum's tone, that she didn't believe she was ever coming back. Of course she was willing to sacrifice herself to ensure her daughter stayed safe.

"Where is Maple?" Anna shrieked. Billy rolled his eyes upwards and gave one jolted nod upstairs.

"It was you, wasn't it?" Billy looked confused by Cameron's accusation, "that jumped the fence at your house. You were there. I knew I saw someone." Another rise smile from Billy. "Wendy and I must be leaving now."

"You said you wouldn't hurt her!" Anna yelled, as her raspy voice cracked, tears filling her eyes.

"And I won't. I'll return her safe and sound. If she can find her way home that is." A wicked laugh before he grabbed Wendy and headed for the back door. Cameron still holding Anna back. He whispered in her ear, "Trust me. Let them go. I won't let him take her. I have a plan." Anna did trust him. She put all her trust in him. She whispered back with a vicious tone, "They're leaving the house..."

"Let them," he assured her, "Slowly follow them. He'll use the side entrance to get to his car. He will be so fixed on you that he won't see me coming. I'll cut him off in the driveway. Go... Go!" Anna kept her distance but followed him. Out into the garden, and as Cameron predicted down the side path, through the wooden gate and out into the drive way, he weaved his way through the bushes and flower pots. Anna panicked when she couldn't see Cameron. Where is he? she thinks. Tears flood down her face. Where is he? He was almost at the car. She wanted to do something. She wanted to run and grab her mum; she didn't. She just stopped and watched as Billy Crimley, whom she had always known as Clive Johnson, put Wendy into the back of his car. His eyes glued to Anna the entire time. He slammed the door closed.

"See you soon Anna... Oh maybe not!" He laughed again. He opened his driver door. Anna distraught. Cameron grabbed his ankle, from under the car and pulled him to the ground, the knife fell from his grasp. Cameron rolled out and imposed himself on top of him. Unlike Clive Johnson, Cameron was much bigger and stronger than Billy Crimley. He held both his wrists down on the pavement, as Anna rushes over. She unties her mum and uses the rope to tie up Billy. They tied him to his car door handle. "Maple..." Cameron reminded Anna. She ran into the house to find her aunt beaten and tied to a radiator. Luckily the heating hadn't come on yet, on the autumn evenings.

38

Go Get Your Dream

It was the morning after the night before. Sunshine soared through the crack in Cameron's bedroom window. It was 7:38 AM. He leapt from his pit with a spring in his step, took himself into his en suite. A new lease of life today. Monday's often a day of dread for Cameron; not today. An expression of joy on his face as he caught his eye in the mirror, while manoeuvring his tooth brush around his mouth. A splash of water on his face before heading to the Mini-Mark. A fry up was in order this morning. Cameron was going to enjoy every last bit of it. He stacked his basket with goods, he wouldn't usually indulge in. Bacon, sausages, eggs, beans and hash browns. He even loaded in the finest chopped mushrooms he could find. He wondered if he could make them as well as his mum did. He washed the pots, pans and plate by hand. Humming the lyrics of Frank Sinatra, My Way; his arms, elbows deep in foaming suds. He dried and packed away. The kitchen was spotless. Just the way he liked it. The humming during cooking was now a full-blown concert in the shower; all of Frank's classics were coming out, 'Strangers in the Night' was his favourite. His love for Frank Sinatra was one of the few things, he and his dad had in common. Chequered shirt, chinos and laced up leather shoes assembled, he was ready for the day. He was eager to see Anna for lunch in Maicon's. He only had one thing to do first.

'Hey Nat, it's Cam. How have things been? Would you like to meet up for a drink one evening? I could meet you in Putney? I need to see the rents at some point, so while I'm in town! Let me know ☺*'*

The morning sunshine had disappeared and grey gloomy skies clustered, this however did not dampen Cameron's mood. He made a haste on as he headed for Maicon's.

'Morning Jeff! We still on for beers tonight? I thought we could hit up the cinema before and catch that new Batman film. My treat!'

Maicon's was busy today. Prime lunch time hours. Anna was already waiting, at their usual table by the window. Two lattes and two pan au raisins sat on the table with her. Cameron could not control his face as he fiercely smiled across the cafe. He gave a dorky wave and headed straight over, keeping his eyes on Anna, as he weaved through the traffic, of coffee drinking customers.

"I have big news!" he said without even a hello. His smile stretching from ear to ear.

"Cam... We're leaving." A sadden response also absent of a welcome. Cameron's smile vanished, he smirked and chuckled twice.

"What do you mean you're leaving? Who is we?"

"Me, Mum and Auntie Maple. Maple decided this morning, we can't stay here. We have family up in Hartlepool- Maple and Mum's cousins; we are going to stay with them until we find somewhere permanent. We leave this afternoon." She struggled to keep eye contact with him, with fear of bursting into tears. She looked down at her hands as she twiddled her thumbs on the table. Cameron was stunned to silence. Like a ton of bricks had just fallen on top of him. "Say something."

"I... I can't... What? You're leaving?" confusion written all over his face. Processing wasn't coming easy.

"It's for the best Cam, get away from everything that's happened here. We will sell the house. That way we can pay for the right care for Mum. Family there can support us as well. I'm sorry Cam." Cameron grabbed her hands across the table. Neither said a word, as they looked each other dead in the eye. Tears gathered on the surface of Anna's bottom eyelids. A strong blink released the liquid which streamed down her nose and collected in the corner of her mouth. Cameron didn't know what to say. This was all completely unexpected.

"I will come back and visit you. But I don't know when that'll be. And I don't know how often." Cameron nodded as to show her he understood, but he still couldn't find his words. "The police were round this morning." She pulled her hands away from his. Cameron fought back the tears, a shake in his voice was evident how upset he was.

"Any news?" he looked out the window to ease the pain.

"Clive Johnson crumbled and confessed everything. He'll get less of a sentence 'cause he cooperated. Billy Crimley is being charged with all sorts. Mainly kidnap and attempted murder. Turns out they met in Scotland, when Billy ran from down here. Clive was working in a care home, when Billy was somehow successful in getting a job at the same place. They became close and after time, Billy told Clive all about his unlawful past times. Clive liked the sound of this and wanted in. They moved down here on Clive's clean record and lived in Billy's old house. Billy would find them, take them, and hurt them."

Cameron interjected, "Who is them?"

"Old people. He had a thing for them. He liked to abuse them. Clive would tend to them afterwards. Or so he says."

"Fucking hell!" Cameron gulped. "Sorry." Anna shrugged it off.

"Anyway, Clive says sometimes Billy even molested them. Real sicko." She took a mouthful of coffee. "He's saying nothing apparently. Billy Crimley."

"What a scumbag. He'll go down for a long time."

"I hope so," Anna said. "Clive has evidence for over 5 cases of people they took." Cameron shook his head in dismay. "What was your news anyway?" she asked Cameron. Hoping this would bring cheerier news. He snapped out of his thoughts, puffing out his cheeks.

"Well... I quit my job..." Anna smiles at the news

"Wow Cam!"

"Yep, this morning. Walked straight in and quit." Anna slowly nodded her head in appreciation.

"That's great Cam. What's the plan next?" He collected his thoughts again.

"Well I have a friend. I saw her at the wedding. He dad is an editor of a newspaper. He's always liked me. So I'm hoping he can get something for me. Sport writing or something. It'll probably be an intern type thing if anything. But got to shoot my shot."

"Definitely. I'm so happy for you Cam." They both drank their coffees. "I have to go. I'm going to miss you Cam. Stay in touch."

"Yeah I will." Anna got up from her chair and grabbed her rain mac. She rubbed her thumb across the stain, left from her and Cameron's first encounter. "I got you something." She handed him a rectangular box, covered in rustic brown wrapping paper. "Open it when I've gone." She leant down and gave him a kiss on the cheek. "Bye Cam, go get your dream." He tore the wrapping paper once the café door shut behind her. He lifted the lid of the box, which was no bigger than an A5 book. He pulled out and held out in front of him, what was inside. Before him was a royal blue and white dream catcher, with beautiful grey and white feathers dangling low beneath it. His beaming smile was back. Neatly he packed it away, back inside the box. Upon checking his phone he saw that Natalie had replied to his message. He opened it.

'Friday? Xxx.'

www.ingramcontent.com/pod-product-compliance
Lightning Source LLC
Chambersburg PA
CBHW071141180726

48291CB00007B/2284